Charming Dave

At the End Zone, Book Three

by

Doreen Alsen

Charming Dave: At the End Zone, Book Three

Cover Art by *Kim Mendoza*

The Wild Rose Press
PO Box 708
Adams Basin, NY 14410-0706
Visit us at www.thewildrosepress.com

Publishing History
First Champagne Rose Edition, 2011
Print ISBN 1-60154-994-6

Published in the United States of America

Her eyes twinkled.
"I bet you say that to all the girls."

"I've never said it before to anyone." Which was true.

"Well." Ainslie's smile wilted a little. She tilted her head toward her front door. "I've got to get inside. I promised I'd be home in time to listen to Patsy read." She went up on her toes and placed a kiss on his cheek. "Good night."

"Good night." He watched her walk up the three steps up to her porch and reach for the doorknob. Giving him one last look, she nodded.

Then, he remembered. "Wait! Your herbs!"

She came back to him. "Patsy would never forgive me if I didn't come back with some foliage."

He kissed her cheek as he handed the clay pot over. "Now, go away woman, while I still can let you go."

"You're such a bully." She shook her head as she took the terra cotta pot of herbs and walked away. When she got to the top of the stairs, she looked back and blew him one last smooch for the road. He caught it with his hand.

Dave stood there watching her go into her house. Buzzed, aroused, he rubbed his hand over his heart.

Dave wanted more. A lot more.

Dedication

To Lillian Kelly, the best mother in the world.
I love you, Lill!
To Gloria Taves Burhoe and Phebe Rogers,
English teachers at Provincetown Jr.-Sr. High,
who held high standards and
gave us the tools to reach those standards.
And, as always, to Eberhard, Emilia, and Louisa
for all the love, support, and encouragement.

Chapter One

Ah, paradise! Dave Mason sighed as he pulled into the parking lot of The End Zone. Right now, nothing sounded more perfect than a burger and a beer in the company of friends at his favorite sports bar.

Forget the golden arches. He'd take the flashing red neon goal posts decorating the door of The End Zone any day.

He got out of his car and rolled his shoulders, trying to get rid of some of the stiffness that'd been riding him all day. The air was just starting to turn brisk in the evenings and scented with wood smoke and wet leaves. It made for great football weather.

Speaking of football, he pushed open the door to the bar and slipped in. The dining room was packed with people, their conversations loud and enthusiastic. A sense of unlimited warmth and friendliness permeated the room. The bar was full with groups of customers watching various sports events on the several televisions over the bar. He scanned the crowd, finding the friends he was looking for. His mouth split into a grin, until he saw *her*.

The Menace. The Waitress from Hell. She said her name was Ainslie, but he knew better. *Satan* was more like it.

She more often as not got his order right, and when she did manage that basic task, his food had turned cold.

His new favorite sport became avoiding her section.

"Hey, Dave! S'up?" Sandy, his favorite waitress crossed his path.

"Hopefully a burger and a Sam Adams. I'm starved."

Sandy laughed. "I'll let Bobby know. Mike and the gang are over at table twelve."

Dave tweaked her nose. "Saw 'em. Thanks."

"No sweat." Sandy bopped off in the direction of the kitchen.

"Mason! What took you so long?" Dave's best friend, Mike Kelly, hailed him from across the room.

Dave loped over to the table where Mike sat with his wife, Andi, and Gina Francisco, soon to be Gina Ross. Until about a month ago, Gina had worked at The End Zone. Now she was going to Barrett University to get her degree in literature. She had some notebooks and paperbacks strewn all over the tabletop.

Dave turned the chair around and straddled it from the back. "What a day." He loosened his tie. "Unbelievable." Picking up one of Gina's paperbacks, he flicked it a glance before tossing it back on to the table. "What's all this for?"

Gina sniffed as she tapped a pen against her notebook. "It's my homework. I've got my first paper due on Friday. I woulda thought that you, being a high school principal and all, would understand and appreciate my dedication to my studies."

"Oh, I do. I just wonder why you've got an entire library on top of this table. There's going to be no room for the food. Where's the professor?" Gina's born-and-bred-in-England-husband-to-be was a professor at Barrett University.

Gina rolled her eyes in the direction of the bar. "Checking out the replay of the Manchester United/Bayern München game."

"*Gesundheit.*"

Gina punched Dave in the arm. "Bayern-

2

München is one of the baddest, bad-ass soccer teams on the planet, or so I am told, second to only Manchester United."

"Soccer bad-ass is an oxymoron." Mike yawned.

"So speaks the football coach." Gina snorted. "Anyway, my boy is at the bar, dressed like a fan and cheering Manchester United on."

Dave studied the bar. Well, whattaya know. "He's the only one watching. How did he talk Spike into tuning into a soccer game?" The End Zone crowd was a real football crowd, not a whole lot of appreciation for soccer there. "Nice jersey he's got on. Who's number 7?"

"Was David Beckham." She sighed and put her hand over her heart. "Moment of silence, please for David Beckham. Oww!" She glared at Mike as she rubbed her arm. "Do something about him," Gina complained to Andi. "Ian didn't talk to Spike, I did. Please." Gina puffed a breath up that fluttered her red curly hair. "Give him a break. He's trying to fit in. He got the idea about wearing the team jersey from me. He was so into it, he almost did the whole war-paint thing."

"What an animal," Dave said.

Gina put on a purely satisfied smile. "I like that in a man."

"Ewww." Mike stuck his fingers in his ears. "Too much information."

Gina chuckled. "Oh, let me tell you..."

"LA LA LA LA, I'm not listening!" Mike looked at his wife. "Spud, please make her stop."

Andi laughed. "You're a big boy. Deal with it."

"Hm." Dave frowned. "Mike. Did you catch anything of what happened in the boys' locker room today?"

"Nope. I got there too late. But something did go down." Mike scratched his temple. "It's why I sent 'em all to you. And promised to bench anyone from the team if I found out they were picking on that kid." Mike shook his head. "Poor kid. Who would saddle a boy with a name like Ruark?" He pronounced it *Rooark*.

"It moved into chorus. No one was talking, but the atmosphere took a decided hostile tone. And he pronounces it *Rork*." Andi chuckled. "His twin sister is named Shanna. I think she got the better part of the deal."

"They're characters from a classic romance novel." Gina was the definitive expert on all things romance. "It's one of my favorites. I wouldn't name my kids after 'em though. No wonder the kid's getting picked on."

"Ya think?" Dave smiled at Andi. "How did you end up with half the football team in chorus this year, anyway?"

Mike lifted up his hands in the gesture of a totally innocent man. "I guess they're all music lovers."

"Right. You could have left some of those nachos for me." Dave tapped his knuckles on the table, next to the now empty guacamole and refried bean plate in front of Mike. He grabbed a chip, scraped up some beef and cheese, then popped it into his mouth. Man, talk about heaven. On the flip side, where the hell was his beer? "I've got calls in to the parents. I'm meeting with all of them one at a time tomorrow." He looked around again. "Where'd Sandy go with my beer?"

Gina grinned at him, all shiny, sharky, white teeth. "This isn't Sandy's section."

Dave felt his stomach take a dip south. "Don't tell me it's Ainslie's section."

"Okay, I won't tell you."

Dave groaned. Besides being *Beelzebubarina*, Ainslie was, by anyone's reckoning, the absolute worst waitress on the planet. But Bobby had been desperate to replace Gina, and Ainslie had been in the right place at the right time, much to Dave's chagrin.

Great! He might as well go to those golden arches to get his burger, because with Ainslie as his waitress, he didn't think he was going to see his food anytime soon.

****

"Hey, Ains," Sandy called as she bumped the kitchen door open with her hip. "Dave's here, and he's at Mike and Andi's table. I already ordered his Sam Adams."

"What?" Ainslie Logan blinked a couple of times. She was having enough trouble figuring out which orders under the heat lamps were hers, never mind Dave and his beer.

Sandy sidled up to her and started grabbing plates and layering them up her arms. "He wants a Daveburger and fries."

"Comin' right up," Bobby, the owner of The End Zone said as he dropped a basket of fries into the deep fryer.

For the life of her, Ainslie could not remember seeing a Daveburger on the menu, but she dutifully flipped a page in her dupe book and wrote *Daveburger/fries.* "Sandy, I need to ask you a favor."

Sandy stacked one final plate against her biceps. "What can I do you for?"

Ainslie gnawed on her lower lip. She hated asking for favors, but this couldn't be helped. "I have to go to the high school tomorrow for a meeting, and the only time I can get there is a half an hour after I'm supposed to spell you. Can you stay an extra hour for me?"

"Sure." Sandy had already turned and was making her way out of the kitchen.

"Thank you!" Ainslie called to Sandy's retreating back. Getting calls from the school principal's office was just another in a lurid array of new experiences she would have to get used to. Her children did not get in trouble at school. Ever.

Obviously, that had changed.

She couldn't think about it. She pulled what she hoped were her orders off the line and gingerly stacked the hot plates on her left arm. This was the part she hated most. Ignoring the uncomfortable sizzle, she headed out the door into the dining room.

The place was packed. The room buzzed with laughter, conversation, and the blare of televisions. Everyone was having a great time.

Except her. The End Zone was never the kind of place that was her cup of tea. She would never have lowered herself to go to a place like this back in her other life.

Back when she was the queen of Charleston, South Carolina society and had more money than God to spend.

Now she bussed empty beer bottles off tables and schlepped chicken wings and burgers, all for a buck two forty.

She blinked back tears. She would not feel sorry for herself. She had too much pride and not enough time for that.

Besides, she had Dave at table 12 to worry about.

The damn man was beyond tall, dark and handsome. He made Bradley Cooper look like a troll.

And he always, *always*, made her shake in her size 6 1/2 no name sneakers. It annoyed her to no living end.

Because she knew from handsome. Her ex-husband was a prime example of handsome enough to scramble a girl's brains. Look where marrying Bobby Lee Logan had gotten her—here. Out of South Carolina and to the north shore of Boston. Her pretty house gone, all her pretty clothes gone, her

precious babies in public school. No more Junior
League meetings, good-bye Daughters of the
Confederacy. She spent her days cleaning other
people's pretty houses and her nights waiting on
tables. Life was not what it was cracked up to be.

And now she was so distracted by that damn
Dave, she forgot where she was taking the food
burning up her arms.

She needed to lay the plates down and pull her
dupe book out of her apron so that she could get a
clue, but to do that she would have to go back to the
bar where Spike the bartender was glaring at her
over a bottle of Sam Adams.

She *so* should have finished college and gotten a
degree. She'd been her own worst enemy. Former
Miss South Carolinas didn't make money being cute
beyond the age of forty.

They didn't make any money unless they
married rich men. And when the rich men went to
jail for embezzlement and fraud, the beauty queens
were out of time and out of luck.

She swallowed her pride and went back to the
bar. "Where does this go?" she asked Spike as she
tipped her head at the bottle on the bar's pick up
station.

"It's Dave's." Spike inclined her head toward
table 12. "Over there."

"I know where table 12 is." Ainslie bristled.
Even as she did that, she dropped her plates on the
bar and checked her dupe. Ah, sweet information.
"I'll be right back to get his beer," she said as she
stacked the now cool plates back on her arm, "right
after I deliver these meals to table 8."

Spike rolled her eyes. "Whatever."

****

Dave licked his lips. "Where is that woman with
my beer?"

Gina flicked him a glance. "She'll get here. It's

busy tonight, and she's new."

"Humppff." Dave was not amused. "She hates me." He stole another chip from Mike's nachos.

"It's busy tonight. She'll get here."

Ian slid behind Gina and started massaging her neck. "Manchester won. I knew you'd all want to know."

Mike nodded. "Thank God. I'll sleep better tonight, knowing that."

Andi slapped Mike on his arm. "Stop it. Just stop it."

Dave looked around the room. Ainslie dropped off some food at a table nearby. Poor saps. She got the plates down without spilling anything and walked away while the people at the table exchanged meals with each other.

He shook his head and decided to go to the bar and just get his beer and a bowl of pretzels. He needed something to eat before he gnawed his arm off. "Anybody need anything from the bar while I'm up?" Pushing against the back of his chair, he levered himself out of it, turned, and felt something solid hit him smack in his mid-section.

He heard a sharp gasp just before he felt something hot, fragrant, and squishy run down his shirt and into his pants. His arms wrapped themselves around the blockade as it knocked them onto the table where he got a butt load of Bobby's Macho Nachos.

What he got instead, was two arms full of soft, full, feminine breasts pressed up against his chest. Very nice! He looked down to see the startled brown eyes of Satan's sister.

Very nice, only not so much. Damn it!

He couldn't tell who jumped away first, him or Ainslie. She had a stricken look on her face as she clung to a vertical plate that was oozing the remains of a smooshed burger and fries.

Gina jumped to her feet immediately and ran off to the bar. "I'll get some hot water and a couple of towels." Long silent seconds passed before Mike started cracking up.

Asshole. Here Dave was with guacamole and refried beans smeared all over the seat his best pants and his best friend was laughing his ass off.

Ian joined Mike. Figures that the only thing the two of them could agree on was Dave's humiliation.

Ainslie high-tailed it over to the kitchen while Gina returned with that bucket of soapy water and a bunch of towels. She handed him a towel out of the bucket. "Here. You want to get that glop off your pants or it'll stain."

No kidding. "Thanks." He took a breath. He had some sweatpants in his gym bag back in his car. They had a date with the laundry, but they'd do for now. He'd sneak out of the bar, grab his bag, and change his pants. No harm, no foul.

Except for the fact that everyone in the bar was staring at him. *As Stephen Colbert would say, Sweet Jesus Christ on a waffle cone.* He started to leave when Bobby came barreling out of the kitchen. He had another Daveburger in his huge hands.

Bobby was the size of the Berlin Wall. Everyone skittered out of his way. "I'm really sorry." He dropped the plate with Dave's food on to the table.

"No big deal."

Bobby practically started wringing his hands like a grandma church lady. "Ainslie is really sorry. And you've got Daveburgers on the house for the next month. Of course I'll pay for the dry cleaning."

Dave bet Ainslie was really sorry. A damned sorry excuse for a waitress. Bobby was looking at him so hopefully and was such a good guy, Dave just gave it up. "Thanks."

"No problem." Bobby grabbed Dave's hand and shook it. "Whatever you want, you got it." He disappeared back into the kitchen.

Dave looked at the burger. He'd lost his appetite. He'd just get Sandy or Spike to wrap it up so he could take it home.

"Hey! Where you going?" Mike demanded. "You just got here."

Dave shook his head. "I've got some work to do at home. If you think of anything else about that incident in school today, give me a call." He pulled his shirttail out of his pants to cover the guacamole decorating his ass and turned tail to get the hell out of there.

So much for paradise.

****

"What are you doing?" Bobby growled at Ainslie as he came back into the kitchen.

"Cleaning out my locker." Ainslie swallowed back a sob. "I'm fired, right?"

Bobby scowled. "No."

Ainslie shook her head to clear the noise buzzing in her ears. "Pardon me?"

"I'm not gonna fire you." He moved back behind the cook line.

"Why not? I just spilled food all over one of your best customers."

"Gina told me it was Dave's fault. He got up without looking to see if you were behind him. Besides you've got customers." He put a plate under the heat lamp. "Now, here's your order. Pick up." Conversation done, he turned around and dropped a basket of wings into the deep fryer.

Drenched in gratitude, Ainslie let out a sigh of relief. Never in her life had she been so grateful to one man. It gave her back some small faith in the species.

She could do this, she could make it work. She had to. Failure was not an option.

Chapter Two

"So, do you want to tell me why, for the first time in your life, I have to go talk to the principal?" Ainslie put a bowl of cereal down in front of her boy, Ruark, then looked at the clock. "Shanna," she yelled. "It's getting late! You're going to miss the bus!"

"Momma?" Patsy, Ainslie's youngest child, sat at the breakfast table like the little angel she was. "I don't wanna go to school."

"What's that, silly? You love school." Ainslie frowned at the clock again. "Shanna! If you're late, you're going to walk to school!"

"The other girls won't play with me. They say I talk funny." Patsy put on her Olympic gold medal pout. "They say my name is stupid."

Ainslie sighed and looked at her six-year-old daughter. She didn't doubt her story for a minute. Public schools were full of mean girls out to get the new kid. "You are named after the greatest singer who ever lived, Patsy Cline. Your name is beautiful." Ainslie rinsed her hands off in the kitchen sink. "What else did they say?"

"That my clothes are ugly and my pants are high waters. That's why I didn't get invited to Britney Saunders birthday party."

Ainslie had been eyeing those pants, hoping to put off a shopping trip for some new things for Patsy until she had a little bit more money. "I'll figure something out, precious. Do you want me to talk to your teacher?"

Patsy shook her head. "She won't do anything.

11

She hates me."

"Now, sweetie, she doesn't hate you, I'm sure of it."

"I think she does. She's always tellin' me I use words wrong and only calls on me when I don't raise my hand." Patsy stirred her cereal. "I want to go home. I want to go back to my old school."

It wouldn't help matters if Ainslie admitted that was exactly what she wanted too. "Things will get better, I promise. Now eat up, so you're not late for the bus." Oh, damn, the bus. Where was Shanna? "Shanna!"

"I'll see you, later, Momma." Ruark slung his backpack over his shoulder and headed for the kitchen door.

"Wait a minute! You didn't tell me why I have to visit the principal today!" The outside door closed, and Ruark was gone.

"Momma, I don't feel good," Patsy whined. "My stomach hurts."

"What?" Ainslie threw Patsy a look, just as the child threw her breakfast up all over the kitchen floor. A moment later, the bus blew its horn, making a kind of last call. Shanna managed to fly down the stairs just as the bus rolled away.

"Sorry, Momma," she mumbled as she grabbed a Cookies and Cream Luna Bar out of a cabinet. "Can I get a ride?"

Ainslie felt despair gurgle up behind her eyes. "Sure. Go help your sister get cleaned up." She was pretty sure Patsy had made herself sick—sick with worry. Well, they all had to face their new lives.

"Ew!" Shanna looked at her sister. "You're *so* gross."

"Can you do it without detailed commentary, sugar?"

"But Momma, I'm too sick to go to school." Patsy stood there in all her miserable glory.

And it might have worked if Ainslie hadn't seen her angel baby hide a triumphant smile. If little Patsy could play her at age six, Ainslie was going to be toast when she was sixteen.

"Just hush, please, and go get changed. You're going to school." She turned her back to the girls and wet a dishtowel with hot soapy water so she could clean the gloppy mess.

One day at a time seemed like a luxury. She went from minute to minute, praying for some peace. Remembering her appointment with the principal and Ruark's reticence, she didn't hold out too much hope for an easy rest of the day.

She cleaned the mess and ran upstairs to grab a change of clothes for her meeting with the principal. When in doubt, she could always count on her Chanel suit. Karl Lagerfeld had designed it just for her. This was the one piece of her designer wardrobe that she wouldn't take to the consignment shop for the money to make a rent payment. She grabbed her make-up bag and her Christian Louboutin sling backs. She would get changed at the Brewsters after she cleaned their beautiful house, get to school, talk to the principal, take Ruark home, change into her End Zone uniform and only be an hour late for her shift.

God bless Sandy, that's all she had to say.

About halfway to Patsy's school Ainslie remembered to remind Shanna to pick up her sister.

"I can't, Momma. I have cheerleading try-outs." She was using her holier than thou voice. "Ruark has to watch Patsy today."

"Ruark can't, sugar. Remember?" Ainslie's hands tightened on the steering wheel. "We've got that meeting with your principal."

"But if I don't go to practice today, I won't make the squad." Shanna wailed, the perfect sound of fifteen-year-old angst.

"Then take your sister to practice with you." Ainslie sighed. "I'll pick her up on my way from the Brewsters." She glanced in the mirror and caught Patsy sticking her tongue out at Shanna.

"Momma!" Shanna's voice held the perfect blend of dismay and outrage. "She's such a brat. She'll ruin everything!"

"No, she won't. She'll behave."

"She better, or else I'll shave her head bald while she's sleepin'"

"Momma!" Patsy screamed. "She's gonna shave my hair all off!"

Ainslie banged her hand on the steering wheel. "She'll do no such thing. Shanna, apologize to your sister."

"Whatever. I'm sorry I said I'd shave you bald, okay?"

"I don't believe you." Patsy was adamant.

"Patsy, sweetie, everything's gonna be fine. Shanna was just picking on you. You should be a big girl and just ignore her." Ainslie shook her head. "Can you do me this one favor without riling up your sister?"

"'Course I can, Momma," Miss Sweetness replied. "Since I'm babysitting for the brat, can I get a new dress for the dance next weekend?" Ever the operator, Shanna knew when to pick her moments.

"No, and stop calling your sister a brat. I don't have the money right now. I promise I'll get you a new dress soon."

"I've got to get new outfits first," Patsy chimed in, twisting the knife.

That was true. Patsy was way past due for some new things. It was times like this she *so* regretted giving all Shanna and Ruark's baby things and outgrown outfits to charity when they had outgrown them. Back then, it never occurred to her to keep used clothes for a new child. Ainslie mentally did an inventory of that designer wardrobe of hers again. She guessed a trip to the consignment shop was in order. It was the vintage Dior gown's turn to go.

Tears stung her eyes. It was so shallow, she knew, but she loved that gown.

"Momma?" Shanna's voice broke up her pity party. "Do the Brewsters have a daughter named Cecily?"

"I believe they do, sugar. Why?"

"Can you not let them know I'm your daughter?"

Ainslie nearly drove off the road. "What?"

"Well, she's really a snob, and she's the head cheerleader, and if she knows I'm the daughter of her cleaning lady, I won't get onto the squad."

Ainslie was robbed of all power of speech. Stunned, she focused her attention on the road as she blinked away tears.

"Okay, Momma? I know it's a lot to ask, but I really have to get on the squad."

They got to the high school none too soon. Shanna opened the door and slid out. "Thanks for the ride. I'll see you when you pick up Patsy." She slammed the door shut and melted into the crowd of students rushing to class.

Ainslie had to sit there a minute, as she had a little trouble breathing. Her beautiful baby girl was ashamed of her. It just didn't bear thinking about.

"Momma, can you take me to school now?" Patsy nagged from the back seat. "I'm gonna be late."

"Can't have that now, can we sugarplum?" She gathered her wits about her and put the car into gear. It was only the morning, and already the day had gone to hell in a hand basket.

****

Ruark, his guts churning to beat the band, sat outside the principal's office. A janitor in the hall pushed around a great big broom. Teachers were coming in and out, laughing with each other as they

15

picked up their mail and messages. Every once in a while, one of them would slide him a look.

He just sat there, fighting the urge to puke.

The group of jocks who had beat him up yesterday in the locker room hung around the hall outside the principal's waiting room. When they'd beat him up, they'd been sure to leave marks where no one could see them. Like they practiced it a lot and did it for fun.

He was so terrified he shook, he hadn't been able to eat, and he wanted to bolt in the worst way. All of that would shame his momma more than she was already shamed. A real man would do what he had to do. He would not add to Momma's burden. He would not be like his father.

He just wanted to get this whole thing over with. As in done. Period. Finished.

Mrs. Rockland, Mr. Mason's secretary, looked over at him with a kind look on her face. "Mr. Mason will be out of his meeting soon. Is your mother on her way?"

Ruark nodded. He didn't trust himself to speak. Alden Bradford was giving him the death stare, promising retribution for telling the truth.

Actually, death might not be a bad option right now.

Mr. Mason breezed into the office, checking his watch as he did. He was dressed in a nice suit, off the rack obviously, but it fit him well. He smelled really good, too, Ralph Lauren's Polo, and his hair, as usual, was awesome, even though he didn't use any product.

Mr. Mason was totally hot. Ruark shifted in his chair to hide his shameful reaction to the principal. In that moment, he couldn't have hated himself more.

Mr. Mason smiled and looked at him. "Hey, Ruark. Is your mom here yet?"

"No, sir." Ruark could feel himself blush. He hoped with no little bit of desperation that Mr. Mason couldn't tell what he was thinking and feeling.

"Then I'll just go make a few phone calls while we wait for her." He looked at Mrs. Rockland. "Buzz me, please, when Mrs. Logan gets here."

"Sure thing." Mrs. Rockland nodded at Mr. Mason as he disappeared into his office. She gave Ruark a look. He was deathly afraid she could read his mind or something equally embarrassing.

Soul deep guilt swamped him. He drowned in it. He just hated that he was adding to his mother's problems. It broke his heart to see her working so hard, to see her give up everything just for him and his sisters. He tried to talk her into letting him get a job, but she was totally against it. "Don't worry 'bout a thing, sugar," she'd told him. "You just worry about school."

If she only knew what-all he had to worry about, she'd have a heart attack.

He heard a familiar *click-clack* and looked up. There was his momma.

His *real* momma. Dear Lord, she was dressed in her Chanel suit, the one Uncle Karl designed, her Louboutins, and she was made up to perfection. Her short, dark hair was just the dignified side of messed up.

Sucking in a deep breath, he watched her come into the office.

He wanted to cry with relief. He knew it was only temporary, but for now, she was the momma he missed. He stood up, like a gentleman should.

"Ruark, sugar, sorry I'm late." She kissed his cheek. She smelled like *Nocturnes de Caron* again, not like the bleach or the beer and the grease he was getting used to.

"Mrs. Logan?" Mrs. Rockland also stood up. "Mr.

Mason has been waiting for you." There was just the smallest touch of scold in her voice, Ruark thought.

If his momma heard it, he couldn't tell. "I'm so sorry, ma'am." Her voice oozed southern charm. "The traffic was horrendous."

Mrs. Rockland sniffed. "Please have a seat. I'll let Mr. Mason know you're here."

"Thank you so very much." She lowered herself into a chair with all the grace of a prima ballerina. "Don't worry, baby," she said to Ruark as she patted his knee. "It's going to be okay."

Ruark mentally crossed his heart, as if wishing could make it so. He was pretty sure, however, that nothing was ever going to be okay ever again.

****

Ainslie smoothed the skirt of her suit, even though there were no wrinkles to smooth out. Her mother's intuition on full alert, she knew beyond the shadow of a doubt that her boy was just terrified. She could practically hear his heart beating out of his chest. "I got here as soon as I could, baby," she told him. It killed her to think he was sitting there, scared silly and waiting for her.

"'S'okay, Momma." Ruark looked at her, but she noticed that he avoided her eyes. "I wasn't waiting long. Besides, I'm not a baby. I can handle bein' by myself for a coupla minutes."

"Shush, you. You'll always be my baby."

He turned red, like he always did when she said things like that. "You look real pretty today."

She chuckled. He had too much charm by half. He was going to be a lady-killer someday. "You keep sweet talkin' the girls like that, and you'll have to beat them off with a stick."

Ruark didn't react to that, just looked away from her. She'd obviously embarrassed him again.

All her attention was focused on Ruark, so she didn't hear the door to the Principal's Office open.

"Mrs. Logan, I'm Dave Mason, the principal here."

She stood while extending her hand, grabbed a look at Principal Dave Mason, and fell back in her seat. Standing right in front of her, holding her boy's future in his hands, was Grumpy Dave, her personal Scrooge at The End Zone.

The very same Dave Mason whose butt she'd knocked onto a platter full of guacamole and refried beans just last night. Oh, this could not be good. He hated her.

Ainslie wasn't that fond of him either.

She pasted on her best Miss South Carolina smile and extended her hand as she stood. "It's so good to finally meet you, Mr. Mason," she lied through her pearly whites. She took consolation in the fact that he looked nearly as pole axed as she felt.

"Yes, well," Mr. Mason ran his hand down his tie before he shook her hand. "Why don't we go into my office?" He swept his arm out toward the office door.

"Certainly." She grabbed Ruark's arm and held on for dear life.

Principal Dave Mason's office was an education about the man. His degrees hung on the wall, along with other awards and citations. No picture frames sat upon a very organized desk. The chair behind that desk had seen better days, and she imagined if any woman could stand to put up with him, one of the first things she'd do is get rid of that ugly maroon chair.

He gestured to the guest chairs in front of his desk. "Please, take a seat."

She sniffed as she took a look at them. They were only marginally better than the chair behind his desk. Ruark used his manners and helped her into a ratty chair before sitting down himself.

How could such a polite, well-raised boy be in trouble at school? There must be some mistake.

"Thanks for coming in today." Principal Dave smiled as he sat behind his desk. "There was an incident yesterday in the boys' locker room, and I'm hoping Ruark can help us get to the bottom of it."

Ainslie bristled at the insinuation that her boy was part of an *incident*. "Are you accusing my son? Because I have to tell you, Mr. Mason, that Ruark is a good boy. He's *never* been in any trouble his whole life."

"I'm not accusing Ruark at all. He was in the locker room when something went down, and I'd like to know what *he* knows about it." Dave, *Mr. Mason* she corrected herself, looked from her to Ruark, who was dead still in his seat. "Did you see anything?" Mr. Mason asked Ruark, his tone of voice gentle and encouraging.

"No, sir." Ruark wouldn't look at Mr. Mason, a sure sign he was lying.

"If you know something, sugar, you need to tell Mr. Mason."

"I don't know anything." Ruark insisted.

"Ms. Adams thinks some of the other boys were giving you a hard time." Mr. Mason looked at Ainslie. "Ms. Adams is Coach Kelly's student teacher."

"You have a female student teacher in the boys' locker room?" Ainslie couldn't quite believe it.

Mr. Mason shook his head. "No, which is the reason I need to question all the boys." He again turned his attention to Ruark. "You don't have to worry about getting into trouble. Anything you tell me and your mom is confidential."

Ruark swallowed hard and shook his head as he studied his shoes, the picture of utter misery. He was trying very hard to be brave, and she knew there was a story here, but her boy wasn't going to spill it here and now. "Ruark, would you please go out and wait for me. I want to have a private word with Mr. Mason."

Ruark jumped up and ran out the door like the roadrunner hightailing it away from an acme anvil. Ainslie took a deep breath and turned her attention to Mr. Mason. "I think you and I need to have a talk about my boy."

Chapter Three

Dave watched Ruark scurry out of his office, but really never took his gaze off the in control, totally-take-no-prisoners woman sitting in front of him. No way was this woman the ditzy waitress from The End Zone.

There had to be an evil twin lurking around somewhere.

"Just what type of *incident* are you talking about, Mr. Mason? Is my boy in any danger?"

Whoa! "He's not in any danger," Dave hurried to assure her. "Addington High is a safe school. But I'm certain he knows something about what happened, and I want to get to the bottom of it."

"He's not going to tell you anything today. This is a new experience for him, and he's feeling quite humiliated." The new Ainslie, Mrs. Logan, informed him.

"He's gone through a lot this past year, and he won't respond well to an interrogation." She sniffed. "He's a very sensitive boy, and I won't let you harass him."

What did she want? For Dave to take the kid to the park for a ride on the merry-go-round? "Coming to my office to talk to me is not harassment," he said, speaking in his best I-am-king-of-the-school voice. "Would you rather I'd brought him in with the boys I thought were causing trouble?"

Mrs. Logan, uh, Ainslie, sighed. "Do you know anything about his history? Why he's here instead of the safe, secure private academy he'd been going to since kindergarten?"

"I personally don't, but I'm sure it's on file in the Guidance Office."

She blushed. "Actually, it isn't. That was a rhetorical question. I'd hoped our troubles could have stayed in Charleston and we could begin a new life here." She sat up straighter. "Ruark and Shanna's daddy is Bobby Lee Logan."

Huh? Who's Bobby Lee Logan...?

"Of the Cooper Logan Investment Firm? Crook extraordinaire, second only to Bernie Madoff, who I'm sorry to say, I entertained once in my home." She snorted. "I should have had the caterer put rat poison in the paté."

She looked at him directly, chin high, color flaring on her cheeks. He felt like he had fallen down the rabbit hole into some alternate universe where truly horrible waitresses turned into super-heroes.

Absolutely delicious, mouth watering super-heroes with bee stung lips and thick eyelashes over gorgeous brown eyes.

Then what she had told him lazered through the testosterone haze clouding his vision. Bobby Lee Logan—the great-great-great-great grandson of Robert E. Lee, as he would tell anyone who would listen—had stolen hundreds of millions of dollars from his investment corporation and its customers. He was in jail. The money nowhere to be found. Bobby Lee, good ol' boy and Son of the Confederacy, refused to tell the authorities what he'd done with it.

"How did you end up here from Charleston?" Dave asked her. "Didn't you have any family at home?"

Ainslie sighed and sat back in her chair. "The shame was too much for the children to bear. And even though we sold absolutely everything of value we could, we couldn't live the way we had before Bobby Lee went to jail. We'll never be out of debt, unless Bobby Lee tells where the money is, and he won't." She rubbed her hands on her skirt. "I had no idea what Bobby Lee was doing. There was always money, I didn't question where it came from." She shrugged. "This has all been too much for the children," she repeated. "They're not used to me working, and they're spoiled, I'm the first one to admit it. It used to be a hobby of mine." She gave a half-hearted little laugh, like she was trying to make a joke.

Dave cleared his throat. "Both Shanna and Ruark are very smart and well-behaved. She seems to be fitting in with the popular crowd, which I guess works for her."

Ainslie grimaced. "She does like to be in the center of it all."

"Ruark, on the other hand, seems to be having a pretty rough time of it." Dave tried to get her to look into his eyes, but she was in avoidance mode.

"Ruark lost so much. Not just his daddy. They got along once Bobby Lee got over the fact that music was *it* for Ruark, not sports." She did look Dave in the eyes this time. "He has a beautiful voice. Like an angel." She smiled. "I know I'm his momma, so I have some bias, but the boy has a rare talent. He was in a school specializing in the arts and was studying with Miles Maxwell."

"I'm sorry, I don't know who Miles Maxwell is."

Her eyes bugged out of her head. "Only the best bass in the world. You know? Opera?"

He didn't know opera from nano technology. "I'm sorry, I don't really follow opera." See? He wasn't so proud he couldn't admit to something he didn't know.

She smiled. "He has sung every bass role in just about every major opera house in the world. He's in Charleston as Artist in Residence at Mayfield University. Ruark auditioned for him, and Max took him on as a private student." Her mouth flattened

24

out. "Taking that away from my boy was the hardest thing I've ever had to do. He acts so brave, but I know he's dying inside." She looked down and blinked away tears from her eyes.

Oh, he was such a sap for brave women fighting back tears. He was also in a position to help her with her son, if only she'd let him. "Mrs. Kelly, you know, Andi?" He picked up a pen and tapped it on his desk blotter. "Mike's wife? From The End Zone?" He could tell by her blank stare that she wasn't going where he led. "She's the vocal music teacher here. She's actually mentioned Ruark to me."

Again, she went bug-eyed. "Oh lord love a duck, do all my children's teachers eat at The End Zone?" Horror dripped off her in agonizing drop after drop.

"No." He said, trying to lighten the mood. "I'm pretty sure Mr. Randall from the chemistry faculty has never eaten there."

His insides turned to ice when she dropped her head into her hands and shook. Oh, crap. "Don't be upset. I was only trying to be funny."

She lifted her head and looked at him with dry eyes. "Good thing you're a principal and not a stand up comic."

"Yeah, it was a tough career choice to make." He wanted to grin. Mrs. Logan was funny and sassy and in total control. "Look, I really want to bring Andi in on this. I'm sure she'll be more than happy to work with Ruark."

Mrs. Logan pursed her lips together. "Chorus is probably the only class he likes." She frowned. "He's a very private kid. He doesn't talk a lot about his feelings, but he's my boy, and I know him. His daddy going to jail really hit him hard."

Dave nodded. "So I'll talk to Andi. In the meantime, I'd really appreciate it if you could try to find out what happened in the locker room yesterday."

"I can try." She shook her head. "He can be really closed mouth when he wants to be. Maybe Shanna knows. Now my girl, she has no trouble talking."

"Any information would be great." He smoothed down his tie. "I won't put up with harassment in my school."

"I appreciate that." She looked at her watch, sighed. "I've got to go. I'm already going to be late for my shift as it is."

Without thinking, without hesitation, he leapt out of his chair and crossed around his desk to offer a hand to help her up. Mrs. Logan inspired gallantry.

If she was surprised at his Prince Charming routine, she didn't show it. Her big brown eyes were just gorgeous. He could stare into them all day. With a gracious smile, she took his hand and let him help her out of the chair. "Thank you for letting me know about Ruark."

He cleared his throat, his mouth suddenly dry, his palms suddenly sweaty. "I appreciate you coming in and working with us on this." He stuck his hands in his pockets. "We really believe in the team approach around here. Parents are partners, not problems."

She looked at her watch again. "I have to go. Sandy's waiting for me to relieve her."

He walked to the door and held it open for her. "Thanks for coming in."

She nodded, and just like that, Mrs. Logan walked out of his life. He wondered how much Ainslie took after her alter ego.

****

Shanna mopped perspiration off her forehead with a scratchy, no-thread count towel. She sighed. The dance routine to *Toxic* was so hard. But she had to nail it to get on the cheerleading squad.

She was one of the best cheerleading flyers in the state of South Carolina. Her daddy had been so proud of her.

Out of the corner of her eye, she saw Patsy the brat looking at herself in the mirror and trying to do all the moves. It was *so* embarrassing. Where was Ruark? He was supposed to be here ages ago to get Patsy.

She picked up her water bottle and squirted some water into her mouth. It was warm and tasted, very slightly, of chlorine and plastic. In her old life, her real life, she would have had a brand new bottle of Smart Water. In this messed up excuse of a life, she had a water bottle that she filled up with tap water.

Ugh.

"Hey." Shanna looked to see Cecily Brewster behind her.

"Hey."

"You're lookin' good out there." Cecily smiled really wide. "Much better than anyone else."

"Thanks." Okay. How did she say thank you without sounding stuck up?

"Yeah." Cecily looked over to where Patsy was showing off.

Shanna wanted to sink into to floor. Patsy was currently trying to do a Russian jump. She looked totally spastic.

"Your little sister is cute. I only have a little brother, and he's a such a pain." Cecily took a slug out of her own Vitamin Water bottle.

"I told her not to get in anyone's way. My brother will be here soon to take her home."

Cecily perked up. "Your brother is really cute."

What? "He's okay, I guess."

Cecily nearly swooned. "He looks so much like Zac Efron. I've heard him sing in chorus. Does he dance?"

Zac Efron? Ruark? Someone should just shoot her now.

In the meantime, Cecily Brewster was staring at her intently, waiting for info on her dorky brother. Shanna reached up and tightened her hair tie. "He's big into music."

"Omigod, his voice is so beautiful," Cecily chirped. "I get chills when I hear him sing."

Some of the guys from the football team, led by Alden Bradford, marched into the gym, for all intents and purposes watching the cheerleading tryouts.

Except not. Alden was watching her. It gave her a funky, fluttery feeling in her stomach. Her pulse was doing a little happy dance.

Unless he was watching Cecily. In which case, life sucked hard.

Alden elbowed one of his buddies, told him something that got a laugh, and jogged over. Shanna couldn't worry about that, because she was having trouble breathing.

It totally had nothing to do with the cloud of *Axe* that surrounded him. She stifled a cough.

"Hey," Alden said. "You girls are looking good."

"Um." Shanna wanted to stay and bathe in the light that was Alden Bradford, but Patsy came out of nowhere, dragging her backpack. "Ruark's here. We're going home."

Shanna looked over where Ruark waited for Patsy. "'Kay. Stay out of my room."

"Kind of hard when it's my room too." Patsy scampered away and left with Ruark.

"We should get back to practicing." Cecily nudged Shanna with her elbow.

Alden smiled, and Shanna's insides did a belly flop. "I'll see you later," he promised.

Shanna was tongue tied, which had never, ever happened before. "Okay," she managed to squeak out.

O.M.G! Her heart did a little cheering routine of its own.

Finally! Her life was turning around.

Chapter Four

Dave figured the best place to catch up with Andi would be at The End Zone, and he was right. She and Mike were usually there on Wednesday night, grabbing a quick bite before going to choir practice.

He couldn't help grinning like a fool at the memory of how Andi sucker-betted Mike into joining her church choir. Damn, but it was a thing of beauty seeing Mike humbled by a woman.

He was, however, not just looking for Andi. He hoped to see a certain waitress with big brown eyes and a voice that dripped Southern Comfort.

"Hey, Mr. Mason! Lookin' for Coach Mike?" All perky and chirpy, Chelsea Adams, Mike's student teacher, bounced up to Dave, a big smile on her face and a tray full of drinks in her hands.

"Hey, Chelsea. When did you start working here?" And how had he missed it?

"Tonight's my first night." She made a sassy face and stuck her tongue out. "Gotta pay for school somehow."

"Look at it as an investment in your future." He gestured toward Mike and Andi. "I want to catch Mrs. Kelly before she leaves for her rehearsal."

"Can I bring you something to drink?"

"I don't want to make extra work for you."

"Oh, it's no trouble," she burbled like a bubbler.

"I guess I'll have a Sam Adams, then."

"Coming right up!" Chelsea bopped away.

Though it was a slow night, the noise level at the bar was pretty high. Dave was glad Mike and

Andi hid away in one of the booths, which provided a little more privacy and quiet in the otherwise noisy bar. They were holding hands across the top of the table and looking at each other with love-goofy eyes, all romantic-like.

Of course, that probably meant they *wanted* some privacy and quiet and wouldn't welcome his joining them like they might on another night.

Oh, well. He would have left them alone if he hadn't made a promise to Mrs. Logan to talk to Andi. He pulled up a chair from a nearby table and straddled it. "Andi! Just who I was looking for."

Mike scowled at him. "Go away."

Andi, on the other hand, smiled. "Hi Dave. What can I do for you?"

"I had a meeting with Ruark Logan's mother today. You'll never guess who she is." Dave stole an onion ring off the platter in the middle of the table.

Mike moved the plate out of Dave's reach. "You interrupt us to play guessing games?"

"No. Actually I do need to talk to Andi about Ruark."

"Did he shed any light on the locker room situation?"

"No, but maybe Andi can get something out of him." He looked at her. "He's having a lot of trouble adjusting and the family situation is difficult."

Andi's eyebrows raised. "Is he in a bad home?"

Dave shook his head. "No, but it's a broken home. His father is in prison for embezzling and swindling a lot of money. You know, that guy from down south?" He scratched his nose. "Bobby Lee Logan?"

"Oh, dear." Andi's eyes clouded up. "Ruark's got a gorgeous voice. Really remarkable."

"Yeah, well one of the things he left behind in Charleston was a special private school for the arts and a real high power voice teacher. I wonder if you can kind of take him under your wing and help him transition better."

"Of course." Andi smiled. "You mentioned his mother."

Just at that precise moment, a huge crash came from the bar. Ainslie was in the house.

He looked over his shoulder and, yep, Mrs. Logan had definitely left the building. "That's her."

"Who, her?" Andi looked over his shoulder.

"Ruark's mom. Ainslie is Ruark's mom."

"You've got to be kidding me." Mike shook his head.

"Nope. Apparently they had to sell all their worldly possessions and move here to start over where no one knows them."

Andi's eyes filled with sympathy. "It explains why she's such a bad waitress. She's probably never had to work a day in her life before this."

Chelsea appeared with Dave's beer and a grumpy look on her face. "Sorry I was so slow with this. Ainslie dropped a pitcher of Miller Light all over the bar." She gifted him with a smile that bared a tad too many teeth.

"'Kay. Can I get anything for you, Coach?"

Mike shook his head. "Nope, I'm good."

"I'd like a re-fill on my Diet Coke." Andi's voice stalled Chelsea's exit.

"Oh, yeah." She flicked Andi a cursory glance and smile. "Sure thing."

"Thanks," Andi said to Chelsea's retreating back, her tone crusted with sarcasm. "That girl's a barracuda."

"You got nothing to worry 'bout, Spud." Mike brought Andi's hand to his mouth and pressed a kiss into her palm. "I have your name tattooed across my butt in great big letters."

"Now, that's a sight I hope I never see." Dave took a swig of his beer. Nice and cold, the tiny bubbles fizzed and stung his tongue, just the way he liked it. "It'd be great if you could take the kid under your wing," he said to Andi.

"I'm always happy to help out a kid, especially one with so much talent."

"He's that good?" Dave fiddled with the label on his beer bottle.

"Oh, yeah. So much potential." She smiled. "He sight-reads like a demon. Keeps to himself, though. I thought he was shy, but from what you're saying, he's just having a really hard time. I'm more than happy to work with him."

"Great. I'll let Mrs. Logan know I talked to you. She'll be relieved." He winced when he heard a crash from the kitchen. "She could use a little good news, I think."

"Mrs. Logan, eh?" Mike waggled his eyebrows. "Not Bride of Satan?"

Dave watched Ainslie trundle over to a table of rowdy kids from Barrett University. She was in the typical End Zone uniform of a logo tee-shirt and khaki pants. Gone were the expensive suit and skyscraper heels, but she still moved with the same grace and dignity she had earlier in the day in his office. Odd that he hadn't noticed how elegantly she moved before this.

And it looked to him like she had her hands full with those college kids. A couple of them tossed peanuts at each other and one had definitely sucked down too much beer. They were giving her a hard time about being so slow in getting their food out. In Dave's opinion, they weren't being very respectful, and if the drunk kid got any more obnoxious, he might have to be taught a lesson.

He forced himself to look away and turn his attention back to Mike and Andi, who were both staring at him with expectant looks on their faces. "What?"

"Did you hear a word we said?" Mike wanted to know.

"No, sorry." Dave felt his face turn red.

"Spud here was just telling you that we'd both look out for him."

Dave opened his mouth, but clenched his jaw when he heard a burst of laughter coming from the college kids' table.

"What the hell?" Mike said as he looked beyond Dave at the loud table.

Dave turned and looked then, and his temperature rose about hundred degrees. The morons were laughing as they flicked popcorn at Ainslie while she struggled to put their orders on the table.

Well, that had to stop. Didn't those kids give a damn that Ainslie was someone's mother? Dave knocked over his chair as he got up and marched over to teach those kids some respect.

****

"Come on, kids. Please cut it out." Ainslie wanted to conk those college kids' heads together. These Yankees had no manners. She would roll up and die of shame if she was their momma.

A big, blond guy tipped back in his chair and laughed as he pitched another handful of popcorn at her. Okay, that was it. She wasn't going to give them their food until they could behave themselves. She opened her mouth to tell them so when the kid in the tipped chair fell backward with a huge *oomph* followed by a loud *thunk*.

Dave Mason appeared out of nowhere to catch the frat boy, standing over him. Only Ainslie could see Dave unhooking his foot from the bottom rung of the chair. His face formed stern lines, his mouth hard, his knuckles white on the boy's shoulder. "Oops! Didn't you ever hear your mom tell you to keep all four on the floor? Lucky for you I caught you before you got hurt." Dave let go, and the kid fell and took one the chair legs in the area of his kidneys.

"Yo, dude!" The popcorn throwing idiot struggled to get off the floor. "Who the hell…"

"Shut it." Dave's voice held total authority. No one disobeyed him. "Here's what you're going to do. You're going to apologize to Mrs. Logan here, then leave and never come back."

"You got no right to kick us out." One of the other guys stood up.

"No, but I do." Bobby was on the scene, wielding a spatula. "This is my place, and no one treats my waitresses that way." He motioned with his head to the door. "Get out."

Chelsea was breathless as she bustled over. "Hey, Bobby. These guys are friends of mine from school. They won't act up anymore."

Bobby snorted. "Some friends." He pointed his spatula at the door. "There's the door. Use it." He turned to go back to the kitchen but looked at Chelsea. "And I mean it. They don't come back. Ever. And since they're your friends, you can clean up their mess." He looked at Ainslie. "You go to the break room and take fifteen minutes. That's an order. Chelsea will cover your tables until you come back." He stomped back to the kitchen.

Chelsea turned bright red and raced off in the direction of the bar. Dave stayed where he was, like an avenging angel. Ainslie couldn't take her eyes off him. He'd actually defended her. No one had ever come to her rescue like that before.

Of course, she'd never been treated so appallingly badly before. Damn Yankees.

"Aren't you forgetting something?" Dave asked the jerks as they shuffled past her. When all she got in response was a dirty look, he grabbed the kid by the shoulder. "*Yo, dude.*" He imitated their frat boy tone of voice. "You need to apologize to Mrs. Logan."

The kid jerked his shoulder out of Dave's hand. "Who's Mrs. Logan?"

"The lady you insulted." It looked like Dave wasn't letting the kid get away with anything. Her heart thumped extra hard. Lord have mercy, he was off the chart sexy when he went all alpha male.

Rawr!

The kid looked at Ainslie, murder in his eyes. "Sorry." He pushed the kid ahead of him. "Let's get out of here."

The only sounds in the restaurant came from the TVs above the bar. Ainslie didn't know what to do next. She looked at Dave, who was staring at her. The anger left his face, replaced by an intensity that made her breath hitch in her throat. She opened her mouth to say thank you, but nothing came out.

He reached out, took her tray out of her hands, and put it on the table. "Are you okay?"

She nodded.

"Good." Something in his eyes softened. "Bobby was right. You should go on back to the break room and take fifteen minutes."

She realized she was holding her breath and let it whoosh out of her. "I have to clean up this mess."

He shook his head. "You heard Bobby. Chelsea's going to clean it up. They're her friends."

Chelsea chose that moment to show up carrying a bus bucket. "I got it." She grimaced. "Sorry 'bout that. The guys get rowdy, but they don't mean any harm." She busied herself busing the table.

Dave still looked at Ainslie. "Go on. Chelsea's got it."

She thought he might touch her, but he put his hands in his pockets instead. She should have felt relieved, but instead she felt regret. He was her children's principal. She had no business wanting him to touch her.

Although a little bit of male comfort would go a

36

long way. It had been ages since she'd been touched by a man.

"You've had a long day. Go take a couple of minutes." He continued to look at her in that intense way he had. It caused her to shiver from the top of her head to the tips of her toes.

She forced herself to look away. "Okay. Thanks. I mean, thanks for coming to my rescue."

He scratched his temple. "Yeah, ask anyone. I'm a regular Sir Galahad." He smiled at her. "Go."

****

"We've got to get going," Mike told Dave when he got back to their table. "Thanks for the show."

"Those buttheads were way out of line." Dave dropped into his chair. His adrenaline had stopped pumping but he was still wired.

"Absolutely." Mike helped Andi out of the booth. "You know I would have held your coat, but it looked like you had everything under control."

"All in a day's work," Dave said. His hands were trembling. He hid them under the table. "I've had more trouble with period six lunch."

"You coming with us?" Mike slipped his arms around Andi's back.

"No, I'm going to wait here." Dave reached for his warm beer. "Those assholes may be waiting for her when she gets off."

"That's probably a long time to wait." Mike's brows slammed down over his eyes.

"Mike," Andi kissed her husband on the cheek. "Let's go. Dave's a big boy."

The big boy stared at the table in front of him. "Good night."

Mike and Andi left, and he slid into their booth, into a place where he could brood and watch Ainslie Logan.

Someone needed to look out for her, for her children's sake. He cared about all his students, and her kids were having a hard time of it.

Chelsea came up to the table. "I'm covering Ainslie's tables until she gets back. Do you want to order some food?" She pasted on a smile that reeked of embarrassment.

"Uh, sure." He rapped his knuckle against the table. "Whatever Bobby's got on special tonight is good."

"You want bread or soup with that?" Chelsea asked as she scribbled on her order pad.

"Whatever's best." Dave saw that Ainslie had come back out on the floor.

It was a crime she had to work so hard. Her kids needed her now more than ever. New school, new city, new life. Kids didn't like change. They needed consistency and a stable home environment. How Ainslie was holding it together was beyond—

He looked up to see Chelsea staring at him. "What?"

"I want to apologize for my friends again. They were celebrating winning an intramural ping pong tournament."

Dave flashed her his best principal glare. "Don't apologize to me. Apologize to Ainslie."

"I did." She stepped away from his table. "I'll go put this order in."

Whatever, Dave thought. He couldn't take his eyes off Ainslie. She didn't quite look like the power mom she was earlier in his office. Still, she was beautiful, he realized. Incredibly beautiful. Why hadn't he seen it before this?

Because he was an insensitive doofus. It shamed him that he had been so impatient with her.

That was going to change as of now. He watched her march to the kitchen and felt bereft. What was up with that? He shook his head at himself.

Then, like he'd conjured her up, she was there at his table bearing food.

"Here's your order." Ainslie put a big plate of greens with some grilled chicken on them, along with a side of sourdough bread.

His order? He didn't order this. "What *is* that?"

"A grilled chicken Caesar salad."

Salad? No way. "I didn't order salad."

Ainslie's face fell. "Chelsea told me you ordered the special. Please don't tell me I got it wrong. This is tonight's special."

At least there was bread. "Oh. Thanks."

"Um, do you want another beer?"

"No, thank you. How about a Coke?"

"Comin' right up." She left, and he was alone again to brood about her.

He ripped off a hunk of bread and gnawed at it. The crust was crunchy, the insides chewy. Ainslie was at the bar now, picking up drinks. She must have gotten it wrong because when she wasn't looking, Spike picked up one drink and exchanged it for the right one. Ainslie smiled at Spike and trundled off with her drinks, obviously not noticing the switch.

Yeah, she and her family needed some protection, and he was just the man for the job.

Chapter Five

Ainslie could feel Dave watching her. He had eaten the chicken off his salad as well as all the bread in the basket. Chelsea was hovering, but he didn't seem to notice.

No, sir. He was focused on Ainslie's huge butt and mascara-smudged face like he was some hungry jungle cat and she was a hyena.

Okay, who had watched *The Lion King* one too many times?

She groaned. Her feet hurt from being on them this very long day. The night was dragging out even longer. Hand to God, she was weary, both physically and emotionally.

Hard-wired to keep plugging away, she knew how to put one foot in front of the other, but some days it was so difficult.

"Ainslie." Bobby's deep *basso profundo* vibrated from behind her.

She turned around. "What do you need?"

He smiled. "It's getting pretty quiet. Why don't you go on home? Get some rest."

She would dearly love to do that, but she needed the hours. "I can finish my shift."

"I'm gonna pay you for the hours you were scheduled to work. Consider it combat pay."

Pride versus relief flooded her. She chose to take Bobby up on his offer. "Are you sure?"

"Absolutely. Chelsea can finish your tables and put your tips aside for you."

"Okay." This was Christmas, New Year's Eve, Easter, and her birthday all rolled into one. She exhaled with a *whoosh*. "Thank you."

"No prob. Go home and get some rest." Bobby turned back to the kitchen.

She did all her end of shift duties at the speed of light, gave Chelsea a status report of her tables, and punched out.

As she went through the dining room, she noticed Dave was gone. Of course. He didn't have her sideshow of a life to study any more. She pushed open the door and took one step into the balmy Indian summer night.

"Hey." A very male voice came from right next to her.

She *eeped* and jumped into the air, her heart doing palpitations the whole while.

"Whoa, there." Strong hands darted out to catch her.

She whipped her head around. Dave owned those big, male, warm hands. "Let go of me!"

He did. "Don't be afraid. It's only me."

She was shaking so hard that her teeth sounded like castanets. "What are you doing out here? You scared me to death!"

He rubbed a hand across his chin. "Sorry about that. I only wanted to get your attention."

"It worked! Now if you're done terrifying me, I'm going home."

"Let me walk you to your car." He touched her arms again, this time as gentle as a whisper across her skin.

"There's no need," she said.

Dave looked around the parking lot. "I'm not sure if those ass . . . uh," he looked sheepish as he corrected himself, "those jerks from before are hanging around."

She could feel her eyes widen. "That's ridiculous." Her skin tingled when he shook his head from side to side. "Isn't it?"

"Better safe than sorry." He squeezed her arms. "Which one is your car?"

She took a minute to remember where she had parked it. "Over there. The Volvo wagon." Fifteen years old, she'd bought new when she had owned the world. Now she had to pray every time she got into it that it would start.

"Volvos are good cars." Dave gripped her elbow lightly as he shepherded her to her waiting vehicle. "They last a long time."

"This one has no choice," she muttered as she rummaged around in her purse for her keys. Damn it! The smell of the man next to her, the clean, woodsy scent of his after-shave, just swamped her, even though he hadn't applied it with a heavy hand. Her hands shook like she was in Antarctica.

She found her keys, fumbling while she stabbed them at the lock.

"Let me." He reached down to take them from her. She jerked up and somehow their heads collided with a *thunk*.

"Ow." She straightened up, rubbing her head. "Sorry."

He winced as he palmed her keys. "Totally my fault." He handily opened her door. "Your carriage awaits, my lady." He executed a little bow while making a gallant gesture toward the door.

She let him take her arm and help her into the car. "Thanks for being my body guard."

"No problem." He kept looking at her, intensity firing up those beautiful blue eyes of his. He looked like he wanted to eat her for dinner.

A closed off part of her awoke with a slow shiver. Her nipples actually started to tingle. She licked her lips.

His gaze tracked the movement of her tongue. Blowing out a gusty breath, he closed the door after she slid in.

"Thanks again for riding to my rescue." She smiled as she rolled her window down. "Both times. You're a prince."

He grinned like a pirate. "And don't you forget it."

She laughed and started the car up. He was really outrageously handsome with bright blue eyes, thick lashes, and that killer body. He definitely looked like he had muscles in all the right places.

Not that she wanted to see him naked.

Okay, she lied. What woman wouldn't want to see him naked?

A really, really dead one. Ainslie for sure wasn't really, really dead.

"W-w-well." Was she stuttering? Of course not. She never stuttered, was never at a loss for words. "I've got to get home. Thanks again, for, you know, being my knight in," she cleared her throat, "shining armor."

"Good night." He rapped his knuckles on the roof of the car. "Sweet dreams."

She nodded and put the car into gear. As she drove off, she checked her rearview mirror to see him get into his own car. "Sweet dreams to you," she whispered to his disappearing presence.

****

"Hey, Ruark. I brought you some ice cream."

Ruark looked up as his twin sister came into his room. He sighed. He had to get Salinger's *The Catcher in the Rye* read before he tackled his bio lab report. Man, Holden Caulfield was a whiny brat.

"Thanks. That's really nice of you." Ruark wasn't fooled. Shanna wanted something from him.

He should make her work for it.

Shanna sat on the edge of his bed and fluffed her hair. "Yes, it is."

"What do you want? Why don't you have any homework?"

Shanna looked outraged. "You're so mean! Can't a girl bring her brother ice cream without wanting something."

Ruark put *The Catcher in the Rye* down. "When the sister in question is *you*, then no. Save us some time and just tell me what you want."

"Oh, okay." She bounced on the bed. Taking the spoon, she dug into the ice cream. "I need a favor."

"Duh."

Shanna wrinkled her nose and spoke around the ice cream in her mouth. "I want you to ask Cecily Brewster to the Homecoming Dance."

Oh, crap. No freakin' way. "I don't go to dances, you know that."

"Yeah, but can't you go this time? You're a really good dancer. Cecily really thinks you're cute, and if you ask her out, I'll get on the varsity cheering squad for sure." She pouted. "I'll never ask you for a favor again."

Ruark shook his head. "I don't want to go to the Homecoming Dance. I hate school dances."

"But you love to dance! You took all those classes back in Charleston." Shanna sniffed. "You know how important it is for me to get on the varsity squad. You know I'd do the same thing for you." She put another spoonful of ice cream in her mouth.

"I don't want to be a varsity cheerleader." No way he was going to that dance. He'd shove pencils under his fingernails before he'd go there.

"Ha, ha." Shanna frowned. "What's wrong with Cecily? You could be *sooo* popular right away." She casually frowned at the nail polish chipping off her right hand. "It's totally win/win."

If only it were that easy. He looked at his twin and begged her to see him the way he was. She checked out her manicure, no clue as to what she was asking of him.

She wouldn't understand, even if he came out

and the truth whomped her upside the head.

He so wished she knew without him telling her. She was his twin. They'd shared a womb, why couldn't they share the truth? He slanted her a glance.

She was sitting there, pounding down the ice cream she had brought to him, a bribe at best. He knew she loved him. He loved her. He was lucky to have his family, or at least what was left of it.

"You know I'd do the same thing for you," Shanna wheedled.

"You'd hook up with Cecily?"

She slapped his arm. "No, stupid head. I'd say yes if one of your friends asked me out, if you, you know, needed me to."

Shanna was selfish, but she wasn't mean. If he asked Cecily out, it didn't mean he had to kiss her. Just touch her when they danced.

That he could do. He might as well make his sister happy. "I'll ask Cecily to the dance."

Shanna looked up from the ice cream. "What?"

"You've got chocolate on the corners of your mouth. I said I'd ask Cecily to the Homecoming Dance."

Shanna wiped her mouth with the back of her hand. "Thank you *soooooo* much!" She grinned. "I totally thought it was going to take more to get you to do this! You are the best brother in the entire world!" She launched herself at him, grabbed him around the neck and noisily kissed his cheek, her mouth cold and fragrant from the mint chocolate chip ice cream. "I love you!" She jumped off the bed, keeping the bowl of ice cream with her. She pointed the spoon at him. "You rock!"

He looked back at *The Catcher in the Rye*, but he couldn't concentrate on it anymore. He thought of Cecily. If she wanted him to be her boyfriend, she was totally out of luck.

Of course, Cecily was going to want more than he could give. It'd be a major pain in the butt.

"I promise I'll never ask you for another favor." Hopeful was Shanna's middle name.

He so missed his old school, where he was out and had friends. He felt understood there. He could talk to kids there.

He could tell James that he thought the principal was hot, and he had a crush on him. He could talk to Matthew about Lady Gaga's outfits and hair; then they would dance around the music room while they played *Telephone*.

Now all that was gone. His *gaydar* hadn't pinged at all here in Addington. Not even once. His life sucked. Totally, absolutely.

That didn't mean Shanna's life had to suck. He held up a finger. "Just the Homecoming Dance. That's it. I'm not going to date her."

"Thank you soooo much! I love you!" Shanna smacked him again with an ice cream kiss. "Cecily's so nice. You're going to have a great time."

Ruark sincerely doubted that.

Chapter Six

Ainslie bit her lip as she wrestled her vintage Dior couture gown out of its bag. Tears were threatening behind her eyelids. She loved this gown.

Purchased for a fundraiser for the Sons of the Confederacy Scholarship Fund, a quasi-fancy dress dinner dance, she'd spent over $3,000.00 for the dress. She hadn't even blinked an eye at the cost of a one of a kind, vintage Dior.

What she wouldn't give to have that money back.

"That's a beautiful color," Mimi, the owner of Sweet Dreams, the best consignment shop in the Boston area, cooed. "The fabric is almost like tissue paper."

Ainslie got the entire dress out of the bag. The color of a peacock's tail, the gown was made of silk, with a bustle that exploded tulle ruffles from the waist to a small train. The heart-shaped bodice had tulle straps over the shoulders.

The waist had been teeny tiny so Ainslie had fasted and ran her fanny off the month before the event so that she could fit into it. Even so, she had needed a pair of Spanx.

Two pairs, if she was being honest.

"It's a real Dior," Ainslie said. "My stylist was very persnickety about getting the real thing."

Mimi put both hands over her mouth, her eyes full of awe. "Hm." She walked over to her computer. "Let me check a few things. I'll be right back. Please," Mimi smiled, "have a look around."

Ainslie meandered over to the junior formals.

She didn't have to worry about examining all the dresses with a magnifying glass. Mimi only took the best to sell.

A deep purple dress caught her eye. The color was a good one for Shanna, but as she took it off the rack, she saw it was one of those trashy dresses in which the back of the dress consisted of laces which held the dress on the girl. She shoved it back into the rack.

Every dress she looked at had something wrong with it. Ainslie considered giving up, when a shiny swatch of emerald green caught her eye. She pulled it off the rack and sighed.

It took her breath away. Beads cascaded from the bodice to the bottom, in swirls of green. They caught the light in pings and pops, and played hide and seek with it. The neckline was up and straight across her shoulder bones. No sleeves, but cut modestly into an A-line, there was nothing revealing about it. The length was short, but not too short. It wouldn't ride up her baby's tushie while she danced.

The color was bold, but Shanna looked best in bold colors, deep, saturated jewel tones.

Ainslie looked at the price tag. Oh, she hoped Mimi would be generous about buying the Dior.

Maybe Mimi would put it aside until Ainslie could bring Shanna in to see it. No use in spending money if Shanna didn't like it.

Mimi came back in. "That's a great dress! I just got it last week. It's only been worn once."

"Oh, really?" No use in looking too eager, but only having been worn once was a big selling point. "Maybe you could put it aside so I could bring my Shanna in to look at it?"

Mimi took it from her. "Of course." She hung the dress on a rack behind the checkout counter. "Now about the Dior." Mimi perched the cat's eye glasses she kept on a string around her neck on her nose.

"It's a beautiful dress, and you've kept it in such great condition. It's obviously Dior. The size of it is an issue. Most of my clients run to larger sizes and alterations on this dress would be nearly impossible. I'm going to have some trouble turning it around." She grimaced. "I hate to tell you this, but I can only give you $500.00 for it."

Ainslie's stomach took a nosedive. She had so hoped for more money. "Are you sure?"

Mimi nodded. "I'm sorry. You can, of course, take it somewhere else if you think you can get more money for it."

Ainslie thought briefly about taking the dress to a museum, but they would expect her to donate it to the collection. Mimi offered the best deal she could realistically get. "I'll take it," she said, her voice heavy with misery.

"I'll write you a check." Mimi hustled to her desk and got to work, while Ainslie fingered the delicate fabric one more time.

She gave herself a big kick in her hiney. She couldn't afford to get maudlin about a dress. She'd suck it up and do what she needed for her kids. $500.00 was enough to get the green dress and some new things for Patsy, as well as new kicks for Ruark.

Besides, when Shanna saw the dress, she'd be so excited. That would make absolutely everything worth it.

****

Ruark shuffled through the kids in the school cafeteria, ready to beat feet and get out of there.

His sister sat with Cecily, who gave him a big hopeful smile. Yeah, he was so not going over there. He hadn't asked her to the Homecoming Dance yet. He hoped she'd get asked by someone else first, leaving him off the hook.

He pulled his iPod out of his pocket and fiddled with it, trying to find the playlist he wanted to listen to. He was totally into Wagner these days and was studying *Die Meistersinger von Nürnberg.*

Out of nowhere, a foot came out to trip him. He caught himself before he fell, but his iPod hit the cement floor.

Alden Bradford said, "Oops." He stomped his foot right on Ruark's iPod, smashing the screen. Ruark flinched, while Bradford's buddies surrounded him.

Crap. "No problem," he murmured as he bent to pick up his Pod.

Bradford kicked it out of his reach. Ruark stood. No way he was going to play this. "You're going to pay to replace this." Even as he said it, Ruark knew it sounded stupid.

Bradford laughed. "Whatever, faggot."

"Everything okay here?" Mr. Mason appeared out of nowhere.

"Hey, Mr. Mason." Bradford smiled a sharky smile. "Ruark here dropped his iPod. We were helping him pick it up." Bradford handed Ruark the destroyed mp3 player.

"That true, Ruark?" Mr. Mason looked him in the eyes.

Ruark's stomach hitched. "Yeah." He put the iPod into his pocket. He would never say differently, lest he get his ass kicked.

"We're going to the gym to shoot some hoops. Want to come, Ruark?" Bradford knew Ruark didn't want to shoot hoops. It was all an act for Mr. Mason. Ruark nearly rolled his eyes.

"No, thank you." Ruark just wanted to get out of there. He'd go hide out in the music room.

"Then how about you all move along." Mr. Mason said this to Bradford.

"C'mon," Bradford said to his cronies. They slithered away, like the snakes they were.

"You okay?" Looked like Mr. Mason wasn't going

to let this go.

"Sure. I'm going to Mrs. Kelly's room to work on some stuff." He started to make his getaway.

Mr. Mason stared at him hard, like he was trying to read Ruark's mind. "If you have any problems, you know you can come to me."

"Sure." Ruark crossed his fingers. "I've got to get to the music room. Mrs. Kelly is waiting for me."

Mr. Mason looked like he wanted to say more, his mouth all straightened out into a thin line. "Okay."

Ruark scampered away, tossing his dead lunch into a wastebasket. He knew where he could go.

The music room. Mrs. Kelly was totally cool. She'd let him just hang out and do homework, or go over parts and stuff. It was the closest thing to his old school he had, and he cherished it.

He pushed open the door. The sound of Schubert's *An die Musik* filled the air. Mrs. Kelly was standing beside the piano while Jessica, the student accompanist, played Schubert's beautiful *Lied*.

"Ruark! Good! I'm glad you're here." Mrs. Kelly beamed. "Jessica and I are going over this Schubert song. I think it would be great for you to sing in the New England solo competition."

"I know it." Ruark's heart pounded. "I worked on it with my teacher in Charleston."

Mrs. Kelly's face lit up. "Oh, good." She picked up the *International Edition* of Schubert's *Lieder* transposed into the lower key. Handing it to him, she said, "Do you want to go through it with Jessica?"

Oh dear Lord, he did. It had been so long since he'd sung anything besides bass parts in chorus. He took the book. "Yeah, I can do that."

"Good." She smiled. "Just let Jessica know when you're ready.

He opened to the right page and got his breathing on track, in, out, no noise, just soft cleansing air. Nodding at Jessica to start, he readied himself to sing.

He lost himself in the sheer joy of making sound. He opened up his rib cage and let the air flow into him, then turned it around so it could flow out. The sound was warm, the sensation rich. Ruark opened his mouth and sang for pure joy. He let his voice float on the air.

"Du holder Kunst, in wie viel grauen stunden, Wo mich des Lebens wilder Kreis umstricht, Hast du mein Herz zu warmer Lieb entzunden, Hast mich in einer beße Welt entrückt."

Oh, how true those words were. They expressed everything music was for him. *Beloved art, in how many gray hours where I found myself tied up in the wild circle of life, have you my heart to warmer love led, and made my world a better place.*

The song ended, and he just stood there and continued the deep, cleansing breathing. Looking up, he saw Mrs. Kelly wiping her eyes.

"That was so beautiful. Your German is very good."

He shrugged. "A lot of kids in my old school thought it's an ugly language, but I like it."

"That's wonderful." Mrs. Kelly beamed. "So will you sing this song for the solo festival?"

"Absolutely." Finally. Something to live for. "I'd love to."

****

Dave didn't quite know how he found himself in the parking lot of The End Zone. He'd just gotten in his car with every intention of picking up his laundry and dry cleaning, going home and hunkering down with some new paperwork the Commonwealth of Massachusetts demanded.

Yep! That's what Dave intended. Well, as the old

saying goes, the road to hell was paved with all that crap.

If he kept eating here every night, he was going to be blimp sized and have a heart condition.

But he was worried about Ruark and wanted to talk to Ainslie. He was only at The End Zone to talk to her so she wouldn't have to try to finagle more time off work. Being considerate of the mother's work schedule would no doubt translate into a better home situation for the child.

Yep! That was his story, and he was sticking to it.

He yanked the keys out of the ignition and got out of the car. The parking lot looked empty. Hopefully he could catch Ainslie and grab her for some conversation.

He jingled his keys. He felt pretty freakin' nervous and he didn't know why.

No, he was not nervous. He met with parents of troubled children every day. He just didn't go out of his way to meet them at their place of business. He certainly would not speculate why Ainslie and Ruark Logan were different. They weren't.

He was just doing his job. Teachers never punch a time clock.

****

Leaning against the bar, Ainslie stifled a yawn. The End Zone was dead. She reached into her apron pocket and tried to estimate how much she'd made in tips. It felt distressingly light.

While she hated when the bar was so busy and so loud she couldn't think, she hated even more being away from her children and not making any money. She should be at home, listening to Patsy rattle on about her day and making sure Shanna did her homework instead of frittering away her time on Facebook. She would give a million dollars to be there, enjoying hearing Ruark practice.

Well, Ainslie had no patience and zero tolerance for self-pity. She refused to indulge in a pity party, no matter how much her feet hurt.

The nerves on the back of her neck started to spark.

She turned around, albeit reluctantly. She didn't know whether to be thrilled or terrified to see Dave Mason come through the door.

Thrilled, because the man was more handsome than he had a right to be, or terrified, because when he looked directly at her, she felt a distinct *click*. She couldn't have pulled her gaze away from him, never mind run and hide in the kitchen, even if she wanted to.

She didn't want to.

It had to be her hormones kicking up trouble.

"Ainslie." He walked right up to her. "I wonder if you've got a minute?"

Her mouth went totally dry. "I, uh..."

Spike breezed by. "Why don't you take your break?" She put a frosty Sam Adams down in front of Dave. "I can cover your tables."

Ainslie looked over at the two deuces in her section. Everyone had their food and just needed maybe a refill and a check. "If you're sure it's okay."

Spike nodded. "I do." Looking at Dave, she grabbed a dupe pad. "Do you want anything to eat?"

"Yeah, sure." He frowned as his stomach growled. "Does Bobby have fish and chips on the menu tonight?"

"For you, sure. Haddock or sole?" Spike asked.

"Haddock." Dave cleared his throat, focused those amazing blue eyes of his back on Ainslie. "It's about Ruark and something that happened at school today."

Ainslie's heart gave three big, painful thumps. She rubbed the heel of her hand just above where her chest hurt. "Is he in trouble?"

"Not with me. Listen," he said, as he looked around. "Let's just go someplace quiet where we can talk."

"Why don't you go into the break room?" Spike suggested, sympathy in her gaze. "It's quiet, and you'll have tons of privacy. Shush." Spike put her finger in front of her mouth. "Just go. I'll watch your tables." Spike nodded at Dave. "I'll bring your food to the break room."

Ainslie didn't have to be told twice. Tables be damned. Ruark was in trouble, and she needed to do something about it. "Come on," she told Dave.

She pushed open the kitchen door, feeling Dave's presence behind her. Her stomach fluttered, but whether because of her baby's trouble or his school principal's presence behind her, she didn't know.

Probably both. She gave herself a mental slap across the face. Ruark was in trouble. She had no business lusting after his principal, no matter how drop dead gorgeous he looked.

He smelled really good, too. Ralph Lauren's *Polo* if she didn't miss her guess.

She nodded to Bobby as she tromped through the kitchen. "I'm taking a break. Dave and I are going to talk in the break room."

Bobby nodded like he was used to her giving orders. "You need to eat something. What do you want?"

"Not hungry, but thank you." Ainslie couldn't eat a bite.

Bobby pulled a basket of fries out of the deep fryer. "Wrong answer. Never mind. I'll take care of it."

"Thanks, Bobby." Ainslie stopped and looked back at Dave. "We can talk in here."

Chapter Seven

Dave followed Ainslie into the break room. It was certainly a side of The End Zone that he'd never seen before.

One thing was for sure—Bobby was not going to win any prizes for interior decorating. The room was tiny, with institutional green walls plastered with memos to the help, held up by yellowing pieces of scotch tape. A small table was off to one corner, a refugee from a 50's era garage sale, with wobbly aluminum legs and a discolored, black flecked, cracked Formica top. The vinyl on the chairs was full of holes and bits of foam rubber poked out of them.

Ainslie dropped her cute little bottom down onto one of those chairs. She sighed. "So, tell me about my baby boy."

He much preferred the way she looked at him when he first came into the bar.

What was that about?

Oh, hell, he had to get over this crazy pull he felt toward her. He wasn't there to check out her amazing ass, or stare into her beautiful eyes. He was there to talk to her about her kid.

So he took a deep breath and sat down on one of those decrepit chairs. "Look, I don't want to add to your burden, but I..."

"My children are not a burden." She looked pale, but there was steel in her voice.

"I never said they were. Children are a gift. I love them, and if I didn't, I'm really in the wrong line of work." He softened his tone. "You have great kids. My job is to help." He reached his hand across the table and put it over her fragile looking hand. It was so cold. "We're a team, whether you like it or not."

A gust of air left her, leaving her looking more alone than ever. "My children are my life." She pulled her hand out of his and put it in her lap.

"Trust me, I believe you. If I didn't, I'd be talking to social services instead of being here."

She dropped her head into her hands. He watched her with a sinking feeling. "Please don't cry. I'm not going to call social services. You're a good mom."

"Dave, please." Ainslie shook her head. "What happened today?"

She looked sad. A blunt, simple word, but all encompassing. "I think he's getting bullied. He's obviously miserable."

Her eyes widened and flashed with anger. "Who's doing this?"

"That's what I need you to find out."

"He's a sensitive boy." Her mouth flattened into a straight line.

"That's clear. There're more than a few girls crushing on him, so that's going to make more than one classroom Casanova jealous."

She laughed. It sounded like liquid gold. "Classroom Casanova?"

"You know what I mean."

Bobby took that moment to come in, bearing fish and chips and Chicken Alfredo. "Soup's on!"

Dave smiled. "This looks great." The fish looked fresh, the beer batter a golden brown. He couldn't wait.

Ainslie frowned at the pasta. "I can't possibly eat that."

Bobby didn't care. He dropped it down in front of her. "Eat what you can. I've got a bunch of wings I made by mistake. They're in a bag in the cooler. Pick 'em up on your way out."

Ainslie raised her eyebrows. *Eau de distress* wafted off her in waves. "I haven't finished my shift."

"We're slow tonight. After you're done with Dave here, you should punch out and go home."

"Bobby, I need..."

"You need to go home." Bobby was formidable when he wanted to get his way. He handed her a couple of fives. "Here're the tips from your last two tables. Punch out, and check in with your kids." He smiled one of Bobby's frightening smiles, the real toothy one designed to make alligators swim away in fear. "You're no good while you're worrying. We're dead tonight and not gonna get busy. Go home." He moved back toward the kitchen. "Don't forget the wings." Bobby left.

After an eternity of uncomfortable silence, Dave poked his fish with his fork. "Looks good."

Ainslie pushed the plate of pasta away from her. "So, tell me about my boy."

No sugar coating it for this mom. Dave drew his courage to the sticking point. "I didn't get there in time, but I definitely interrupted Ruark getting harassed by some other kids." Dave sprinkled too much salt on his fries. "I think you should ask about his iPod when you get home."

"Oh, no, not his iPod. He loves that thing." Her voice quivered, most likely in distress. "It's old and doesn't do the games and videos, but it's his most precious possession." She shook her head. "If you're so sure about it, why can't you go to the other children's parents and get them to replace it?"

"Yeah. You'd think I could do that. But I got there too late to see how it really went down." Dave rubbed his chin. "These kids have mad skillz, as they say. And Ruark was really tight-lipped about the whole thing. Which is where you come in."

She swung her head, clearly mourning. "I barely see my baby these days, never mind have a meaningful conversation with him." She stabbed her fork into the pasta, mushing it all up. "I hate this. I used to know the family tree of each and every one of his friends. I even knew the pedigree of their dogs."

"I can help you with that. Be a chaperone for the Homecoming Dance. You can be my date." The words flew out of his mouth before he could stop them.

She goggled at him. "Your date?" she squeaked.

"So to speak." But the more he thought about it, the more the idea appealed to him, the more *she* appealed to him. "I need chaperones, you need to meet his friends and some of the other parents."

"I'd need to get the time off. When is it?" Ainslie bit her lip. "I don't even know if Ruark is going. Shanna is, but Ruark hasn't said a peep."

"You could meet Shanna's friends too. It's a win-win situation." Why did he suddenly feel so desperate to get her to help chaperone that dance with him?

"It wouldn't really be a date, right?" Ainslie pocketed the money Bobby had put on the table, then stood. She looked at him with those amazing brown eyes. Fringed by long, dark lashes, they were wide and wary.

He supposed he couldn't blame her.

"Well, no, not really." Dave stood and nearly sent his chair flying behind him. His hands felt like they were six sizes too big and covered with thick, wet woolen mittens.

Her eyes widened, something he didn't think possible, at the crash of the chair. She caught her generous, lush lower lip one more time between her teeth.

From zero to sixty, just like that, he got a lead pipe hard erection. He wanted, *needed* to kiss her. He took a deep breath and held it. Not trusting himself, he busied himself with righting the chair he'd toppled.

59

It took several tries, and the whole time all Ainslie did was stare at him with those incredible eyes and that *come get me* mouth.

Something inside him snapped with a sharp *thwang*. He moved around the table and lifted her chin with his right index finger. "I'm gonna go to hell for this," he whispered. Then he kissed her.

And kissed her.

And kissed her some more.

Her lips softened under his, so he pulled back ever so slightly, to tease her, to make her want to chase him. She did, parting her beautiful lips, an invitation on a rose velvet pillow for his tongue to come in and feast.

Not being a stupid man, he did just that. He used the tip of his tongue to tease her mouth more open. She sighed and settled into his arms.

She fit like she was made for his embrace. His aching arms closed around her. "Mm," she hummed as she laced her arms around his neck. Crushing her breasts against his chest, she made him feel like Superman.

"Hey Ainslie! I wonder if..."

Ainslie tore her mouth away from Dave's and jumped two feet backward. "Oh my God." She slapped a hand over her mouth.

Chelsea stood there like a pig poisoned, her jaw slack and hanging open. "Um, hey, Ainslie. I, uh, wanted to know if you can trade shifts tomorrow."

"I've got to go." Ainslie pushed her way out of the break room. She ran as if the devil was lighting matches under her feet.

Dave started to follow her, but Chelsea got in his way, so he had a hard time getting around her. She stood there looking at him with clear disapproval on her face.

"Excuse me," he said as he dodged left.

"Sure." She crossed her arms under her breasts.

She didn't break any speed records getting out of his way.

He couldn't worry about that. He had a woman to chase.

Chapter Eight

Ainslie still trembled when she pulled into the driveway of the tiny house she rented. She took a minute and rested her forehead against the steering wheel.

Dear Lord, she'd kissed her children's principal. What kind of mother was she?

A horny one.

Christ on a cracker, she had to pull herself together, focus on her children, and not men who were too handsome by half and could win the world's best kisser award, hands down.

Of course, it had been a very long time since she'd been involved in recreational smoochage.

A very long, long time.

The children had left the porch light on, as usual. She felt a huge surge of love, all warm and gooey, run through her just thinking about them. It about took her breath away. She smiled as she opened her front door.

The smile disappeared as soon as she got inside. Shanna held a sobbing Patsy in her arms. Shanna also had tears in her eyes and was white as a sheet. Ruark's jaw clenched tight, and his eyes sparked with anger.

"What's going on?" Ainslie dropped her purse and went over to Patsy and Shanna.

Patsy flung herself into her mother's arms. "The man on Youtube said our daddy is a crook," she wailed.

"Shh, baby, shh." Ainslie rubbed her cheek over the top of her little girl's head. "What man?"

"Camilla Jackson sent me a link to a video." Shanna swabbed tears out of her eyes. Camilla had been Shanna's enemy since their junior high days. "She's so mean. It had a bunch of people who gave money to daddy's company."

"The people he stole from, you mean," Ruark snapped.

Shanna wiped her nose with her sleeve. "It had pictures of us too."

Tears threatened to spill out of her eyes. Ainslie refused to let them fall. She needed to be strong for her babies. "How did Patsy see it?"

"She looked over my shoulder at the computer. I didn't mean for her to see it." Shanna looked down at her feet."

Patsy engaged in a fresh, feverish bout of weeping.

"Hush, baby." Ainslie hugged Patsy tighter as she looked at Ruark. "Can you please dial it down until I get your sister calm?"

"Whatever." He turned his back to her and stalked out of the room, toward the kitchen.

"They called him a thief and wished that he got the death penalty for taking all those people's money." Shanna sniffed. "They showed pictures of him in prison. He looks like a million years old. And now, all the kids at school are gonna know about him." She flopped down on the couch. "You promised if we moved up here where no one knew us everything would be okay. But nothing's okay."

"Oh, sweetie." Ainslie's heart shattered into a million pieces.

"I hate him." Blunt and to the point, Shanna frowned and swiped at moisture in her eyes again. "I wish I'd never been born," she snarfled.

"Oh, baby, no!" Ainslie put Patsy down, sat next to Shanna and threw her arms around her. "I would be so sad if you weren't here."

"Oh, Momma!" Shanna burst into tears, a full blown, gasping, snotty mess.

Patsy reached over and rubbed Shanna's back with a tentative hand. Ainslie smiled at her. She had never been so proud of her little baby girl.

The three of them sat on the sofa, clutched to each other, crying and comforting. At that moment, not only did Ruark come out of the kitchen, sandwich in hand, but the doorbell clanged. "I'll get it," he said, shaking his head, most likely at the three teary females in his life.

Ainslie gifted him with a wet and grateful smile.

****

Ruark shuffled to the door. No one ever visited them. They had no social life at all. His life sucked, sucked, suckedity, sucked, sucked. Damn, what he wouldn't give to open the door and have Prince Charming there, with his white stallion, ready to take him away from all this bullcrap.

He opened the door only to find the man of his dreams on the other side. Speak of the devil. "Mr. Mason," he stammered. His voice broke, just like it had when it was changing. His face heated up.

"Hey, Ruark. Is your mom home yet?" Mr. Mason looked a little shy. He held up a plastic bag holding take out containers.

He still smelled good, though.

Without a tie, and with his shirt unbuttoned a couple of buttons, he was rumpled and adorable. He was also looking past Ruark to where the females in his life were a veritable water works.

"Uh, yeah. She just got home." Ruark eyed the take out bag. It smelled and looked like Bobby's chicken wings. His stomach growled. Bobby's wings were made of awesome.

Mr. Mason must have heard his stomach. "Bobby made too many wings by mistake. Your mom forgot to take them when she left." He held the bag out to Ruark.

Ruark grinned as he took the bag. "He does that a lot."

His mom came to the door. "Mr. Mason, thank you for remembering the wings. Ruark, darlin,' Can you take these into the kitchen before they go all cold?" She held her head high, even though she was blushing.

"Sure." Ruark's throat closed up tight, so he had trouble swallowing. His feet felt like lead boots. "G'night, Mr. Mason."

Mr. Mason was staring at his mom. It was pretty intense.

"Good night, Ruark." He finally looked at Ruark and smiled. "Enjoy those wings."

Momma pulled the door almost shut.

As if he could enjoy anything right now. He hightailed it into the kitchen.

The wings didn't smell so good anymore.

****

"Thank you for bringing the wings, Mr. Mason."

"No problem, Mrs. Logan." He cleared his throat and looked at his feet. "We've got some things to talk about."

"No, we don't." The proof of that was in her house, miserable and needing her.

"I don't regret kissing you." Dave took hold of her hands. Warm, strong and reassuring, she couldn't have let go, even if she'd wanted to.

She didn't want to.

"I want to kiss you again." He gently pulled her in toward him. Dipping his forehead to gently rest on hers, he murmured, "And you want to kiss me again too."

Lord have mercy, she did want to kiss him again. It'd been so long, she'd forgotten long, slow, sweet kisses existed.

Something unfurled in her body, forgotten and

rusty, in hibernation for too long a time. It swamped her, set every nerve in her body to tingling.

Dave touched his lips to her forehead, the tip of her nose, the sensitive spot behind her ear. How had he known how much she liked that?

His eyes locked with hers. Caught in a dream, she lifted her mouth to his and let him lead the way.

The minute his lips met hers, everything went blank. Nothing mattered except kissing Dave Mason. He seemed to know every single, amazing thing that pleased her. His tongue tickled her lips, and she opened up and let him in. Every nerve sizzled.

He broke off the kiss and rested his cheek against the top of her head again. His breathing was ragged. "We're going to have to deal with this," he whispered.

"Yeah," she managed to make her voice work. "The kids are in crisis mode, so I've—I've got to go be a mom."

Dave's eyes glittered like two cobalt balls, hungry and full of lust. "You're a good mom." He touched her cheek.

Breathe, Ainslie, breathe. "I don't feel that way."

"Well, I see all kinds of moms every day, and I know a good mom when I see one." He brought her hand up to his mouth and tucked a kiss into her palm. "We're not done, not by a long shot." He gave her a hot look. "I can be very persuasive when I want to." He kissed her forehead. "Good night."

And off he went, jauntily whistling *Dixie*.

She turned to go into her house, her legs as wobbly as a newborn colt's. Taking a cleansing breath before going in to deal with her babies, she realized that Dave Mason was a dangerous man.

She opened the door and heard Patsy sobbing quietly into Shanna's arms. Ruark was standing by the window, all pale and stiff.

They'd gone through so much. Her heart broke for them.

Pangs of regret pinched her.

She couldn't afford a dangerous man. She had to focus on her family.

Chapter Nine

"So, want to tell me what happened in school yesterday?" Ainslie dropped a slice of raisin bread into the toaster. The scent of cinnamon filled her tiny kitchen. It was the best way to get Patsy down to breakfast.

Ruark was the only one of her children in the kitchen at the moment. He intensely studied the cereal in his bowl, ignoring Ainslie completely. She dropped a hand on his shoulder, frowning when he flinched.

"Ruark, honey, I know something happened because Mr. Mason came to The End Zone last night to tell me so."

Ruark glanced up at that. His eyes were bright and icy. "Nothing happened."

"That's not what Mr. Mason said. He told me that he thinks somebody destroyed your iPod." Her right foot beat out her frustrated impatience.

His mouth tightened into a little line. He looked so much like his daddy. "I'm sure."

Okay, she was going to have to do this the hard way. "So, you won't mind letting me see your iPod, so I can see for myself."

He stood. "It's in my locker at school."

"Make sure you bring it home, then."

"Whatever. I gotta go." With that, he was gone, *poof*, like trace of smoke.

It wasn't like him to be so cold toward her. She prided herself in being open, for having her kids talk to her. In this case, her boy was downright rude to her.

And that wasn't like him. She raised him to be polite, a true southern gentleman. An honest kid, not like his thief of a daddy.

Of course, he no doubt had bad feelings about Bobby Lee. Who wants a daddy who's a crook? She didn't blame him. She herself had bad feelings toward Bobby Lee. The video sent to Shanna just brought those emotions back.

Poor kid. She had to put him first and foremost. Ruark was a sensitive kid, an artist, and he felt things deeper than most people.

****

Dave decided he had to be very visible in the cafeteria during Ruark's lunch period. Finding out what was happening with him had become a personal quest.

It didn't take a Ph.D. to figure out why. He was falling in love with Ruark's mother.

He'd been waiting all his life to fall in love. So far, he'd failed spectacularly at it. He'd learned the hard way to not date anyone he worked with. Things hadn't ended well with math teacher Laura Plunkett. It was difficult for her and he felt sorry for that. However, he'd been doing both of them a favor when he'd ended it.

He was where he wanted to be career-wise. He loved kids, he loved being a principal. All he needed now was a woman to fall in love with.

To start a family with.

Just at that particular moment, Shanna Logan walked by with some of the cheerleaders, dressed in their uniforms for the pep rally that afternoon. She was laughing, quite a different state from last night.

A beautiful girl, she would grow into an amazing woman, resilient and strong. He could imagine Ainslie like that, full of life and promise.

Out of the corner of his eye, he caught Ruark scurrying out of the cafeteria. The boy glanced

Dave's way, scowled, and moved out of the room faster.

Curious, Dave made a circuit around the lunchroom and down the hall of the performing arts wing of the school to the music room. He peeked through the window of the door to see Ruark laughing at something Andi said.

Well, that was good, wasn't it?

"Hey, you checking out my woman?" Mike appeared out of nowhere and punched Dave in the arm.

Dave chuckled. "You wouldn't have had a chance with her if I'd turned on the charm."

Rubbing his jaw, Mike snorted. "Ah, the notorious Mason charm. Heard you were turning it on big time in the break room at The End Zone."

"News travels fast." Dave knew exactly who was spreading the word—Chelsea Adams. "Never thought you'd be gossiping with your student teacher."

"You know I never gossip. She was telling the other student teacher, and made sure she talked loud enough for me to hear." Mike shook his head. "What the hell were you doing playing tonsil hockey with Ainslie Logan?"

"None of your damn business."

"Just two weeks ago, the sight of her made you crazy, and by crazy I mean the bad kind."

"Two weeks ago, I didn't know a thing about her. Now I do, and I want to know more."

"She's not your usual type. For one thing, she's older. Then, there's the kids."

"Bite me," Dave said, "I happen to like kids."

"Apparently. Well, you should probably find another place to hook up, one that's not Bobby's break room. Not a whole lot of privacy there, bro."

"Good point."

Mike went into the music room.

After one last glance to check how Ruark was doing, Dave went back to patrol the cafeteria. Why did falling in love have to be so complicated?

****

Ainslie pondered over Ruark and his problems all afternoon. Her head hurt from thinking about it. It clouded over her thoughts nearly as much as remembering kissing Dave Mason the night before.

What in the world had she been thinking?

Clearly, she was letting her hormones do the thinking for her. That was never a wise choice.

She busied herself with filling saltshakers. It made for an interesting task, as she couldn't help but hear the conversations at tables nearby.

She dearly hoped Dave Mason didn't show up at the bar tonight, although she wanted to hear about Ruark's day in school.

Speaking of which, one of the nearby tables was filled with Dave's friends, Gina and Ian Ross, as well as Andi Kelly. Maybe she could get info about Ruark from her.

"Hey, Ainslie!" Gina smiled at her. "How's it going?"

"Pretty good." She screwed the top off the saltshaker.

Andi and Ian were engrossed in a conversation. Well, at least Andi was. Ian took notes while she talked.

"Don't mind them." Gina waved a hand. "They're brainstorming ideas for this year's Ballet Guild fundraiser.

"Really?" Ainslie felt a smile grow across her face. In her old life, she was the queen of organizing fundraisers.

Andi glanced at her, brows furrowed across her forehead. "Hi, Ainslie." She blew out a breath. "We want to do something different this year, but nothing really tickles my fancy."

"What do you have?" Ainslie nodded to Ian's list.

Ian handed it to her. "It's pretty pitiful. We usually have a gala dinner dance with an auction, but we've noticed a drop in attendance."

"You could just tweak that idea a little. I was on the board of the Charleston Opera Theater, and we had great success with what we called the 'Mirror, Mirror on the Wall Ball.'"

"Ooh," Andi crooned. "What was that?"

"We put out a call for local artists to design one of kind mirrors and put them up on the walls. We made it a fairy tale theme, because there're so many operas based on fairy tales. People came dressed as their favorite fairy tale or mythological character." Ainslie had gone as Cinderella's fairy godmother. She'd had so much fun.

Bobby Lee had gone as the wolf from *Little Red Riding Hood*. It had fit him to a "T." "As people mingled, they bid silently on the mirrors on the wall. We made a mint."

"Omigod!" Gina grinned. "This sounds like something *I'd* have fun at." She pointed at Ian. "Make it happen."

Ian took his glasses off and cleaned them with his tie. "It sounds intriguing."

"Oh, pooh. It sounds great, doesn't it Andi?" Gina turned to a higher power.

"I think it sounds fabulous!" Andi chuffed a laugh. "We could even use the fairy tale theme, because there are lots of ballets built on fairy tales. Maybe expand it to include legendary lovers, or something like that." She looked at Ainslie. "Can we steal it?"

"Of course. I wouldn't even mind helping planning it, if you wanted help." Ainslie mentally crossed her fingers. She so missed her charitable work.

"The rest of the Board will have to vote on this."

Ian tapped a finger on the table.

Gina laughed as she punched him in the shoulder. "You just don't want to have to wear a costume. It's beneath your dignity and all that *stiff upper lippiness* you put on."

"I just don't enjoy a fancy dress ball," Ian bristled.

"Oh, you're so cute when you're pompous." She leaned over and gave him a brief kiss on his mouth. "We have to fix that." She snapped her fingers. "I know! You can go as Grumpy the Dwarf."

"I am not dressing up like a dwarf," he grumbled.

"No?" she asked. "How about going in drag as Little Red Riding Hood?"

"Not on your best day." Ian said, but his eyes twinkled.

Ainslie listen to them chatter and tease each other. Left out, even though the Mirror Ball idea came from her, she went off to fill more saltshakers. An acidy little sphere of dejectedness churned and rolled around in her stomach. She bit her lip.

A cool hand touched her shoulder. Andi Kelly smiled at her. "Are you sure you want to be on the planning committee?"

More than almost anything in the world. "Of course." That scratchy ol' ball in her belly unraveled.

"It's a great idea," Andi said. "Thanks for being willing to be on the committee. May I e-mail you to give you planning meeting dates and such?"

"Absolutely," Ainslie said. "I'm glad I can help." She smiled at Andi.

"We've been needing a shot in the arm. The committee has blinders on when it comes to thinking outside the box. You'll be a great addition to the group."

"Well, I don't know about that." Ainslie shrugged and put the salt carton back in the wait station. "I'll be glad to meet new people and do some good." That was so true.

"Trust me," Andi snorted gently. "You're going to be just what the ballet board needs."

The acid ball started to whirl again. "I don't think I can join the board. I don't have the wherewithal to donate anything but time."

"No worries. Your time and ideas are worth more than a monetary donation." Andi looked at her watch. "I've got to go. Here, let me give you my card. Can you write your e-mail on the back of it?"

"Sure." Ainslie took the crisp rectangle from her and pulled a pencil from her apron pocket.

Andi took it back from her and smiled. "I've got to go so I'm not late for a rehearsal. You'll be hearing from me!" With a quick wave, she was gone, leaving Ainslie staring at the door.

Finally! A bright spot in this twilight zone her life had become. A chance to claim some of her old life back. One thing she could do is plan events that made a lot of money.

She wondered if Dave Mason had anything to do with the ballet. Probably not. She *really* needed to stop thinking about the man.

What she couldn't figure out was whether Dave Mason was a bright spot or just one more complication to drag her down.

She placed her finger tips on her mouth. He definitely brought one part of her back to the land of the living. The man sure could kiss.

She wanted to kiss him again, to run her hands over his sure-to-be excellent body and explore every muscle and ridge up close and personal.

Shivering, she shoved those delicious, scandalous thoughts to the back of her mind. She was not a too young, too naïve Miss South Carolina, fooled by a handsome face and a hot body.

No matter how tempted she was.

Chapter Ten

"Mm-mm. I am *so* going to get a piece of that." Alden Bradford, a.k.a. Butt-munch, let his intentions known to his buddies about his next victim, his voice set to creepy. "She *is* prime."

Ruark did his best to ignore Bradford and his buddies. It was especially hard, since his locker was in the Phys. Ed wing.

The way to the gym was full of kids dressed all up in school spirit crap. Pep rallies were mandatory. It would be the first one he'd ever gone to.

Rah-rah.

The football team wore its team jerseys, though they looked a little small without the shoulder pads, sort of like what his sister looked like back in the day when she was dressing up in their mom's clothes. The cheerleaders also wore their uniforms, and other kids had decked themselves out in green and white, some with the Addington Minute Men logo on them.

Someone hand him a barf bag. Please.

Sports were supposed to build character, right? Not give cretins *carte blanche* to disrespect women and girls.

"Hey, Shanna," Alden said.

Shanna? *Shanna*? As in Ruark's twin sister Shanna? That jerk better not be going after her.

"Hey, Alden."

Ruark heard a very familiar voice. Damn. He knew Shanna's voice better than anyone else's in this world. Dread radiated through him, from the tips of his toes to the tips of his ears.

A realization reached out and whomped Ruark upside the head. Shanna was the girl Alden hoped to get a piece of.

Not if Ruark had anything to say about it. He pushed his locker door shut. "Hey, Shanna."

She turned to look at him, murder in her eyes. "Ruark. What?"

"Am I picking up Patsy, or are you?"

Shanna rolled her eyes. "*You* are." The word *doofus* was implied. "You can't bail on me, not today."

"I wasn't going to bail." Although he would if it would get her away from Alden, he'd bail, big time.

Alden threw his arm over Shanna's shoulders and hauled her close to him. "Shanna," he said with a smirk, "want to tell your brother who's the lucky guy taking you to the Homecoming Dance?"

No freakin' way. No, no, no, no, no. He was not letting his sister go anywhere with Alden Bradford.

"Hey, Ruark!" Cecily bounced up to him. She was just as perky as Shanna was, decked out in her Minuteman cheering uniform, just as cute.

Just as air-headed. Just as clueless.

"Hey, Cecily," Ruark answered as a plan took shape in his mind. "I've been trying to run into you. Has anyone asked you to the Dance yet?"

"No." Her voice held a hint of breathlessness, her face turned a pretty shade of pink.

Ruark grimaced inside. He would do whatever he had to, to keep Shanna out of Alden Bradford's slimy grasp. "Would you like to go to the dance with me?"

"I'd love to!" Cecily just vibrated with excitement.

What did he just do?

Glancing at Shanna, he saw her grin. She should smile. He did what she'd been begging him to do for awhile.

It was worth it to see the look on Bradford's face. *Choke on it, butt-face.* "Maybe we can all go together."

Shanna and Cecily squealed. "That would be so much fun!"

Alden grunted. It wasn't a pretty sound.

Shanna just glowed with happiness.

The things Ruark'd do for his sister.

"We can get ready at my house," Cecily trilled. "My mother came back from a Manhattan business trip and brought me some fun new make up from Sephora."

Ruark watched a little panic come from his sister. No one else would have seen her reaction.

But he knew. Shanna loved Sephora. She'd made her stash last as long as she could, because there'd be no replacing it once it was gone. A lot of it was getting dried out. Shanna was not a "maybe it's Maybelline" type of girl.

Another cheerleader came up to them. Raurk couldn't be bothered to learn her name. Except for Shanna, they all looked alike. "Hey! Where have you been? Coach wants us down in the gym now."

"See you later." Shanna waved as she and Cecily bopped off with the other girl.

Raurk watched them go, a feeling of relief because his sister was safe for the moment. At least she was until he told her what he'd overheard. She'd see reason. Maybe.

"Think you're all that, asshole?" Alden sure didn't sound like a very happy camper.

Which made Ruark feel all warm and toasty inside. "No," *Uh, yes, that would be a ten-four, buddy.*

Alden got all up in Ruark's face. "Better watch your back."

He watched Alden and his no-neck buddies lumber off, one of them flipping Ruark off as he went.

Burn! Except, not so much.

What he had to do was get Shanna to see the light.

Sh'yeah. Easier said than done. She was more stubborn than a pit bull.

****

"Hey, Dave," Spike greeted him with a smile. "What can I getcha for? Sam Adams?"

Dave slid onto a barstool while he tossed his keys next to a bowl of pretzels. "Yeah, thanks." He popped some of the salty goodness into his mouth. "Ainslie around?"

Spike opened Dave's beer and put it on the bar in front of him. She raised and lowered her eyebrows. "Ainslie, huh?"

"Yep." He knew Spike. The less he said, the better off he'd be.

"She's not on tonight. Do you want any food to go with that beer?"

"Sure." He tapped his finger on the bar, a rapid beat that reflected the rhythm of his heart. He was thirty-four, not twelve. He had no reason to feel so nervous about a woman. "A Daveburger sounds good."

"Coming up." Spike grinned at him. "Rumor has it you asked Ainslie to the Homecoming Dance. That's so cute! Are you gonna get your dad to give you the keys to the car?"

Aww, crap. Cute. That's all he needed. "Very funny. I needed another chaperone for the dance, she wants to meet the kids *her* kids are hanging out with." He shrugged. "It's a win-win."

She laughed. "Yeah, and you didn't ask her so you could spend time with her. That would have nothing to do with how much time you're spending *here.*" She rapped her knuckles three times on the bar and shook her head. "The Tooth Fairy will be

78

right out with your food, Sunshine." She loped off to the kitchen.

Okay, he was spending a lot of extra time at The End Zone. It had nothing to do with seeing Ainslie. Nope! He loved the food and didn't have much time to use his kitchen skills.

Although if this kept up, his cholesterol was going to be off the charts. He needed to dial back on the fried food.

Spike came back, still chuckling. "Ready for another beer?"

Picking up the bottle and swirling the inside contents, he shook his head. "Not yet. I'm good. Hey!" He might as well put it all out there. "Do you think you could let me know what her nights off are?"

Spike frowned. "I don't know. Her nights with her kids are real sacred to her."

"Please?" he wheedled. "I'd really like to get to know her, you know, take her out, stuff like that."

Spike stared at him. "Stuff, huh?" She *so* wasn't going to let him off the hook. "What girl in her right mind would give up the chance to go do *stuff* with you?" She laughed. "'Kay, Prince Charming. Be right back."

It didn't take long for Spike to come skipping back with information and Dave's burger in her hands. "She's off on Wednesday. Other than that, the only other night she's got open is the night of the dance." She dropped the burger in front of Dave, then pulled out ketchup and mustard bottles which she slapped down in front of him. "Whatcha gonna do?"

Dave cleared his throat while he opened the ketchup bottle. "I thought dinner would be a good place to start."

"Works for me. Where to?"

"Aren't we nosy tonight?"

"Yeppers! I want all the gory details." Spike laughed. "Take her to Hope Monahan's and ask to sit in the tavern. It's all romantic-like in there, especially if you can get a table near the fireplace."

"Yes, Ma'am." Dave saluted. Spike was right. The tavern at Hope's was as romantic a place as you could want. He tweaked Spike's nose. "When did you go all mushy?"

"When the big guy back there in the kitchen finally opened his eyes and saw the best thing that'd ever happened to him." Spike had a big thing going on with Bobby. It made both of them way more mellow, now that they'd hooked up. She looked real hard at Dave. "Here's her land-line number. Why don't you call her now?"

"Like this minute?" Dave felt a slight hitch in his breathing.

"No, twenty years from now when you're both old and decrepit and think a fierce game of Bingo is just barely more exciting than checking out the early bird specials at Friendly's™." She shook her head. "If you don't have your phone on you, you can use our landline." She pulled a phone out from under the counter. "No time like the present." She leaned against the bar, put her elbows on it, and cradled her chin in her palms.

****

"I got it," Patsy yelled as she sprinted from her spot in front of the TV to the phone in the kitchen.

"Turn a little to the right," Ainslie murmured as she punched another straight pin into the hem of Shanna's Homecoming Dance dress. Fortunately, for all concerned, Shanna loved the dress from Sweet Dreams. It just needed a little bit of hemming. Ainslie had conceded to Shanna's desire to have the dress a little bit shorter. A half inch made all the difference. Short enough to make Shanna happy, long enough to make Momma happy.

"Mo-omma! Phone's for you!" Patsy bellowed from the other room.

Ainslie frowned. "Who is it?" Dread pooled in her stomach. She never got phone calls unless there was an emergency. Please don't let it be Bobby Lee calling from prison.

"I don't know!" Patsy turned back to the phone and made her voice all sugary sweet. "Who may I say is calling?"

Ainslie sighed. At least Patsy was remembering *some* of her phone manners.

"It's a man. He says he's Dave Mason."

Shanna gasped. "Why is the principal calling?"

Ainslie moved to a standing position, cracking and popping joints as she unrolled herself. "I just have to go find out."

Patsy handed the phone to Ainslie then danced into the living room. "Bet you're in trouble." She smirked at her older brother and sister.

"Not me," Shanna retorted. "It has to be Ruark."

"No way." Ruark slumped back into the pillows of the couch, pointed the remote at the TV and flipped by channel after channel.

Ainslie took a second to catch her breath. She finger combed her hair, even though Dave couldn't see her over the phone. Why did this man make her so nervous? "Hello?"

"Hi, Ainslie, it's Dave."

"So Patsy told me." She bit her lower lip. "Is there some sort of problem?"

He chuckled. "I hope not. I'd like to ask you to dinner Wednesday night."

What? "I don't think I can. It's one of my few nights off with my children." She smashed her eyebrows together. "How do you know I have Wednesday night off?"

"I went to The End Zone and begged Spike. She thinks it would be a good idea for you to have dinner with me."

"Oh, really?" Someone needed to have a talk with Spike.

"It would really be nice to know something about you before we chaperone that dance. Less awkward and all that. I could have you home again real early."

"Hm." At a loss for something to say, Ainslie's heart did a big ol' belly flop. If it weren't for the children, she'd say yes in a New York minute.

"Please? I do promise I'll have you home early so you don't spend too much of your family time with me." He cleared his throat. "I wish more of my parents believed in family time."

Oh, no. That wasn't playing fair. "If you're sure you won't mind an early night, then yes, I'll go to dinner with you." She said it before she talked herself out of it. It had been so long since she'd spent time with a handsome man who made her hormones sing out "Hallelujah!"

"Great! How about I pick you up at six?"

"Six is perfect."

"Okay, then. I'll see you Wednesday. Enjoy the rest of your evening."

"Sure. Good night."

The phone clicked as Dave hung up. Ainslie cradled the receiver between her breasts, partially to slow her heart down.

She gathered her wits and moved back to the living room to finish pinning Shanna's dress. *Keep things normal.* If she didn't act like it was a big deal, the kids would be okay with it.

Three intense faces greeted her.

"What did Mr. Mason want?" Ruark re-focused all his attention back on the TV.

"Nothing bad, sweetie." She sighed. "You know how I'm chaperoning the dance on Saturday. Mr. Mason just wants to take me to dinner to discuss it."

"Dinner?" Shanna's eyes got as big as Frisbees.

"You're going out to dinner with the principal of the school? Way to go, Momma! He's *soooo* hot for an old guy!" Her voice squeaked a little at the end.

Oh, Sweet Baby Jesus in a Manger. "Yes. And I won't lie to you. It is a date. A casual date, nothing special."

Ruark turned up the volume on the TV.

Patsy stuck her thumb in her mouth. Ainslie's heart sank. She'd stopped sucking her thumb when she was four. She began to do it again when Bobby Lee went to jail. She hadn't done it since the move north.

"It'll be okay, baby." Ainslie sat down beside her little girl, pulled her onto her lap and stroked her soft, buttercup yellow hair. "It'll be just fine. Ruark and Shanna will be here to take care of you, and you'll have fun. I'll even order a take out pizza for y'all."

Take out pizza had been unheard of since Bobby Lee's arrest. Ainslie simply couldn't afford it. It was a bribe through and through, but Ainslie wasn't going to let guilt stop her. She really *did* want to have dinner with Dave Mason. She wanted to very much.

The thumb stayed planted firmly in Patsy's mouth. Ruark's gaze lazered on the TV. Shanna said, "Real pizza?"

"'Course, baby." Shanna was the easiest of her children to bribe. "It'll be fun. Won't it be fun, Patsy?"

Patsy, taking a cue from Shanna, nodded.

"Okay, now. Why don't you go on and get ready for bed." She let Patsy slip from her lap. To Shanna she said, "Come on back over here so we can finish pinning up your hem. It's such a pretty dress, and you look so pretty in it."

Ruark got up. Shutting off the TV, he tossed the remote onto the couch. "I'm going to bed."

Doreen Alsen

"Well, sure, sugar. Sweet dreams." Ainslie angled her cheek for her bedtime kiss. It didn't come.

She let it go. He was a young man now, not a boy. He probably needed some space.

"Momma?" Shanna ran her hands down the emerald satin of her dress. "I really like the dress. Thank you."

Wow. Just...wow. "You're welcome."

Shanna giggled, then got serious. "I think it's kind of cool you're going on a date with Mr. Mason."

"It's not a big deal."

Shanna smiled. "Whatever you say, Momma. I think it's romantic."

Romantic? Of course, Shanna would think a date with Dave Mason was romantic. Ainslie really needed to nip this in the bud. "Sorry, sweetie. Move along. No romance to see here."

Giggling, Shanna moved another quarter turn. "'Course it's romantic, Momma."

Ainslie slid the last pin into the dress. "All done! Why don't you take this off so I can take up the hem."

"Sure, Momma! Thank you so much for this awesome dress!"

Ainslie smiled as Shanna hopped off the hassock. "You'll be the prettiest girl at the dance."

Shanna flung her arms around Ainslie's neck. "It's all 'cause of you! You're the best mom in the entire world!"

Ainslie swallowed hard against the tears lodged in her throat. Never had a dress meant so much.

It never would have meant *anything* in Charleston. Shanna had two closets full of clothes. A new dress for the Homecoming Dance wouldn't have made a ripple in the pond.

But this one emerald green, pre-owned satin dress made her big girl just shine.

Ainslie would do whatever it took to make them

happy and give them back a portion of the wonderful life Bobby Lee the Wonder Dad stole from them. Ruark and Patsy were a bit harder to please, but eventually they'd find something to make them happy. And perhaps she could find some happiness for herself that would be part of the whole package.

A picture of Dave Mason floated into her brain. He was handsome, charming, caring and great with children.

He was younger than she was. She frowned at that thought. She shouldn't put too much into this. It was one dinner date.

She had only dated one man in her entire life; Bobby Lee. She'd only slept with one man her entire life; again, Bobby Lee.

She felt like a silly school girl, not a grown woman. Pitiful. Just pitiful.

It was just dinner! She should keep things in perspective.

****

A couple of hours later, the house quiet, the last piece of clean underwear folded, Ainslie stretched the kinks out of her muscles. Ready for bed, she began her nightly routine.

First she tiptoed into the girls' room. Shanna had fallen asleep while reading *Puddin' Head Wilson*, which had to be an English assignment, because the only things Shanna read on a regular basis were *Elle* and *Marie Claire*. Ainslie bent to kiss her forehead before she turned off the reading light.

Patsy had long been down for the count and slept fiercely, her brows furrowed and that thumb jammed in her mouth. Ainslie bent and kissed her as well, with gentle fingers rubbing the lines away.

Ruark's room was next. She opened the door, causing a flurry of covers over the boy's head.

"Ruark?" The lump under his bedclothes went very, very still.

She mentally sighed. "I know you're awake. I love you." She bent over him and kissed the top of his head. "I'll always love you."

Suddenly exhausted, she made her way to the bathroom. The morning came way too early.

Chapter Eleven

Dave considered himself to be a man of the world, someone who had been around the block a time or two or three. He'd taken women to dinner before. But none of them had ever been married to a kajillionaire. What could he bring Ainslie that would in any way, shape, or form, measure up to what her ex-husband gave her?

Never mind that he didn't know how far to take it when she had very vulnerable children at home. How much was overkill?

Well, he was about to find out. He pulled up the parking brake. He adjusted his tie and bounded up to the front door of the little bungalow where Ainslie lived with her children. Rolling his shoulders, he took a deep breath and pushed the doorbell.

A flurry of footsteps came from behind the door. It cracked open, and a little blonde girl peeked at him from the inside. Her thumb was stuck in her mouth like a cork in a wine bottle.

"Hello," he said in his friendliest voice. "I'm Mr. Mason."

The child nearly broke his nose when she slammed the door shut. Okay, this might not go the way he wanted it to.

After more bumps and some clumps coming from inside, the door opened again, and this time, a gracious Shanna Logan appeared. The little girl, Patsy, stood right behind her, eyes wide and suspicious. Shanna, however, turned her mouth into a warm smile. "Hi, Mr. Mason. Momma's not quite ready yet, but please come inside and wait for her."

"Thank you, Shanna." He stepped across the threshold. Ainslie's heart gave a great big thump. Dave held out two mini flower bouquets he'd gotten on the advice of his florist, one in each hand. "These are for you girls."

Shanna's eyes absolutely sparkled as she accepted the nosegay. "Oh, a *tussy-mussy*! It's beautiful! Thank you!"

"You're welcome. What did you call them again?"

"A *tussy-mussy*. That's what they called them in the olden times, so they wouldn't know how bad everything smelled." She brought the sweet little package of roses, ribbons and a doily up to her nose and inhaled deeply. "It smells so good. Go ahead, Patsy! Check yours out."

Crouching so that he was face level with Patsy, he held out the flowers. "I made sure there were a lot of pink flowers in here, because I bet pink is your favorite color."

Patsy just stared at him, mouth slack around her thumb. Shanna reached down and yanked Patsy's thumb out of her mouth. "Please don't suck your thumb in front of guests. It's rude." Looking up at Dave, she shook her head sadly. "I apologize for my sister."

Dave just kept looking at Patsy, just kept holding out the little bouquet. "That's okay. Why don't you take the flowers now, and if you don't want to keep them, you don't have to."

Patsy nodded and took the flowers. "Thank you, Mr. Mason." Following Shanna's lead, she buried her head in the bouquet and sniffed loudly.

Dave smiled as he stood up. At the same time, Ruark ambled out of the kitchen. "Hey, Ruark."

Ruark barely spared him a glance as he dropped onto the sofa. "Hey."

"I've, uh, got something for you." After patting his jacket pockets a couple of times, he pulled a CD out of the left one. "Mrs. Kelly says your favorite singer is Miles Maxwell, so I picked up a copy of his newest CD. Is *Boris Gudonov* a favorite opera of yours?"

Ruark stood. "Max was my voice teacher in Charleston. I got a copy of the demo right after he finished recording it." Dave forgot that back in Charleston, Ruark had a world famous bass as a teacher.

The kid wasn't going to give him an inch. "Well, I hear those demo things don't last long, so you can listen to this after it wears out." He held out the CD.

Ruark took a couple of reluctant steps toward him. Dave gave him the CD, and held out his hand to shake.

Shaking Dave's hand, Ruark looked directly at him, albeit reluctantly. "Thank you."

"You're welcome."

"May I get you something to drink?" Shanna jumped into hostess mode. "Please sit down."

His butt nearly made it into the offered chair when Ainslie made her entrance. He just managed to stay on his feet.

As before, Ainslie's transformation from End Zone waitress to woman in charge kicked him in the gut. She had that just-out-of-bed tousled hair, those big, velvet brown eyes, all pulled together with an angelic smile. "I'm sorry I kept you waiting."

"It was worth it. You look beautiful."

"Thank you. You don't look so bad yourself."

Patsy went up to her mother and held up her flowers. "Look, Momma! See what Mr. Mason gave me and Shanna."

****

Ainslie looked at Patsy, who had her nose buried deep in a sweet little tussy-mussy and her heart went *kerplunk*. How could she possibly resist a man who brought her girls flowers?

Short answer, she couldn't.

She could barely see anything because of the sudden stars in her eyes. "It's very pretty, baby. Can I have a little sniff?"

Patsy held it up. Ainslie took the adorable bouquet of flowers and inhaled deeply. Over the bouquet, her gaze caught Dave's. The look in his eyes made her feel all squiggly wiggly. She took another deep inhale and caught the scent of little tea rose buds. "Mm." She handed the flowers back to Patsy. "It smells like roses."

Patsy nodded as she took back her tussy mussy. "I counted. There are ten pink ones." She turned and looked up at Dave. "Do you have flowers for my momma?"

Tears pricked at Ainslie's eyes at the look on her daughter's face.

So earnest, so hopeful.

"You know, I just might have something for your mom in my car. It's a surprise." He winked.

"Can I come with you and see the surprise?"

Shanna scoffed. "No, Patsy. You know you can't go with Momma on her date. No kids allowed."

"That's okay, sugar," Ainslie intervened when Patsy began to pout. "You can see my surprise when I get home."

"But I'll already be in bed, then." No doubt about it, Patsy Logan had a killer boo-boo lip.

"I'll be home before bedtime, and I'll tell you all about my surprise, and you can read a little bit to me from your library book."

"'Kay." Ever the drama queen, Patsy sighed mournfully.

"Give me your hand, baby." Ainslie placed a lipstick kiss on Patsy's palm. "If you miss me, just check out the palm of your hand." She turned to Shanna. "I've got the cell so call me if there's an emergency."

Shanna rolled her eyes. "We're not babies, Momma. We can take you being away a couple of hours. We take care of ourselves every night when you go to work."

"You're right, sugar, but I'm your mother, and it's my right to worry about you." She grabbed up her purse. "I'll be home before you miss me." She reached for her coat, only to find Dave holding it out for her to slip into.

Oh, the simple courtesies, how she had missed them. "Thank you," she murmured as she slid her arms into the sleeves.

His eyes twinkled. "You're welcome." He tapped his watch. "We have a reservation for 6:30. Are you ready?"

His grin was infectious. She found herself also grinning like a fool. "Okay." Turning back to her children, she said, "I'll be home soon. Call me if there's a problem. Promise?"

Shanna nodded. "Have a good time, Momma!"

With that, Ainslie turned around and left her children to go out to dinner with a man who was not their daddy.

****

Damn, Ruark thought. He wished Patsy wouldn't make so much of those stupid flowers. Obviously, they were a bribe.

It didn't matter to him one way or another if Mr. Mason brought him Max's recording of *Boris Gudonov,* even if his own had died ages ago. He couldn't be bought.

Patsy spun and danced around the room with her flowers, while she sang a very bad, very out of tune version of *Here Comes the Bride.* "Just shoot me now," he mumbled. "You know Mr. Mason only gave you those flowers to bribe you."

Patsy stopped whirling. "What's a bribe?"

Shanna frowned. "What are you doing, Ruark?"

He stood up. "I'm telling her the truth." Turning to Patsy, he said, "A bribe is something someone gives you to make you like him."

"Ruark, stop it!"

"Think about it, Patsy. He wants you to like him so you won't mind staying by yourself when he takes Momma to the Homecoming Dance."

Patsy's lower lip began to quiver. "Momma won't leave me alone. You're going to stay with me."

Ruark shook his head sadly. "I'm going to the dance too. I'm taking one of Shanna's friends."

Shanna stomped her foot. "Ruark, why do you have to be this way?" She went to Patsy and hugged her. "Nobody's leaving you alone. I know Momma's getting a babysitter for you."

"Who's it gonna be?"

"I don't know yet, but I know she wouldn't leave you here alone."

"I don't wanna be by myself. It's scary."

"It's gonna happen all the time, now that she's dating Mr. Mason. They're gonna keep goin' on dates until she marries him, and she'll forget all about us for her new family."

"Ruark, stop it!"

Patsy was on the verge of tears, but he couldn't stop himself. "We'll be orphans because Daddy's in jail for life. We'll have to go to foster care."

"I don't want to go to foster care. I wanna stay with Momma." Patsy hiccupped, a prelude to a crying jag.

"That's enough! Don't listen to him, Patsy. He's being a brat. We won't be orphans, and Momma won't leave you alone." Shanna glared at Ruark. "Why don't we leave Ruark here to be his mean ol' self, and I'll listen to you read."

"'Kay." Patsy sniffed while she followed Shanna into their bedroom.

Ruark slumped back onto the couch. His

stomach felt full of slithering snakes and iron butterflies.

He shouldn't have riled Patsy like that, but he could not stand for Momma to date Mr. Mason.

Chapter Twelve

"So, where's my surprise?" Ainslie put on her seatbelt while Dave opened the driver's side door. She'd nearly swooned when he helped her into the car.

In her other life, men treated her like spun glass. This new life—not so much.

Until now.

Dave reached into the backseat and pulled out a clay pot filled with different herbs. It had a big blue bow around the rim of the pot. "Spike mentioned that one of the things you miss is having an herb garden." Handing it to her, he shrugged. "I thought you might be used to getting roses. I wanted to be different."

Taking it from him, she brushed her fingertips over some spikes of rosemary. Pungent, rich, the scent filled the car. She *had* missed her little garden of herbs. "I love it! Thank you!" Remembering, she smiled. "The grounds around our home were landscaped and maintained by gardeners, but I had one small corner, just for me." Bobby Lee hadn't understood her desire to muck around in the dirt, but she had loved that little herb patch. She laid a hand on Dave's arm. "Thank you."

"You're welcome." He looked relieved as he put the car into gear. "Do you think Patsy will be disappointed?"

"I don't think she'll be able to think beyond that sweet little tussy-mussy you brought her." She felt a smile bloom on her face as she remembered Patsy's happy grin. "Those are the first flowers she's ever gotten. You won yourself a fan there."

"I'm honored. She's a sweet little girl."

"Oh, don't let her fool you. She can be quite a handful when she sets her mind to something."

"Then she's a normal, well-adjusted kid."

"Yeah, I guess she is. I hope she is." She watched his face while he drove.

Such a handsome face. Eyes as bright a blue as she had *ever* seen, his every feature put there by God made a girl swoon. His body wasn't bad either. Clearly, the man worked out. His long, perfect fingers tapped absently on the steering wheel.

She imagined those long, strong, capable fingers could wreak havoc with a girl's self-control and composure.

She'd heard that self-control and composure were over-rated. She remembered the old saying about the size of a man's fingers being an indicator of the size of another part of his body.

He glanced over at her and caught her staring at him. "What's wrong? You're looking at me like my skin suddenly turned green."

Ainslie felt a blush spread across her face. She would not admit to speculating about the size of his penis. "Oh, no. I was just looking out your window to see if I could guess where we're going."

"Ah." A smug looking smile spread across his face.

She could tell he knew exactly why she'd been staring at him, damn the man.

"We're going to Hope's. Have you been there yet?"

She chuffed a laugh. "The only restaurant I've been to in ages is The End Zone."

Dave pressed his lips together and nodded. "Well, Bobby's food is good, but Hope's exists in a different dimension. She's a genius."

"I'm looking forward to it even more then."

"I hope you'll like it there." He pushed down on his blinker and maneuvered the traffic to make a left turn.

He *was* handsome, no doubt, and there was no question about her well being when with him.

And he brought her baby girls fussy, wrapped in doilies, little bouquets of flowers.

They pulled into the parking lot outside of a cozy little cottage with a friendly looking front garden and a yellow glow from candles in each window. A simple sign in cranberry with gilt lettering on the gate proclaimed the restaurant *Hope's*.

"It looks charming." Ainslie smiled at Dave.

Dave smiled back as he got out of the car. "I'm glad you think so."

She undid her seatbelt while he made his way to the passenger side of the car. He opened the door and helped her out.

Dave kept hold on her hands, pulling her closer to him. "I have to get this out of the way, or else I won't be able to concentrate on anything else." Lifting her chin with one finger, he kissed her.

His lips were firm and smooth and coaxed her lips open with the tip of his tongue. She couldn't help but respond to his kiss. He tasted like peppermint and dazzling magic.

Dave pulled away and rested his forehead on hers. It was a good thing he was holding her up because her knees wobbled a little. "Let's go in." He bent down and stole another kiss.

Oh, Lordy. "Okay."

The man grinned like a pirate in a cave full of booty.

"C'mon, let's go eat." He laid a hand at the small of her back as they walked up the flagstone path leading to Hope's.

****

Man, he shouldn't have kissed her. He'd wanted

to get it out of the way so he could concentrate on getting to know her without any latent testosterone sizzling through the air.

Bad idea. He'd had no way of knowing how potent Ainslie Logan was. She should come with a warning label. If he got this hot under the collar after one simple kiss, making love to her might just cause him to have a heart attack.

Yep, he decided right then and there, heart attack be damned, that making love Ainslie Logan was definitely part of his plan. Not tonight, but eventually. Hopefully very, very soon.

Being a weeknight, Hope's looked fairly deserted. He opened the door into a comfortable parlor, reminiscent of a time long past. Furnished with overstuffed chairs and a settee, the walls were mostly shelves, laden with books in case a customer had to wait for a table. Mismatched shades topped the lamps, which glowed with a homey, welcoming light. A quiet soundtrack of classical guitar music filled the small room, accompanied by the rhythmic cling of silverware hitting plates and the murmur of intimate conversations. Delicious, mouth-watering scents wafted from the kitchen.

The hostess, a woman whose daughter had just graduated from Addington High last spring, looked up from the reservations book and smiled. "Mr. Mason! So nice to see you!"

Dave nodded back. "Mrs. Gale. How's Melissa doing?"

Mrs. Gale's smile grew broader. "Just great! I think she just might make the Dean's List over at Barrett."

"That's pretty impressive, being her first semester and all."

"She gets that from my side of the family." Mrs. Gale picked up a couple of menus and a wine list. "You have a table in the tavern, right?"

Doreen Alsen

"That's the plan." He smiled at Ainslie and guided her ahead of him as Mrs. Gale led them to their table.

Tucked away in a corner that was close enough to the fireplace without getting overheated, their table stood next to a bay window that looked out over a pond and Hope's gardens. She mostly had mums going on and some tiny pumpkins. The evening sun would set right behind the gardens and wash them in pink and magenta light.

He helped Ainslie into her seat then took his own as Mrs. Gale put down the menus in front of them. "I'll make sure Nicole knows you're here." She left.

"This is lovely," Ainslie said as she looked around. She might have been blushing, but he couldn't tell because of the candlelight and the glow from the fireplace.

"It's all new. Hope got her start catering out of her kitchen when her husband died on 9-11. Her business just kept growing until it was more than she could handle in her kitchen, on her own."

All the color drained out of Ainslie's face. "Oh, no!" she gasped. "How horrible for her. I can't even imagine that kind of loss." She sighed. "It's impressive how she moved on. While it's small comfort, how lucky for her that she had a skill she could fall back on when her husband died." She hid behind the hand-written menu. "So, what's good?"

Well, fabulous start, asshole. He wanted her to have a good time, not dwell on her current job situation. "Hard to say. It's all good. Or so I've been told."

Right in the nick of time, Nicole, as promised, glided up to the table, bearing a plate of cheese and crackers. "Hi, Mr. Mason! How are you?"

"Great." Nicole had graduated from Addington High about two years ago, if his memory was correct.

98

"Have you had a chance to look at the wine list?" Nicole asked Dave.

Ainslie looked at him. "I really better not have any. I have so much to do when I get home."

"Hope has very nice Mosel Riesling from a little winery in Trier. One glass wouldn't hurt," he wheedled. He knew jack squat about wine. He'd known the subject would come up so he asked Ian Ross for advice.

"Oh," Ainslie said. "Is it from the Reichsgraf von Kesselstadt *Winzerei*?" She smiled at him. "It *is* a wonderful wine. You're right. One glass wouldn't hurt, I guess."

He handed Nicole the wine list, happy for something to do. Of course, Ainslie knew about good wine. He hoped to hell it was from the *Rikesgraff fonn Whereever*. "We'll have a bottle of the wine and a bottle of Pellegrino as well."

"Very good." Nicole scratched her pencil on her order book and took off.

"So many things to choose from. It's difficult to know where to start," Ainslie murmured. "It all sounds so delicious."

He couldn't take his eyes off her. Forget the menu. *She* was the most delicious thing he'd seen in ages. He wanted to devour her in little bites and sips, so he could savor her.

Make it last a long time.

He had to loosen his collar as he dragged his eyes away from her and focused them on the menu.

Dave looked up to see Ainslie looking at him. Her eyes were big, brown and beautiful. It took him a moment to remember how to speak. "She's, uh, well known for her shrimp in puff pastry."

Ainslie wrinkled her nose. "I'm sorry. I'm allergic to shellfish. What else is good?"

"Oh." He just wanted to lean over the table and kiss the tip of that cute little nose. "I always do the shrimp things."

"I guess you need to try something else. You know, take a walk on the wild side." Her eyes twinkled and sparked with humor.

"I suppose I do." He closed the menu and reached for a cracker and a slice of cheddar. "Why don't you decide for both of us?"

She grinned. "Okay. I hope you like grits."

"Hope doesn't make grits."

"I bet she would if I asked her." She tilted her head. "Don't you like grits?"

"I've never had them. I'm not real adventurous with foreign food."

"No!" She slapped a hand over her heart. "Really? I never would have guessed."

He narrowed his eyes. "Are you making fun of me?"

She shook her head, innocence personified. "Of course not. But you *are* the most predictable customer at The End Zone."

"I'm not. I mix it up all the time." He was totally appreciating her teasing him. He didn't expect it.

"Your idea of mixing it up is having onion rings with your Daveburger instead of fries."

"I get wings every once in a while."

She laughed. "You big ol' maverick, you."

Nicole came back to the table and delivered their wine and Pellegrino. She showed the wine to Dave. When he nodded, she went ahead with the ceremony of opening the bottle and presenting the wine. "Have you decided?"

"Do you still want me to order for you?" Ainslie grinned. "You can't complain. You've got to eat it all."

Dave inclined his head, like a king granting a boon. "Go ahead."

"You asked for it." She smiled at Nicole. "We'd like to start with the baked brie. Then, we'd like the

Chicken Dijon with grits instead of the wild rice?"

Nicole tapped her pen on her order book. "Grits." Looked like Nicole had the same queasy reaction as Dave did when it came to the "g" word. "I can ask. Bleu cheese or the house vinaigrette on your salads?"

"House. I'm sure it's delicious." She handed both her and Dave's menu to Nicole. "Thank you!"

"Very good." Nicole hurried away.

Ainslie laid her elbows on the table, linked her fingers, and rested her chin on her fingers. "How's that?"

"Brie and grits. What's not to like?"

"That's the spirit." She picked up her wine glass and swirled around the pale liquid in it. Bringing it to her nose, she sniffed the fragrant wine. "This smells lovely, delicate with a small hint of apricot."

Dave picked up his glass and sniffed it. He couldn't smell anything but wine, philistine that he was. So he held the glass over the table. "To grits."

She clinked her glass against his. "To grits."

****

Ainslie smiled as she sipped her wine. "This is good."

"You better hope the grits are."

"Hush, you. You're going to love them." He was so cute when he was grumpy. "I make a mean bowl of grits."

"One of your best dishes?"

"My only dish, actually." She felt her body go warm, shame at admitting this next bit. "We had a housekeeper who cooked for us most days." Dear Lord, she'd been so spoiled. "On the days she took off, she always left casseroles and such in the freezer."

"You have other talents, I imagine."

She grimaced. "I guess you could say that. Most of the time I was out and about, going to meetings of one committee or another. I was the go-to girl if you wanted to have a successful event. And of course, I was always the hostess with the mostest, putting on parties and such for Bobby Lee's business associates." A blue funk threatened her, remembering how everybody thought she had known all along about Bobby Lee.

"How did you meet him?" Dave's eyes looked understanding and safe.

"The night I won Miss South Carolina." She shook her head at herself. "I was so full of myself, and he really turned up the charm to eleven."

Nicole came to the table, delivering the baked brie. The scent of cheese and pastry, accented with the tangy bite that came from the tomato chutney, wafted up to make her mouth water. Heaven on a plate.

"Thanks," Dave said.

Nicole smiled and left them alone again.

"He must have been very charismatic."

"Oh, yes. I was *so* young and stupid. He was this successful man, not too much older than me, who wore designer suits and always had a lot of money to throw around. I never stood a chance." She looked him in the eyes, waiting for him to judge her young, stupid self.

"Okay, you got me at the brie." Dave swallowed a fork full. "This is good."

"Told you." He puzzled her. He didn't react the way she thought he would. She forked up a wedge of the brie and slipped it into her mouth.

He paid special attention to that, his eyes following the movement of her tongue. It sent shivers up her arms.

Dave cleared his throat and wiped his lips with his napkin. "So you fell in love with him."

"I adored him. We'd walk through a store, and I'd notice something, and he'd say, 'Do you like that, sugar? Let me get it for you.' And he did. He took me on trips, to the best restaurants, the opera, ballet, you name it. He took me all over the world, we stayed at all the best hotels, the whole nine yards."

Dave said, "Hard to resist."

Ainslie shook her head. "Especially if you're young and inexperienced. Look…" She put her fork down. "I'm sure all this ancient history is boring."

"Not at all. You're this puzzle I want to figure out."

"Me?" she squeaked. "I'm no puzzle."

He picked up his wine glass and held it up to the light. "I beg to differ. Like, why does a wealthy woman need to move north and work herself to a frazzle with menial jobs?"

"I'm not wealthy anymore. And because I let Bobby Lee take over my life, I didn't finish college. Now I want to earn money the honest way, to be a good example for my children. A fresh start for me and my babies." She clasped her hands in her lap. "I'm sure there's more money. Bobby Lee can't be moved to tell me where it is. It would only go to pay off some of his clients. I wouldn't see a penny of it." She took a delicate sip of her wine. "I wouldn't want to."

"I can't imagine doing that to my family."

"Bobby Lee Logan only cared about Bobby Lee Logan."

Nicole showed up to bring them their salads. Dave looked at his with a touch of disdain. Ainslie laughed. "What's wrong?"

"Why couldn't you order the bleu cheese?"

"I'm broadening your horizons. And protecting your cholesterol."

"My cholesterol is just fine, thank you very much. Since when are tomatoes yellow?" He stabbed a bite of the heirloom tomato on his salad with suspicion then shoved it into his mouth and munched.

"See, not so bad." Ainslie chuckled.

He swallowed. "Not bad." Putting his fork down on his salad plate, he sat back in his chair.

She wanted to change the subject. Her ex-husband wasn't worth a spare thought. "What about you? How'd you get to be such an amazing high school principal?"

"I love kids."

For him, she sensed, it was just that simple. He was direct and to the point. He was honest and didn't pretend to be what he wasn't. She knew that like she knew her children.

"You really do." She smiled, and he grinned at her back.

"Yeah."

"Why isn't there a Mrs. Dave tending the home fires?" It was a fair question. She'd been spilling her guts all night long.

"Haven't met her yet." He picked another tomato out of his salad. "Or maybe I have, and she doesn't know it." He lowered and raised his eyebrows like Groucho Marx.

"No, really. Tell me about you. I told you about Bobby Lee, the Wonder Dad."

"I have a feeling you didn't tell me *all* about Bobby Lee." He toasted her with his wine again. "So, we're even."

"We're nowhere near even." She narrowed her eyes at him. "Spill, Mr. Mason. Let me know why a hot, sensitive guy like you doesn't have a Mrs. Mason and a boatload of darling children himself."

He took a big swallow of Riesling. "I've come close, once, but it didn't work out. Her name was Emma, and I thought we were happy. She just up and left me, no reason at all." He shrugged. "Don't know why. I tried again a time or two, but it just didn't click. You know." He speared a cucumber slice, considered it then popped it into his mouth. "No chemistry."

No way. The man would have chemistry with a cabbage.

"It just never happened. I want a wife and kids, no question, but I never found the woman I wanted to share children with."

She rubbed her hand over her stomach, hoping to alleviate the sudden queasiness creeping over her. Of course, he wanted children, children of his own.

Children she couldn't give him, even if she wanted to.

Ainslie was saved from answering by a woman dressed in a white jacket and black and white checked pants. A chef's toque perched precariously on her head. Carrying two plates, she sidled up to their table. "Nicole told me Dave Mason was here and ordering Riesling and brie instead of his trusty Sam Adams and shrimp puffs. I had to come out and see for myself."

"Hi, Hope." Dave leaned back in his chair. "Please meet my friend, Ainslie Logan. Ainslie, this is Hope Monahan, owner of Hope's."

Hope put the two plates down, one in front of Ainslie, the other in front of Dave. "I've been hearing a lot about you, Ainslie. Andi is totally wild about your Mirror on the Wall Ball."

"It's not my idea, originally." Ainslie could feel her face warm up.

"Are you going to be at the meeting next week? I'm going to talk about the food." Hope waved her hands to indicate the plates of food in front of them. "I couldn't do authentic grits, so I whipped up some polenta to go with the chicken. I used freshly grated parmesan instead of cheddar. It'll go better with the Dijon sauce for the chicken." She chuffed a laugh. "I think I'll need to take pictures of this because no one is going to believe that Dave Mason, food wimp extraordinaire, is eating polenta." She smiled at Ainslie. "I'll see you next week at the meeting."

"Thanks, Hope." Dave said, then looked at his plate like it might jump up and bite him.

Hope got straight A's for presentation. The colorful plate showcased the food, with the chicken placed on top of the polenta, the crisp green beans speckled with red and yellow pepper shoots. "This looks delicious." Ainslie forked up some of the polenta. It exploded with flavor when it hit her tongue. "Mm. Go ahead, try it."

Dave pushed the polenta around with his fork. He reminded her of Patsy, whose diet contained about five items, none of them exceptionally healthy.

"Go ahead. It's not poison. It won't kill you."

"That's what you say."

"It looks like we're going to do this the hard way." She scooped up another forkful of polenta and dipped it in the Dijon sauce. She licked her lips as she held the fork over the table for Dave. He dutifully opened his mouth, and his eyes sparked with light that wasn't interest in polenta. Mesmerized by his gaze, she slid the food into his mouth. Dave put lips around the polenta and swallowed. She watched him swallow, lick his lips. It made her squirmy.

"It's not as bad as it looks."

Ainslie rolled her eyes, breaking the spell. "It's better than okay. It's amazing. You just don't want to admit it."

"But this isn't grits, right? It's polenta. What's the difference?" Dave cut into his chicken and swabbed it into some of the Dijon sauce.

"Polenta's Italian. Grits are southern. It's just a name."

"Okay, you win. Enough about grits. I'll eat them all up." Dave wiped his mouth with his napkin.

That gorgeous mouth, those amazing lips. She

felt a hum run through her body. She shivered. She hadn't felt very sexual since her hysterectomy. Mr. Dave Mason was waking up all sorts of things inside her. She realized he was staring at her, his gaze expectant. "I'm sorry. Would you kindly repeat that?"

He smiled as if he knew exactly what she was talking about. Sipping his wine, he studied her. "Are you going to be able to get to the game on Friday night?"

"Oh, don't I wish. I have to work Friday night so I can chaperone the dance." She shook her head. "I'd love to see Shanna cheer. I'm used to going to all her games and competitions. She says she doesn't mind that I can't get there, but I know otherwise."

"I'm sorry about that."

She shrugged it off. "It is what it is."

"Hm." He speared a green bean and studied it. "They're good kids. You must be proud of them."

Oh, he had no idea. Pride didn't begin to describe what she felt for her children. They were the reason she got up in the morning, the reason for every breath she took.

And as much as she enjoyed his company and the way he made her feel, she would give him up if her children couldn't handle her having a relationship with a man who wasn't their father.

Chapter Thirteen

"Thanks for dinner," Ainslie murmured to him as he walked her to her front door. "I had a wonderful time."

"I hope it'll be the first of many."

She stopped at her porch steps, faced him, and took his hands. "Me too."

"C'mere." He coaxed her body in toward him. She didn't put up a fight. Wrapping his arms around her, he dragged her close so he could kiss her.

Her response generous, her mouth softened and warmed against his. Her lips teased his, an erotic game of hide and seek. His tongue came out to play and raised the ante. She melted against him, humming a sweet note of pleasure. Their lips broke apart then came back together, clinging as their passion spun down.

He leaned his forehead on hers. "You really pack a punch. I wish we could explore this further." He pressed his lips to the top of her head, as he nuzzled her hair.

She trembled in his arms. "I need to get in. The children, you know."

He did. Moving her an arm's length away, he said, "You need to go *now* then, while I can still let you."

Her fingers came up to touch his mouth. "Thank you for dinner and everything."

He kissed her fingers. "It was my pleasure. I'll see you on Saturday, okay?"

"Yeah." She dragged in a deep breath. "Saturday."

"I'm counting the minutes."

Her eyes twinkled. "I bet you say that to all the girls."

"I've never said it before to anyone." Which was true.

"Well." Ainslie's smiled wilted a little. She tilted her head toward her front door. "I've got to get inside. I promised I'd be home in time to listen to Patsy read." She went up on her toes and placed a kiss on his cheek. "Good night."

"Good night." He watched her walk up the three steps up to her porch and reach for the doorknob. Giving him one last look, she nodded.

Then, he remembered. "Wait! Your herbs!"

She came back to him. "Patsy would never forgive me if I didn't come back with some foliage."

He kissed her cheek as he handed the clay pot over. "Now, go away woman, while I still can let you go."

"You're such a bully." She shook her head as she took the terra cotta pot of herbs and walked away. When she got to the top of the stairs, she looked back and blew him one last smooch for the road. He caught it with his hand.

Dave stood there watching her go into her house. Buzzed, aroused, he rubbed his hand over his heart.

Dave wanted more. A lot more.

****

"Hello! I'm home!" Ainslie put the pot of herbs down on a side table, slipped out of her jacket, and hung it on the hook beside the front door.

"Momma! *Hic*!" Patsy screeched as she launched her self into her mother's arms. Her face was tear-streaked, her nose was all snuffy, and she had the hiccups—a sure sign she was on the verge of a meltdown.

"Shh, baby. Everything's okay." Ainslie stroked

her girl's pretty blonde hair. "Why are you crying?"

Patsy hiccupped, her little chest spasming with the violence of it. "Don't leave me by myself."

"'Course I won't leave you by yourself. Why do you think such a silly thing?"

Shanna came into the room. "Ruark's been tellin' her that she's going to be left home alone because you're going to the dance with Mr. Mason. I tried to tell her that it's not true, but Ruark's being a butt-head."

That butt-head was nowhere to be seen. Ainslie would deal with him later. "I've got a babysitter all lined up for you, pumpkin. And I won't be gone long anyway. It's all set up." She kissed Patsy's cheek. "Now, how 'bout getting ready for bed, and I'll come and listen to you read."

"I want the song too." Patsy loved "My Favorite Things" from *Sound of Music*. If Ainslie'd sung it once, she'd sung it a thousand times. She'd probably sing it a million times more.

Patsy loved that song to death.

"It's a deal if you add brushing *and* flossing to getting ready for bed."

"Do you want me to help her get ready while you talk to Ruark?" Shanna cheerfully shoved her twin under the bus with nary a qualm.

"No, I'll get Patsy ready for bed. Have you finished your homework?"

"I've still got some reading to do."

"Well, you'd best get to it, angel." She knew Shanna would like nothing more than to see Ruark get in trouble. She was going to be disappointed. "Now, Patsy, scoot. Brush and floss, and I'll be up soon to hear you read."

"'Kay!" Patsy scampered off to her room, all drama gone without a trace.

Ainslie studied her older girl. Shanna looked like she had something to say, but she surprisingly kept it to herself. "Do you have something to tell me?"

Shanna bit her lip. "No, not really. I better go and get that reading done."

"If you need to talk, you know where to find me."

"Sure, Momma. I'll read in the kitchen so you can talk to Patsy in our room." She trotted off.

Ainslie stopped outside Ruark's door, thought about knocking, but then decided not to. She'd get Patsy to bed, then deal with her boy. Something was up there, no doubt.

He probably had trouble seeing her go to dinner with someone who wasn't his daddy. Give him time, and he'd come along.

Oh, how she wished Ruark would come around. She really wanted Dave Mason in their lives.

****

Ruark heard his momma stop outside his door. He hoped she wasn't going to knock and come in, have some stupid conversation about his feelings.

She really didn't want to know how he felt.

He didn't know how he was going to make it through the Homecoming Dance. Having to pay attention to and pretend he liked Cecily, watching his sister dance with his worst enemy, and, worst of all, watching his mother be with Mr. Mason.

He knew he didn't have a chance with Mr. Mason, but he wanted the fantasy. He needed the fantasy. Now it was ruined because Mr. Mason was dating his momma.

And that was pretty much *so* not going to happen if he could help it.

Chapter Fourteen

"So I hear you had a hot date last night." Chelsea nudged Ainslie with her right elbow. They were both in The End Zone kitchen doing side work before their shifts.

"I don't know if I would call it a big date." Ainslie turned off the mixer she'd used to make whipped cream for desserts and for coffee drinks from the bar. Spike was well known for her Irish Coffee. "It was just dinner."

"'Kay, if you say so." Chelsea stopped shoving creamers into their place on the line. "Have you found a babysitter for the Homecoming Dance?"

"No, I haven't. I thought Sandy could do it, but something came up, and she had to leave town."

"I knew that." She leaned against the walk-in. "I can baby-sit, if you'd like."

Ainslie released the beaters from the mixer. "You're not going to the dance?"

"There were enough chaperones, and I need to do some reading for my evaluation by my co-operating teacher. Your little girl is adorable. I'd love to take care of her. And you wouldn't need to pay me."

"Hm." She dropped the beaters into a stainless steel bowl filled with warm soapy water. "You'd do that?"

"I wouldn't have offered if I wouldn't do it." Chelsea sniffed. "If you don't trust me to take care of Patsy, that's okay."

"No, not at all. Patsy's met you and likes you," Ainslie assured her. "I just don't want to impose.

You're very generous."

"I'm happy to do it."

"Well, thank you. I'm very grateful."

Smiling widely, Chelsea reached behind her to tighten the bow at the back of her apron. "Great!" She bopped her way out of the kitchen.

Ainslie watched her go. She was glad Patsy liked Chelsea. It was a burden off her mind.

****

On Friday evening, the cool air had a distinct snap to it. Fragrant with the scent of fallen leaves and the pep rally bonfire, the air crackled in the crisp October night.

Dave found a spot where he could get a good view of the cheerleaders. Even better, Andi and her father, pro-football coach god Deke Nelson, were already sitting there. Dave was relieved. He didn't want people to get the idea that the principal was a pedophile.

"Hi, Dave. Why aren't you sitting with the rest of the brass?"

"Hey," Deke said. "I'm here. I'm brass."

"Hi, Andi, Deke." Dave pulled his camera out of its bag.

"Whatcha got there?" Deke bellowed. His voice had two volumes: Loud and blast. Several parents turned toward them at the sound.

Dave felt his face heat. "Ainslie can't be here tonight and feels bad because she can't see Shanna cheer. I'm taping the girls so she can see them."

Deke cocked his head and looked at him, much like a dog did when he didn't understand his master's command. "You're going to take pictures of the girls instead of watching the game?"

"It's a favor to one girl's mother. I'd do this for any other parent."

"Hunh," Deke grunted as he crossed his arms over his chest and turned his attention to the field.

"The boys looked good yesterday in practice. Oughtta do some damage tonight."

Dave, thankfully, was dismissed.

The girls were facing the crowd, jumping around, trying to get the fans revved. Dave started to shoot.

Beautiful and lively, in her element, Shanna cart wheeled like an Olympic gymnast. She had her mother's dark hair and huge brown eyes. Those same eyes were snapping and sparkling as she egged on the crowd. Dave imagined Ainslie would have been as beautiful and full of life when she was a teen. She was still very beautiful, but she always looked so frazzled and tired.

He'd like to do something about that.

"*Really*. Videoing the cheerleaders for Ainslie." Andi rooted through her purse and pulled out a Chapstick. "That's very nice of you to do." She rubbed some on her lips.

Dave didn't need to look at her to know that she had a teasing smile on her face. "Okay, let me have it."

"Have what? Are you embarrassed? I think it's sweet." She coated her lips with the Chapstick again, then plunked it back into her bag.

He swore under his breath. "That's me." He put down the camera and looked at her. "Don't read too much into this."

Andi pulled her jacket closer. "You're acting positively dad-like."

"You're getting way ahead of yourself."

"Am I?" Andi moved over as Ian and Gina joined them. "Dave here is making a video of the cheerleaders tonight so Ainslie can see Shanna cheer."

"No kidding." Gina reached over and slapped him on the back. "That's so cute."

"No, it isn't." Dave's teeth clenched so hard, he

thought his jaw might break.

"What isn't?" Ian plopped down onto the bench.

"Dave is so cute. He's taping Shanna cheering so Ainslie doesn't miss out seeing her."

"Mate." Ian took off his glasses and cleaned them on his tie. "No words."

"He's a regular boy scout," Deke rumbled.

"Thanks for the support." Dave glowered at them. "This is just me, being a good principal."

"Absolutely," Andi said. The roar of the crowd had her standing. "Time to rumble."

Mike and his assistant coach came out of the tunnel to the gym. Andi put two fingers in her mouth and whistled loudly. Mike looked up, found her immediately, and grinned. Then he went back to serious business.

The cheerleaders set up a big frame covered with green and white spirit slogans, which they held up in front of the hallway to the home locker room. The Minutemen were announced, and the paper burst apart as the players tore it open and ran onto the field.

The girls cart wheeled, whooped, tumbled, jumped, and ran to the sidelines. They kept up a colorful litany of encouragement and whipped up the crowd into a frenzy.

Last season, the Minutemen had managed to lose every game they played, except for one. This year, they were doing better, mostly due to Mike's believing in his team and Deke's timely intervention. Deke's interest in the team, as well as Andi's twin brothers', both pro-football stars, gave the kids a real boost. This year, they'd racked up a couple of wins and were ready to win this game.

Dave really wanted to watch, but he was afraid to take his attention off the cheerleaders. Since Deke was providing very colorful running commentary on the team and Mike's choices, whether good or bad,

Dave could follow the game.

Kinda, sorta.

Half time came, the score 10 to 7, in favor of the Minutemen. The stands emptied out to line up at the concession stand. He was practically alone in the stands, save for Gina and Andi.

The cheerleaders took the field. The music cued, the home team girls went to say hello to their guest cheerleaders.

On cue, hip hop pounded out of the speakers. Girls were tumbling everywhere then stopped and went into formation. They moved in a mix of hip hop dance moves, military precise arm and leg motions, going into intricate pyramids, with the smaller girls perched on the top.

Then things got interesting. Before breaking back into another dance routine, the girls on top were thrown into the air, executed twists that would make a pro diver proud, and were caught by the rest of the team before they hit the ground.

Now Dave knew what "flyers" were.

They were crazy.

They didn't just fly around in the air once. They executed the same daredevil stunts several more times, each time being tossed higher and higher.

The cheerleaders from the visiting team performed a similar routine in front of the Addington side. Dave didn't know if he should video them or not.

Deke plopped down next to him and handed him a hotdog. "So, Ainslie, eh?"

Dave put down the camera and took the hotdog. He'd forgotten that Deke was an End Zone regular. "She's in a tough spot. I like to support my school's families."

"Sure." A large dollop of chili rolled off Deke's hotdog and onto his shirt. He caught it with an index finger the size of a ham hock and slurped it into his mouth. "She's a pretty lady. Terrible waitress, though."

"It's a new experience for her."

"I bet. Met her and her husband once."

That got Dave's attention. Why hadn't anyone told him Deke knew Ainslie? "They're divorced."

"I'd heard that. They were guests in the Galveston Hurricanes skybox once, back in the day when I was still coaching the team. Me and Pammy had both of them over to the house for a barbeque after the game. He was one slick son of a bitch. He tried to get me to invest some money in some business deal he was putting together." Deke looked at Dave. "Something about him wasn't right, you know? I didn't trust him."

Dave nodded, not knowing what to say. It didn't matter. Deke had enough to say for the both of them.

"I don't s'pose his wife knows where any of the money went."

Dave took another bite of hotdog, chewed and swallowed deliberately. "I don't think she'd be cleaning other people's houses and waiting on tables if she did."

"That's what I thought." Deke stood up and braced a hand on Dave's shoulder. "Like I said, she's a pretty lady. And Pammy liked her when we had had them over for cocktails." Pamela Nelson was Deke's wife and Andi's mother. "She's never wrong." He snorted a laugh. "Or so she tells me."

Dave exhaled noisily as Deke lumbered off to sit next to Andi.

What was he, wearing a sign that said "falling in love with Ainslie Logan?"

Chapter Fifteen

Ainslie's head swiveled at the sound of a loud horn barking outside her house. This meant the limo the boys had rented to pick up the girls at Cecily Brewster's house had arrived. "Ruark, honey, the limo's here."

The sound of dragging feet scraped into the living room. "Thanks for lending me the money to chip in for the limo and the corsage," he mumbled, his tone of voice flat.

She sighed. Her boy was so shy about girls. "Let me look at you."

He stole her breath away, this handsome young man who was her son. He'd gotten just enough of Bobby Lee's good looks to be a danger to girls' hearts the world over, with those aquamarine eyes and the dimple off to the right of his mouth that appeared when he smiled.

Dressed in a gray silk suit, with a darker gray shirt and tie, he looked like he stepped off the cover of *GQ*. If a girl had warm blood running in her veins, she would be toast at the sight of him. Her boy was dangerous.

Just like his daddy.

With one difference. She was Ruark's momma and she made sure that she raised him to have a strong moral character. He would not be a thief and he would not take advantage of people. She loved her gorgeous boy, both his looks and his character. "You are so handsome." She gave him a hug, kissed his cheek, then fiddled with his tie. She stopped short of licking her fingers and smoothing down his hair.

He wouldn't appreciate the gesture, since it took him ages and tons of product to get his hair to stand up every which way.

She went up on tiptoes to give him a kiss on the cheek, making sure to wipe off the lipstick mark right. "Go have a great time, honey bunch."

"Yeah." He looked like he was on his way to the firing squad instead of a dance. "See you later."

Ainslie felt tears start to form behind her eyes. Her baby boy was growing up.

****

Shanna put the garment bag holding her dress for the dance onto Cecily's bed. The house was so pretty and full of antiques, art and flowers. Real flowers, not fake ones. Remembering her old beautiful home in Charleston, a pang of longing for her old life nearly made her cry. She would not cry, however. She sucked the inside of her cheek into her teeth.

Puffy eyes and a red nose would not do at the Homecoming Dance. Especially not for Alden Bradford's date. Her heart skipped a beat just thinking about Alden.

He was *so* hot.

She hoped Ruark wouldn't ruin things for her. Ruark hated sports. He could be so stupid sometimes, with opera this and opera that.

He just wasn't normal.

As she bent to unzip her garment bag, Cecily and Priscilla, another cheerleader, giggled their way into Cecily's bedroom.

"Ooh, let me see your dress," Priscilla said as Shanna pulled the dress from the bag. "Omigod, Cece. It looks exactly like your dress from last year."

Cecily came over. "What? Let me see."

Shanna felt her stomach plummet to the floor. Her mom had gotten the dress from a consignment shop. What if it really was Cecily's dress?

Cecily's cast-offs. Shanna Logan was reduced to wearing someone else's old, useless clothes. She would have done better if her mom had shopped at the Salvation Army.

Mortified, Shanna did the only thing she could do.

She lied. "Really? I got this dress in Charleston, right before we moved here." She swore her heart was just going to bust out of her chest.

"It really looks like the same dress." Priscilla reached out and touched the hem.

Cecily rubbed at a place where the sequins were kind of loose. It looked like she knew just where to touch. "Well it wasn't one of a kind. I got it off the rack at the Nordstrom's in Chicago." Cecily tossed off with a wave of her hand. "It's going to look awesome on you, Shan, with your dark hair and eyes."

Shanna nearly wept with relief. "I don't know about that. Where're your dresses?" When in doubt, change the subject.

Cecily crossed to her closet and picked out a gold and silver beaded flapper style dress. "Now, this one *is* one of a kind. Mom and I picked it up last summer in Paris." She held it up against her. "What do you think?"

It was incredible. Shanna knew true envy. It just wasn't fair. She wanted dresses from Paris, trips to Nordstrom's in Chicago. She'd had them once, back when they had money.

At that moment, she couldn't have hated her daddy more.

All she had was Alden Bradford wanting to date her. Ruark better not screw that up.

****

Ainslie had just put on the final touches of her make-up when the doorbell rang. Only two people it could possibly be, Chelsea or Dave. Why was her heart pounding so hard? It wasn't a real date. She and Dave were chaperoning a high school dance.

Patsy beat her to the door. "Momma," she yelled. "Chelsea's here!"

"Hey, Patsy. S'up?" Chelsea slipped off the huge backpack she was toting and rolled her shoulders.

"Watchin' T.V. Can we do our nails tonight?"

"Sure thing. Hi, Ainslie." Chelsea smiled as Patsy scampered off. "You look really nice."

Nice, huh? "I have no idea what to wear to chaperone an occasion north of the Mason-Dixon line." For a dance in Charleston, she would wear a dressy suit, pearls and heels. For tonight, she put on gray, light wool slacks, an ancient, amethyst, cashmere twin set, and a cute pair of flats she'd bought five years ago.

"Well, you look great. Purple is a good color on you."

"Thank you. I've got a list for you in the kitchen. Let me go get it." Ainslie took a deep breath as she trundled to get the list.

The doorbell trilled again. Dave had arrived. No backing out now. She grabbed the list with one hand and rubbed her stomach with the other. She went to answer the door. Again, Patsy beat her to it.

Her heart melted at the sight that greeted her.

Dave crouched as he handed an excited Patsy one of the gaudiest heart-shaped box of chocolates Ainslie had ever seen. Her little girl had never looked so happy.

He stood when he saw her rush in and treated her to one of the most beautiful smiles in the history of the world. Nerves tingling, shivers raced all over her body.

Especially the girly parts. They zipped and zapped like they were plugged into lightning.

Patsy bounced over to her, the lace covered heart box leading the way. "Look, Momma! Mr.

Mason brought me another present!" She hugged it to her heart. "It's so pretty."

"I hope you said thank you."

Patsy wiggled around to look at Dave. "Thank you!"

"You're welcome." Still sending Ainslie that amazing smile he said, "Are you ready to go?"

"I just need a minute." She faced Chelsea. "Here's a list of phone numbers—my cell, Patsy's pediatrician, her dentist, and 911 in case there's an emergency. On the back, there's her night time routine and the list of what kind of snacks she can have before bed, and the list of TV shows she can watch." Ainslie sighed. "Don't let her talk you into letting her eat her weight in junk food. She can have *one*—did you hear that, Patsy? *Just one*—of the candies in that pretty box. The fridge is full of juice and stuff for sandwiches, fruit and veggies. Please feel free. And don't be afraid to call if something comes up."

Chelsea laughed as she took the list. "No worries. I think I can handle it. We'll manage, right, Patsy?"

Patsy was too busy admiring her box of chocolates, carefully opening it, most likely to pick the candy she wanted to eat. "Right."

"Well, okay then. Gonna give me a kiss good night, baby girl?" Ainslie crouched down.

Lips pursed tightly, Patsy kissed her, then went back to admiring her treasure.

"Looks like we're all set, yes?" Dave already had her coat held out for her.

"Looks like."

"Let's go, then."

"Have a good time, you two." Chelsea smiled. "Don't do anything I wouldn't do."

Yeah, right. There were lots of things on Ainslie's list of what to do with Dave Mason.

From the look in his eyes, he knew exactly each and every one.

****

"You look nervous." Dave glanced at Ainslie as he put the car in gear.

"Oh, no, not really." Ainslie grimaced. "Well, just a little."

He smiled. "You'll do fine." She smelled really good—some exotic mix of flowers and spices.

"I really won't know anyone."

"Isn't that the point of tonight? To meet Shanna and Ruark's friends and their parents?"

"Yes, it is." She fiddled with the pretty ring on her right ring finger. "I'm a little uncomfortable about the fact that I probably clean some of their houses."

"It's honest work. You've got *nothing* to be ashamed of." A little spurt of outrage raised his hackles. "Has anyone said otherwise?"

"No." She heaved a sigh. "It's just my own pride talking, I guess."

Dave's hackles lay back down. "Why don't we try this—just relax, don't worry about anything you think people might be thinking about you, and have a good time with your children." And him. He really wanted her enjoy being with him.

"Okay, I'll try." Ainslie smiled at him, a big warm smile that melted his heart into one big gooey mess.

There was no sense fighting it. He had fallen in love with a wonderful, beautiful, amazing woman.

Who also happened to be the mother of two of his students.

There must be some kind of moral clause or conflict of interest, but he wasn't going to think about that now. He was going to enjoy an evening with a healthy, beautiful, unattached female.

Along with about 500 teenagers trying to get

away with all kinds of trouble.

Kinda wrecked the buzz.

He really wanted to make love to her. He'd have to think about how to make that happen. The sooner the better. He'd been having some amazing dreams the past few nights, and he wanted, desperately, to try out some of the things he'd dreamed about.

He glanced over and saw her staring at him, a quizzical look on her face.

"Have you heard a word I've said?" She asked as she shook her head.

He blushed like an eighth grader. "Sorry, I was just thinking of the dance. What did you say?"

"I'm very appreciative of this chance to get an insight into the twins' lives." She put a hand onto his arm. That simple touch sent his whole system into overdrive.

Man, he was gone, totally gone. "I know how much this means to you."

She squeezed his arm. "Thank you." The look in her eyes made him feel like Superman, Batman, and Spiderman all rolled into one.

He liked it.

A lot.

Steering his car into his personal parking space—one of the perks that came with the job—he pulled up the parking brake and turned off the engine. "Ready?"

"Oh, yes." She picked her purse up off the passenger floorboard. "I'm really excited."

"Okay, then. Let's do it."

****

Because she knew he would come over to open her car door and help her out, Ainslie stayed put until he did that. Lord, she had missed the old-fashioned courtesies. Her heart went pitty-pat as she took his hand. It was so warm and strong. "Thanks," she murmured.

He didn't let go of it as they walked to the gym.

Music already filtered out into the parking lot. The only kids there were the decorating committee and their faculty sponsor, so Dave told her.

She'd never been to a dance in a gym. Country clubs, museums, and ballrooms, even Fort Sumter, but never a gym.

"If you want, I can get us the names of the Homecoming King and Queen." Dave said smoothly.

"Oh you can, can you?" The thought of Kings and Queens satisfied the southern debutante in her.

"Yeah, I know a guy who knows a guy." Dave said with a wink. "I do have some pull around here."

"I didn't realize I was spending this evening with a mover and shaker of the educational community."

"You'd best believe it, dumpling. I can move it and shake it with the best of them."

Now, *that* was something she could believe. In fact, a long dormant part of her counted on that. "Can't wait to see you in action."

Chuckling, he let go of her hand to open the door to the gym. Ainslie had expected the gym to look like, well, a gym. Nothing she imagined had come close to what met her eyes.

The bleachers were up and pressed into the wall. In their places stood tables and chairs, like one might find at a Parisian bistro. Small white lights twinkled everywhere, from the basketball hoops to the scoreboards. Autumn colored paper leaves were sprinkled around for some seasonal color, and the refreshment table centerpiece was a huge pumpkin with the school mascot, the Minuteman, carved into it. Light flickered from within it.

She'd expected it to smell a bit like dirty socks and sweaty sneakers. She'd been wrong. Clinging to the air were the scents of cinnamon, nutmeg, and apple cider.

Smiling at Dave, she said, "This is charming."

He raised his eyebrows up and down. "You had doubts?"

"I just didn't know what to expect."

"We are a world class operation here." He stretched his arms out in front of him and fiddled with the cuffs of his shirt. A woman hurried up to them, the decorating committee faculty advisor, if Ainslee had to guess.

"Hi, Dave." Clad in an artsy, bright, silk-screened tunic, the woman had dark brown hair with gray threads shot through it. She wore it piled on top of her head, anchored by a colorful chopstick. "The kids did a great job, didn't they?" Her eyes were curious as she looked at Ainslie.

"They really did. Ainslie, this is Carmen Bartolomeo, our art teacher. Carmen, this is Ainslie Logan. She's Shanna and Ruark Logan's mom."

Carmen smiled as she extended her hand for Ainslie to shake. "It's very nice to meet you. I haven't had Shanna in class, but Ruark is a delightful boy. Very creative."

"Thank you. I know he loves to draw." And he'd never said a word about Ms. Bartolomeo's class. She should have known enough to ask him about it.

"He's very polite and works hard." She looked at Dave. "Maybe you could come over and say something to the committee?"

"Of course." He straightened his tie. "I'll be right back."

He looked comfortable in his world. After Dave shook every student's hand, one of the students said something and made Dave laugh out loud. He said something, and all of the students guffawed.

How natural he was with them. They clearly loved him, and she could tell he felt the same way about the students. She was relieved to have him in her children's corner.

He grinned as he walked back toward her. An answering grin spread across her face. She relaxed, knowing that she and her children would be safe in his hands.

Chapter Sixteen

"I feel lucky *to*night." Alden Brewster leaned back against the supple leather limo seat. He wore his tie loose and wore what appeared to Ruark the school's formal uniform: pressed khaki trousers, blue button down oxford cotton shirts, dark blue sport coats, ugly ties, and boat shoes with no socks.

Ruark couldn't breathe due to the noxious cloud of Chocolate Axe in the limo.

He didn't mishear Alden, though. "Lucky?" Picking at a loose thread on his jacket, all casual like, he looked Alden in the face. "You'd better not be talking about my sister."

Alden bared his teeth in a Chester Cheeto big cheesy grin. "She's totally hot." He shook his fingers as if they sizzled. "Any guy would be lucky to be with her. You don't think I'm lucky to be her date tonight?"

Leo Campanello, part of Alden's gang, snickered.

"I don't think you deserve to breathe the same air she does." Ruark wanted to rip Alden's guts out through his mouth.

"I guess she doesn't agree with you." Alden leaned forward and rested his elbows on his knees. "I think we'll be sharing a lot more than air tonight."

A vein started pulsing in Ruark's temple. "You'll be a gentleman and treat her with the respect she deserves."

"Whatchu gon' do 'bout it, if'n Ah don't, son?" Alden asked as he channeled his inner Foghorn Leghorn. Leo and Kevin, the other one of Alden's buddies in the car, guffawed like hyenas.

Assholes.

"Just watch where you put your hands." If he hadn't wanted to go to the dance at first, Ruark really was glad to be going there now, so he could keep an eye on Alden.

His sister sure had lousy taste in guys.

"Oooh, I'm scurred now." Alden leaned back again. "What you gonna do, faggot? Smack me with your purse?"

Just in the nick of time, the limo turned into the circular drive in front of the Brewsters' house. Ruark figured Alden, Leo, and Kevin would behave once the girls joined them. He hoped. He hated violence. He hated even the thought of violence. He would, however, go after anyone who hurt his sisters.

The limo came to rest underneath a portico held up by fat white columns in front of the entrance to the house. Warm light glowed from within, creating a very homey effect. Pots of orange, red, and yellow mums, along with strategically placed pumpkins and cornstalks, were just enough. Any more decoration would have been tacky.

Mrs. Brewster, looking totally dignified, opened the door before the boys could ring the bell. Hair the color of champagne, make up perfect, dressed in a pair of loden green slacks, a rich cream cashmere turtleneck and a muted plaid blazer, she looked like a cover model for *Town and Country* magazine.

Maybe time with Cecily wouldn't be so bad. If her mom was so classy, maybe Cecily would be.

Mrs. Brewster grinned warmly at the boys. "Come on in, guys." She winked. "I think the girls are almost ready."

"Hey, Mrs. B." Alden bounded up the porch steps. "How are you?"

"I'm well, Alden." She shook the hand he offered. "We missed your mother at bridge Thursday afternoon. I hope everything's okay."

"She had to take my grandmother to a doctor's appointment in Boston. Just a routine check up."

"Well, you just tell her hello for me."

"Yes, ma'am." Alden swung his arm around Ruark's shoulder, like any good ol' boy would. So cool, butter wouldn't melt in his mouth. "Have you met Ruark Logan? He's Shanna Logan's twin brother."

Mrs. Brewster smiled at Ruark. "Oh my, Cecily's date!" She held out her hand out. "I'm glad to finally meet you."

Ruark shook her hand. "I'm honored to meet you, ma'am."

Mrs. Brewster upped the wattage of her smile. "Aren't you the charming one? I suppose all you southern boys are." She turned her head to greet a man who's pressed, brightly plaid pants and emerald green polo shirt screamed "GOLFER!" "Come here, Hank. I want you to meet Cecily's date, Ruark Logan."

Hank came over sporting his best hail-fellow-well-met smile and grabbed Ruark's hand. "Logan. Where have I heard that name before?"

Uh, my mother is your cleaning lady? Holy crud. He didn't care for himself, but all Shanna needed was to have her friends all find out her mother was the hired help.

"He's Ruark Logan, Shanna Logan's twin brother. You know, the little girl who's Cece's new friend." A noise from the stairs grabbed her attention. "Oh, here they are. Hank, do you have your camera?"

He held it out. "Right here, Abigail." He rolled his eyes at the boys. "She always thinks I'm going to forget."

"That's because you always do, unless I remind you," Mrs. Brewster retorted. "Smile, girls! Dad has a camera, and he knows how to use it."

Totally relieved to have the attention off him, Ruark checked out the girls. Shan was cute in her emerald green dress and her make up looked good. Having a mom who was a beauty queen definitely put a check in the plus side of the box. Priscilla Cooke was wearing a god-awful, pink on steroids satin thing. She'd applied the make up with a heavy hand, and the pink eye shadow she wore made her look like one hot, tranny, vampire mess. He couldn't bear to check out her shoes. Josslyn Mills had stuck with a little black dress and it looked good on her. Simple, great lines, none of the frilly crap that teen girls thought they needed on a party frock. Her black patent stilettos worked well with the dress—so fierce!

Then came Cecily, wearing this sparkly, cracked out flapper dress. Or was it supposed to be a gladiator dress? There was *fringe*. It was a flapper costume. There wasn't a single swatch of cloth that didn't look like Tinkerbell had designed it and a unicorn had farted glitter all over it. The same went for the shoes. Though gold, they looked just like a red sparkly pair Shanna used when they were kids and playing *The Wizard of Oz*.

Tim Gunn would be very concerned.

Ruark Logan merely felt miserable embarrassment. Why couldn't Josslyn be the one who wanted to date him? She, at least, knew what not to wear.

She'd probably be the only one at Addington High who'd figure out he was gay.

Nevertheless, he took Cecily's hand as she came down the stairs. "You look very pretty," he lied as he held out the corsage box, opened it, then slipped the flowers onto her wrist. It looked stupid against the dress. What wouldn't?

"Thank you." She admired tight red, baby rosebuds before pinning a yellow rose boutonniere on his lapel. Wrinkling her nose, she murmured, "Let's go. The sooner we get the pictures done, the better. Dad's kind of a dork."

"He seems pretty cool." At least he wasn't a crook like Ruark's dad.

"Well, anyway, I'm excited to get to the dance." She grabbed his hand and pulled him toward the fireplace where the kids were gathering for a group photo. "It's gonna be so much fun." They took their places with the other kids.

Mr. Brewster grinned and aimed. "Say cheese!"

Chapter Seventeen

Ainslie looked at her watch. The dance had started, but the only kids there were obviously freshman. No sign of Shanna and Ruark. She frowned.

Dave came up bearing punch. He held the plastic cup out to her. "I brought you a drink. One of the chaperone duties is to make sure the kids aren't spiking it when we aren't looking. Hey," he said. "What's up?"

"The twins aren't here yet." Her right foot tapped in spite of her trying to keep it still.

"They'll be here soon. The upperclassmen usually get here a little bit later than the younger kids. They're too cool for school."

She smiled wanly. "I guess."

Dave made her take the cup of punch. "Bottom's up."

Obedient, she drank it down. Grimacing, she shuddered. "This is awful. It tastes like melted lollipops."

"That's why I let *you* taste it." He laughed and flinched when she punched him in the arm. "No booze?"

"No booze." She bit her lower lip. "Would you mind if I took a couple of minutes to check up on Patsy?" She knew she was over-protective of her babies, but she couldn't help herself.

"Sure, go ahead. There's other parents here, and the rush won't come for a while."

"Thanks for understanding."

He raised his hand like he was going to touch

her hair, but then he didn't. His blue eyes were soft and understanding. "No problem."

****

"Everything okay?" Dave asked Ainslie when she rejoined him.

"Seems to be." She craned her neck over the increasing crowd of kids.

"They're not here yet. Don't worry." He put his hand on her shoulder and squeezed. "The older kids are only starting to get here." A commotion off to the side of the gym caught his eye. "I'll be right back. A couple of kids want a month of detention. Be right back."

****

"Time to party!" Alden squeezed into the limo as close to Shanna as possible. If he was trying to make Ruark crazy, he was doing a good job.

Alden pulled a flask out of his coat jacket and took a big swig. He held it out to Shanna. "Here you go, darlin'."

Ruark stared at Shanna while she took the flask. She blushed. He knew that she didn't drink. She never drank.

"Shanna, come on."

Alden whispered something in her ear that Ruark didn't catch. She gave Alden a shy smile and took a sip.

As the flask went around, every one of them took a drink. It finally got around to him. "No, thanks," he told Priscilla, as she tried to give it to him.

Cecily took the flask from Priscilla, her eyebrows raised at Ruark. "Not even a sip? Don't you want to have fun?"

Part of the truth was his new best friend. "The alcohol affects my voice. I can't sing for days after I drink." He left out the fact that someone was going to need to be sober if Shanna was going to be stupid.

She pouted. "Your loss." She took a big drink.

The booze went around a couple more times. The girls got annoyingly giggly.

They passed around gum before they got to the dance. Alden had draped his arm over Shanna's shoulders, continually whispering stuff in her ear. From the adoring look on Shanna's face, she was buying every word of it.

Ruark flinched when Cecily rubbed against him. God.

What a nightmare.

****

"Hey, you're here!" Andi came up to Ainslie and gave her a quick hug. "Don't you just love chaperoning dances?"

"I didn't see you come in," Ainslie said. "Where's Mike?"

"Oh, he's in his office getting his speech ready." Andi patted a hair back into its place in her French twist. "Homecoming Dance is the big event for the football program. Between you and me," Andi smiled confidentially, "Mike hates it because he has to make this presentation."

"When does that happen?"

"At 9:30 when he has to announce the Homecoming King and Queen."

"Who picks them?"

"The student body votes on it." Andi stood on tiptoes, smiled and waved. "Here's Mike now. Maybe we can get a head's up on who won."

"Hey, Spud." Mike kissed his wife on the top of her head and totally messed up the hairs Andi had moved into place just a couple of minutes ago. "Ainslie," he said over Andi's head, "Dave around?"

"I think he made a trip to the men's room. Seems someone saw smoke coming from underneath the door."

Mike shook his head. "Kids are so stupid. If

they'd put something along the edge of the door, no smoke would have escaped."

"Got a history with that, coach?" Andi gave Mike a little hip check.

"Never! Remember I was an altar boy. I was a perfect kid."

Ainslie smiled at the two of them and glanced at the gym entrance for what felt like the millionth time.

Hallelujah! Shanna and Ruark were at the door with their dates. They looked so wonderful, so beautiful, to her. Her eyes welled up.

Shanna's date wore a dark blue jacket that looked near to bursting, he was so muscular. Handsome in a football player kind of way, Alden certainly was solicitous toward Shanna, who wore a happy smile and sparkly eyes.

Ruark didn't look as excited. In fact he looked like he was at a root canal instead of a dance, but he was so handsome in that gray suit. She had to admit Cecily's dress was, uh, well, unfortunate.

Ruark glanced over at Ainslie and gave her a smile. He might have crossed his eyes at her, but she couldn't tell because of the distance.

"Those are very handsome children you have, Mrs. Logan," Dave murmured from behind her.

She turned to face him. "All clear on the bathroom front?"

He sighed. "I wish. We'll have to monitor it in shifts, as usual." Dave scanned the dancers, then looked at his watch. "Looks like the gang's all here." He turned to Mike. "Ready to make the big announcement?"

Mike nodded. "Let's do it."

The two walked over to the mic stand. Andi watched them go. "No matter the year, there's always a girl who is so disappointed. Mike hates that." She tapped her foot in time to the music. "I wish they'd just stop this stupid homecoming queen and king thing. The competition brings out the worst in the girls. Of course," she said, "the same could be said about the competition among the girls over the lead role in the musical."

"Being a former Miss South Carolina, I can't say that I don't enjoy all the spectacle and glamour, even at this age, but you're right about how it puts the girls in competition." Ainslie did know from experience that girls could be really vicious.

But deep down, she was a born and bred Dixie debutante and loved the rituals that came with crowning a homecoming king and queen.

Chapter Eighteen

Cecily grabbed Ruark's hand. "I hope it's us."

"Us what?" Ruark wanted to politely extricate his hand from Cecily's, but she had a grip like an anaconda.

"The Homecoming Queen and King. I hope we win."

"I didn't know we were in the running." *Please, kill me now.*

"I put our names on the ballot during the spirit week kick-off pep rally." She bounced on the tips of her rhinestone and gold stiletto sandals.

Ruark longed for a fork so he could poke his own eyes out. Homecoming King? Absolutely no way. Though, in other circumstances, being crowned Homecoming Queen might be kinda fun. This was, however, not other circumstances.

Mr. Mason was doing the talking, and Ruark glanced over to where his mother stood. She looked at Mr. Mason as if he hung the moon. He was pretty sure she'd never looked at his father that way. And, if Ruark could see how much his mom liked Mr. Mason, then the whole school should be able to see it.

He wanted to puke. He loved his mom, he wanted her to find a good man. Just not Mr. Mason. He hated seeing her with him. The whole thing drove Ruark crazy.

He felt Cecily clutch his hand, her gold sparkly acrylic nails biting little crescent shaped grooves into his palm. Hopefully, she wasn't going to draw blood.

Coach Kelly read off a piece of paper. "Best game in years," "worked really hard," "kept their eyes on the prize," blah, blah, blah.

Then he said, "It's time to announce the Homecoming King and Queen."

Cecily looked like she was going to spontaneously combust right there. Just up and go boom. *Flame on!*

Coach Kelly handed a paper to Mr. Mason. Unfolding it, Mr. Mason smiled and said, "Let's give a hearty cheer for this year's Homecoming King and Queen, Alden Bradford and Shanna Logan!"

Wild clapping and whistling burst from the kids as Alden helped Shanna up onto the platform where Mr. Mason and Coach Kelly stood. Ms. Plunkett, a math teacher, also came forward with the chest banners, a crown, and a tiara. She handed them to Dave, who did the coronation honors.

Ruark glanced at Cecily, all set to say "better luck next time." On second thought, he figured that might be the wrong thing to say to a girl who looked ready to rip someone's lungs out of her throat.

Watching Cecily, he saw her literally pull herself together and fix a fake toothy smile on her face, she turned to him. "Aren't you excited! Your sister is Homecoming Queen!"

He glanced toward his sister and her date. Shanna and Alden were holding court. Alden held her too tight against him, to Ruark's way of thinking. That was so *not* okay and had to stop. "Sure, let's go congratulate them."

"Why not?" Cecily grabbed his hand again and pulled him along like he was a little kid crossing the street. The kids parted to let Cecily drag him by, just like Moses parting the Red Sea.

One hapless kid stopped her and asked how excited she was for Shanna. Raurk had never heard a girl growl before.

He just wanted to get his sister home and away from Alden Bradford and his magic flask.

Shanna saw them, her smile huge, her happiness palpable. She threw herself into Cecily's rather stiff arms. "Omigawd, I'm so surprised."

Cecily pulled away and checked her manicure. "I guess you're wearing a lucky dress." She tossed her hair back. "I was Homecoming Queen last year wearing a dress just like that."

Ruark watched as a little bit of Shanna's exuberance popped like a bubble, confronted with Cecily's cattiness. He pried Shanna away from Cecily and gave his sister a hug. "Way to go, Shan. You're really pretty tonight. Momma must be proud as can be."

Cecily grabbed his arm again. "Let's dance."

Ruark did as he was told.

****

Tears of joy formed in Ainslie's eyes. She brushed them away, making sure she didn't smudge her mascara all over her face. Her little girl being crowned Homecoming Queen. Ainslie's southern belle, beauty-pageant-lovin' heart melted like butter in the sun. She tried to catch Shanna's eye, but it didn't happen. Shanna was surrounded by her friends, both male and female.

Alden was holding onto her girl a bit more closely than Ainslie was comfortable with. It set her spidey senses tingling, as one of Ruark's comic book heroes would say. She'd ask Dave and Mike about Alden. She probably should have before she let Shanna go out with him.

Something else to feel guilty for.

But since she cleaned the Bradfords' house as well as the Brewsters', she'd checked Alden out and felt comfortable letting Shanna go out with him. However, she did not want him getting so physical with Shanna. Shanna was too young for that kind of relationship.

Dave and Mike returned after the coronation. Andi smiled. "Good job there, Coach."

"I try." He looked at Ainslie. "That's a beautiful little girl you got there."

Ainslie, flooded with pride, nodded. "My babies are the reason I get up in the morning."

Andi's smile drooped a little. "I can only imagine."

Mike slipped an arm around her waist and hauled her in. "How's about taking a walk around the gym outside so we can catch evil doers."

Andi laughed. "I love nothing better than catching evil doers." She and Mike walked away toward the visitor side door of the gym.

Dave sidled up to her. "Congratulations."

Ainslie grinned. "Maybe I should get her into pageants here." Chuckling, she slid Dave a glance. "Y'all do have pageants here in the north, right?"

"Yes, Ma'am, Ah b'lieve we do."

Dear Lord, that had to be the worst southern accent she'd ever heard. "Stop," she laughed. "Just stop. You sound like a Hop-a-long Cassidy wannabe. I've never heard anyone from the South talk that way."

"I'll work on it. You can teach me." Unrepentant, Dave waggled his eyebrows. "I'm a slow learner. I need a long time to get the facts, but once I have all the knowledge I need, I know exactly what to do and when to do it." She knew that suggestive tone of voice. No doubt there would be more going on than just teaching him how to speak southern.

Lord love a duck, she surely wanted to give him lessons in how to speak with a southern accent.

An accent dripping honey.

All over.

Naked.

In bed.

She did feel very eager to get the clothes off Dave Mason. A flash of sheer heat ran up her body. The tip of her tongue came out to moisten her lips. He watched her, his gaze smoldering.

Dave broke away first, cleared his throat, and fixed his tie, even though it didn't need fixing. "Are you going to congratulate Shanna?"

"I don't want to embarrass her," she lied. She cleaned the houses of Shanna's friends.

But this was Dave. She realized with a jolt that she trusted him enough to tell him anything. "Shanna isn't comfortable sharing the fact that I clean most of her friends' houses.

His eyebrows squashed together like he didn't understand what she was saying. "Well, okay then. Why don't you let me buy you a cup of punch?" He touched her elbow, and she felt electricity zap through her body.

"I know that punch and can say with absolute certainty that it's not a very good incentive."

He looked at her solemnly. She couldn't tell what he was thinking. "Let's go check out the refreshment table again. Sometimes, while all the attention is on the coronation, kids take advantage of that and spike the punch or slip a plate of pot brownies on the table."

A quick spurt of gratefulness overtook her. He wasn't going to make her talk about Shanna's embarrassment over Ainslie being a cleaning lady and a waitress. It was a Charleston thing. They had been on the top of the social circle. It was totally her fault that Shanna was a snob.

Still, it hurt a little bit.

When they got to the table, he greeted the kids standing around. "May I have two of the pumpkin cookies, please?" He handed a five-dollar bill to the girl at the cash box. "I hear they are very good."

The girl laughed, picked up two sugar cookies

decorated with two inches of frosting to look like pumpkins, and put them on a paper plate. "Thanks!"

"Thanks!" Dave said.

"You're welcome! Hope you like your cookies!"

"No problem with that, Liz. I have yet to meet a cookie I didn't like." Dave punctuated that with a smile, then turned and gave Ainslie one of the frosted cookies. "Let's take a walk around the room."

****

"Why are you constantly looking around?" Cecily murmured into Ruark's ear. "You're supposed to be my date, as in like, paying attention to me."

Ruark bit back a sigh as he looked down at the girl who was wrapping herself around him like a vine on a stick. "What? I'm paying attention to you. We're dancing." To a trite and sappy slow song about true love.

"No, you're not. You're too busy trying to keep an eye on Shanna and Alden."

Cecily's pout was nearly as good as Shanna's. What was it with girls and pouting? And what could he say? He *was* more interested in keeping track of Alden and Shanna, especially since he knew Alden hoped to get lucky and Shanna'd been drinking.

Cecily disentangled herself, grabbed Ruark's hand, and dragged him to a corner of the gym where there were few kids. "Look," she snarled, "I'm used to guys treating me better than this. So, if you don't step up and stop embarrassing me by *ignoring* me, I'll make sure everyone knows the truth about you and Shanna."

What the hell? "What do you think is the *truth* about me and Shanna?" Had Cecily figured out he was gay?

"That your mom is my cleaning lady, and the dress Shanna is wearing is one of my cast-offs that I gave to charity." Smug, Cecily crossed her arms under her breasts. "We'll see how popular she is then. She might even lose her spot on the cheering team."

Whoa! Ruark so didn't see that one coming. What a *biatch*. Shanna thought Cecily was her BFF. Showed what Shanna knew.

He pushed aside the relief he felt when Cecily hadn't found out he was gay. Lord help him, but he was going to protect his sister by dating Cecily, more than this one time.

His life sucked. Shanna was dating a guy who loved to humiliate Ruark at every opportunity, most likely looking to score and toss Shanna aside once she put out. With their father in prison, Raurk had to take care of his sisters. And Cecily wanted him to dote on her until she found a new toy and dumped Ruark. That day could not come soon enough.

Sometimes a guy just had to put his own feelings aside and look after his family, no matter what it cost him. He sighed and pulled Cecily's hand, and just for good measure and a great show, he kissed her cheek. He hoped none of the foundation she'd troweled on rubbed off on his lips.

Her eyes glittered, most likely in triumph. If this was the way it had to be to keep Shanna on Cecily's good side, he'd do it.

****

Pinned against the stone wall of the school, Shanna tried to keep from panicking as Alden kissed her really hard. He kissed her so their teeth clicked together, and he stuck his fat ol' tongue in her mouth, like it had a right to be there. His hand had a death grip on her right breast as he squeezed it.

If this was the way northern boys kissed, then she wanted no part of it. Alden had lived in fairy tale prince land in her mind, until he started making out with her.

It was a dance. She had a pretty dress, and she wanted to dance, not be pawed like this.

Turning her face away from him and breaking the kiss, she asked, "Alden, I'm getting cold. Can we go back in and dance?"

"What's the matter with stayin' out here and having a little fun?" He squeezed her breast hard again. His breath smelled kind of boozey, even though he'd chewed an entire pack of spearmint gum.

Her little buzz from the vodka in the limo had burned out an hour ago.

"Nothing. I like it fine," she lied through her teeth. "I just want to go in and dance again, that's all."

He looked at her as if she were speaking Martian. "If that's what you want, sure we can go back for a while." He stood back from her. "We'll still have the after party at Kevin's house to have some fun."

She winced from having been pushed against the wall. She hoped there was no damage done to the back of her dress. Something must be wrong with her. She really liked Alden, he was so hot and all that, so she should like making out with him and stuff. Right?

Really confused and a little bit ashamed, Shanna ran her hands through her hair. She'd have to stop in the ladies' room before going out onto the dance floor. She didn't want her momma to see her like this.

****

Crepe paper drooped and tangled as the clean up crew came in. The last teen had left about a half hour before. The air smelled less like a dozen cheap colognes all mixed together. As the poisonous combination faded, the smell of eye-burning floor cleaner replaced it. Ainslie stifled a yawn as she wiped down the refreshment table.

Another new experience, being part of the

cleaning crew. Dave had to make sure the decorations were down so the gym could be a gym again. Next week was coed volleyball, and the janitors were putting up volleyball nets so all would be ready for the first period on Monday morning.

Andi sidled up to her, wet cloth in her hand. "You have beautiful children."

"Thank you." Ainslie answered her. "I think they're gorgeous, but of course I'm biased." She bit on her lower lip. "I wanted to meet their dates, but it didn't happen. What is your opinion of the kids they were with?"

"They're tight in the popular crowd. Cecily is all right. She's right on top with the uber-popular girls." She wiped at a spot on the table. "Alden is the captain of the football team." She pressed her lips together. "They come from solid families."

But, because she was a mother and her children went out of their way to avoid her, her stomach churned. She sighed, wishing with all her heart she didn't have jobs that embarrassed them.

Chapter Nineteen

"Thank you for the dance. It was so good to see Shanna and Ruark with their friends." Ainslie twirled her thumbs as Dave parked in front of her house.

"No problem. It was one of the best Homecoming Dances I've been to."

"Well, I doubt that. I just loved seeing Shanna get crowned Homecoming Queen."

"About seeing Shanna..." Dave reached into the pocket inside his jacket. He pulled out a DVD. "I, uh, shot this yesterday at the game. It's the cheering squad at halftime."

She looked at the slim box he held out to her. "Cheerleaders?"

"Yep. I know you were disappointed because you couldn't go to the game." He took her hands and pressed the DVD into them. "You wanted to see Shanna cheer. Now you can."

She looked at the DVD and held onto it as if it were made of spun gold. "I can't believe you did this."

"As a reward, you can invite me in for coffee."

Oh, those blue, blue eyes of his. How could she say no when he was looking at her like she was the only woman in the world. "Would you like to come in for coffee?"

"I would love to come in for coffee. Thanks for asking." He was up and out of the car and holding her door open before she had a chance to blink.

She put her hand in the one he held out and wiggled herself out of the seat. He pulled her in for a

147

breath-stealing kiss. "Let's go on in and get rid of Chelsea," he whispered into her ear, after he had playfully nipped at her earlobe.

She shivered. The man was a magician. "As soon as we politely can."

He kissed her again, this time longer, and caused Ainslie to shiver again.

Dave murmured, "I can be polite. Look up polite in the dictionary, and you'll see my picture." He planted a little kiss on the top of her head."

"Ditto." She went up on tiptoes and brushed her lips over his before they opened her front door.

Chelsea sat on the sofa reading a book, all nice and quiet. She looked up as Dave and Ainslie came through the door.

"Is Patsy in bed?" Ainslie let Dave help her out of her coat and thrilled at the courtesy.

"Sound asleep, like the little angel she is." Chelsea stretched as she stood.

Ainslie began to open her purse so she could pay Chelsea, but Dave beat her to it, handing Chelsea a couple of twenties.

"Oh, Dave no," Ainslie protested.

"Let me get this," he said.

Chelsea stuffed the cash in her jeans pocket. "Thanks!" She stood there, apparently not in a big hurry to leave. "Anytime you need a babysitter, you know where to find me," she chirped. "Was the dance fun? Anybody get detention? An in-school suspension? I want details."

Dave rocked back on his heels as he put his hands in his pockets. "Pretty uneventful, no drama, no problems." His face was unreadable. "Which is just the way I like it."

"Oh, sure, me too." She slung her backpack over her right shoulder. "Well, I better go. I've still got some lesson plans to write and e-mail to my co-operating teacher."

Ainslie gave Chelsea a quick hug. "Thank you for taking care of Patsy. It meant a lot for me to see my children and their friends."

"No worries." Chelsea nodded. "See you later."

Ainslie and Dave both watched her leave. Ainslie heaved a big sigh. "Looks like everything went okay."

Dave looked around the room. "We can pop the DVD in, if you want to watch it."

"Please! The DVD player is part of the TV. I'll just check on Patsy."

He smiled at her, his come-get-me smile, which made her insides melt. "I can work a coffeemaker, you know. Check on Patsy and let me get it going."

She nodded, then skedaddled, anxious to check on Patsy.

Opening the door with a tiny creak, Ainslie poked her head through so as not to disturb her sleeping little girl. Ainslie shut the door and followed the rich, nutty aroma to the kitchen and Dave.

It felt odd to see him puttering around her kitchen, though she could get used to it. She leaned against the doorjamb. "Did you find everything?"

He grinned as he turned. "Yes." Moving across the kitchen, he caught her hips and pulled her against his body. His hands rubbed her lower back. If those hands moved any lower, he'd be grabbing her derrière. "I found everything just fine," his voice was a gruff, rusty whisper.

He kissed her, gently, just a mere brushing of their lips, which spun into a long, slow kiss. Her heart started thumping loudly. "I've been wanting to do this all night." Ainslie threaded her arms around his neck, because her legs were about to melt into a puddle on the floor.

Breathing heavily, he murmured against her lips. "Are you okay with this with Patsy around? If you're not, we can stop." He flexed the fingers that were holding her upright and squeezed her bottom.

"She's a very sound sleeper." Could Dave be any more considerate, worrying about Patsy?

"I'm very glad to hear that." Hiking her up with those strong, warm hands of his, he pulled her in close. She wrapped her legs around his while he moved to the kitchen table. He stood between those rickety legs of hers to kiss her again.

Her head fell back, and he took the advantage and kissed the sensitive arch of her neck. Slow and sweet sweeps of his lips traced her throat alternated with quick little nibbles, teasing and ticklish.

Ainslie reached between them to unbutton his shirt so she could feel the muscular, warm skin. She traced the outline of each and every muscle.

When she had finished with his shirt, he murmured, "My turn."

She shivered as he uncovered her and for a moment stood silently, his arms around her waist, her arms clinging around his neck. She had to let go of his neck so he could slip the two purple sweaters over her head.

That done, those magic hands of his moved up her back to the edge of her bra. She shivered, loving the way he touched her. Dave pulled the cups down under her breasts and pushed the straps down her arms.

Dave stopped kissing her, pulling back to see what he'd discovered. Gravity was not her friend. If he expected perky, smooth skinned, and no stretch marked breasts, he was out of luck. Her boobs didn't do perky any more, due to 38 years and the three children she'd breast-fed.

So nervous that Dave wouldn't like what she looked like, she practically choked on it.

"You're so lovely," he breathed in a reverent whisper. "I've lost a lot of sleep dreaming of what you looked like, and you're much more beautiful than I imagined."

Agile fingers rolled and teased her nipples into achy awareness. It had been so long for her, and his hands on her breasts felt so good.

He eased her backward on the table, so her body needed to rest on her elbows. He cupped both breasts, kneading and fondling them. Dave kept his hand on one while he bent his head playing with the hard, wildly aroused, needy point of the other, laving her with sweeps of his generous tongue. Then he tugged her nipple gently with his lips and nibbled on it with playful teeth until she squirmed with frustration and delight. The man had mad skills.

He found another really sensitive spot on her neck and made her moan and wiggle against him.

"Chelsea? Momma?" Patsy said from the living room. "Momma?" Her voice started to take on an edge of panic. "It's scary here alone."

"Oh, God. This was a bad idea." Ainslie slipped off the table, pulled her bra up, and hauled her sweater over her head. "I'm right here, baby." She didn't look back when she opened her kitchen door.

****

Dave looked around. Hearing Ainslie coo and comfort her little girl, he felt a jolt of emotion. He was all the way gone, in love with Ainslie Logan.

Moving into the living room, Dave stood, ready to stay or go, depending on what Patsy needed.

Ainslie didn't miss a beat, she just murmured soft words Dave couldn't hear while she cuddled her daughter on the couch.

The phone rang. "Do you want me to get that?" he called to Ainslie.

She looked at him. "Do you mind? It might be one of the twins, and I'm all tied up with my little pumpkin here." This statement was followed up by a monster burp from said pumpkin.

"I don't mind at all." He took a deep breath

while picking up the phone. "Logan residence."

"Who's this?" Dave recognized Ruark's voice, even though the background noises were loud enough to make it difficult to hear.

"It's Mr. Mason. Is something wrong? Do you need help?"

"I want to talk to my mother."

"She's a bit busy with Patsy right now and can't leave her. Can I do something to help you? Are you in trouble?"

Silence, then a sigh gusted through the earpiece. "The girls got picked up and went to a sleepover at Cecily's house. I don't want to stay here at Kevin's. I need to get a ride home."

"Your mom really can't leave Patsy now, but I can come get you."

More silence, then, "Yes, please. If you don't mind doing this."

"Not at all." Dave would do just about anything for Ainslie and her family. "I can be there in about ten minutes."

"Thanks." Ruark hung up.

Ainslie came into the room carrying a hiccupping Patsy in her arms. "Who was that?"

Dave moved to get his coat. "Ruark. He needs a ride home from Kevin Baldwin's house, since the girls went to the Brewsters' for a sleepover. I'm going to go get him."

"You don't have to do that," Ainslie protested. "I can put Patsy in the back seat while I get him."

"I think you need to stay here with Patsy. Please." He looked at her frazzled, lovely face. "Let me do this for you."

She looked at Patsy, who was still hiccupping and sniffling. Looking back at Dave, she said, "Thank you."

He smiled as he tugged on his jacket. "Be right back."

Chapter Twenty

Dave pulled into the Baldwin's driveway and put the car in neutral. He didn't know whether to wait for Ruark or go up and fetch him. Option two would cause a few eyebrows to rise.

Ruark made the decision for him by hightailing it off the porch. He practically flew to the car, then pulled the door open and slid into the passenger seat. "Thanks for picking me up." Ruark wouldn't look Dave in the eyes. "Is Patsy okay?"

"I think she'll be fine. Your mom has it all under control." Dave put the car in gear. Waves of misery rolled off the kid like Niagara Falls.

Ruark hunkered down in the car while he belted up. He looked straight ahead, discouraging conversation.

Too bad, because Dave knew something was up, and he wanted to get to the bottom of it. Someone had harassed Ruark in school, and Dave had a chance to find out who it was. He figured Ruark was going to have to give up the bullies sooner or later.

Actually, right now would be a really good time. "How was the party?"

"Okay."

"Who was there?"

Ruark shrugged. "Kids."

Okay. Didn't look like Ruark was going to spill his guts.

Ruark cleared his throat and looked out the passenger side window.

"I didn't realize you were friends with the football crowd, at least enough to get a limo with them."

He still wouldn't look at Dave. "The girls arranged it all. They wanted to all go together, so since I was Cecily's date, I got included in it."

"When did you start to date Cecily?"

"Just tonight."

"She's a pretty girl, really popular. I think lots of guys were jealous of you being with her."

Ruark snorted. The sound wasn't polite. It sounded like the only comment Ruark intended to make about Cecily.

Dave glanced at Ruark. The kid looked so angry. "You would probably feel a lot better if you just told me what's going on."

****

Ruark had a ball of barbed wire rolling around in his stomach. He'd happily give Cecily to any guy who wanted her. He kept his face turned to the side because he wanted to puke.

His sister and Alden Bradford, King of the Douches, were together. Alden wanted only one thing from Shanna, and Ruark couldn't do one damn thing about it. And she was drinking to fit in with Alden and Cecily's clique. He had to keep dating Cecily to save Shanna's face as well as keep an eye on her. Bile rose in his throat. He nearly choked on it.

"I want to be back in Charleston. All the people who understand me are there. My music is there." The words blurted out of him before he could stop them.

In Charleston he had a life, friends, really *good* friends who he could be out of the closet with. He wanted to tell his mother he was gay, but she had so much to deal with, thanks to his sperm donor.

Gay or not, he was the man of the family now. He needed to take care of things and not worry her.

Pigs would fly before he could come out to his

mom and sisters. Especially since Shanna was hooking up with Alden Bradford. That would be horrible.

"Have you talked to Mrs. Kelly? It's not too late in the year to start an independent study. She could tailor a program just for you."

"It's not the same." He desperately missed music. Mrs. Kelly was okay, he liked her just fine, but she wasn't a world famous bass. She couldn't teach him what he hungered to know, what he needed to learn in order to have a career as a professional opera singer.

"I think you're selling Mrs. Kelly short." Mr. Mason flicked the blinker when he turned left into Ruark's driveway. "She knows a thing or two about opera."

"Sure, she does, okay. But she's not going to put on an opera so one kid can sing. That's what I want. And you know she can't do that."

"I'm sure she can come up with something. This independent study with Mrs. Kelly is better than nothing but chorus."

What did Mrs. Kelly know about opera, about losing your dreams, your future, the one thing that mattered? Raurk looked out the window again. Mr. Mason was right about one thing. An independent study would be better than nothing. "I can give it a try, I guess."

"Good. I'll talk to her first thing on Monday." Mr. Mason parked his car behind his mom's. Ruark grabbed for the door handle and pushed it open.

"Tell your mother I said good night."

Ruark stopped and looked at Mr. Mason. "Sure." He hopped out of the car before closing the door. "Thanks for the ride."

"Anytime." Mr. Mason smiled. He had such an amazing smile.

That was another dream gone. Ruark knew he'd

never had a chance with Mr. Mason, but still he'd liked the fantasy. He just couldn't fantasize about his mom's boyfriend.

Ruark felt a little queasy because he'd spilled his guts to Mr. Mason. "Please don't tell my mom the stuff I told you tonight, especially about the opera. It'll only make her feel bad."

"Of course. It'll stay between you and me."

Ruark sure hoped that was true. "Thank you for the ride, sir." He nodded once, closed the car door, then turned to go into the house his mom rented for them, his steps heavy and slow. That queasy feeling grew exponentially.

His mother was on the couch cuddling Patsy to sleep. "Hey there, handsome," she whispered. "How was the party?"

He shrugged. "Okay. Is Patsy all right?" She sure didn't look good.

"She woke up and got scared because she thought she was alone." His mom's brow furrowed. "Is Mr. Mason coming in?"

"No." Ruark cleared his throat. "He told me to tell you that he'd call you tomorrow."

"Are you okay?" Momma looked really hard at him. "Did something happen?"

"Uh, no." He crossed his fingers behind his back. "I'm just tired, is all. I'm gonna go to bed."

"Well, good night, then." Her gaze speared him. "Maybe you should take your temperature."

He heaved a huge sigh. "I don't have a temperature." No way he was ever going to burden her with his problems. So he lied. "Nothing's wrong. I'm tired, is all."

Mom shifted Patsy in her lap. "Good night, then, baby. Sweet dreams."

As he walked to his room, he turned his mom's words in his mind. Sweet dreams only dwelled in the part of his life he left in Charleston.

Chapter Twenty-One

"Dear Lord, my feet hurt." Ainslie dropped her butt onto a bar stool. Two competing soccer teams had come into The End Zone earlier, both at the same time, and mayhem had ensued.

It wasn't pretty. French fries as projectile weapons were never a good idea, unless thrown by college kids who'd had one too many cold ones and didn't have to scrape the smooshed ones off of the floor.

Spike wiped down a section of counter. "Tell me about it. My tootsies are tired. Maybe I can talk Bobby into closing early."

The End Zone's big front door opened, and Mike and Andi came in. Dressed up, they looked like they'd been somewhere fancy. Mike loosened his tie as he crossed the room. "Looks like a bomb went off in here."

Spike rolled her eyes. "No flies on you." She grabbed a Heineken, opened it with a *fsst,* and slapped it down on the bar in front him.

When she reached for a glass, Mike stopped her. "I don't need the glass. After the night I've had..." He exaggerated shivering, then took a swig. "I can't wait. I'm a victim of torture."

Andi shook her head, put her hand on his shoulder, and started to squeeze it. "Poor baby." She smiled at Ainslie and Spike. "He had to come to the ballet with me."

"I'm scarred for life." Obviously forlorn, Mike shook his head.

Andi gave him a hip check. "I think you'll live. I

actually need to talk to you, Ainslie."

Ainslie frowned. She'd known something was wrong with Ruark. Maybe something in choir. "Is there a problem at school?"

"Oh, no. Now that Dave's worked out Ruark's schedule so he can start an independent study with me on Monday, I wonder if there are school records from his school in Charleston that can be sent to me. Maybe some notes from his teachers about his progress there."

Ainslie goggled at Andi's serene face. "Really? This independent study is news to me."

Andi shifted her bag from her right to her left shoulder. "I thought Dave had checked with you about it."

No, Dave hadn't said a word. She didn't know whether to be annoyed or relieved. She chose relieved. If anything could start to make Ruark happy, a new class in music would be it. "He didn't, but this sounds intriguing. I'll make some calls tomorrow and get them to fax what isn't in the records I already had transferred. I've got lots of pictures of him in the school opera workshop. I have some DVDs, too, if you think those would help. He sang leading roles in some of their performances." And Max. "You know he did some work with Miles Maxwell."

Andi nodded. "That's impressive. It's a little daunting, to be honest. I'm not a world class *basso profundo*, but I can come up with something to keep him challenged and happy. Speaking of projects, are you available to have lunch Tuesday at Esmeralda's with the team planning the Ballet Gala? You're the one who came up with the Mirror on the Wall Ball idea. We really need you to give us some guidance on what will work and what won't."

Ainslie's heart beat hard and fast. "Lunch?" She'd make it work. She only had the Brewsters' house to clean. She could do it in the morning, then re-arrange the rest of her day. "Sure."

"Great! About 1:00? There's only a half day of school."

She'd forgotten all about that. One or both of the twins would have to stay home with Patsy. "I'm sure I can make it. Thank you."

"No, thank *you*. This is going to be a wonderful event." She elbowed Mike in the ribs. "Come on, buddy. Let's go home."

He chugged the rest of his beer and put the bottle down. "'Bout time. Later, ladies."

Poof, they were gone.

Ainslie grinned at Spike. "Wow. Ruark is just going to love this."

Spike polished a wine goblet. "Hope it works out for him. He's a good kid." She slipped the glass into the rack hung from the ceiling. "Everyone says Andi's a good teacher."

Ainslie slid off the barstool. "I better get back to wiping down tables. Can I get a clean cloth?" She picked up her spray bottle of table cleaner and the washrag Spike handed her. She hummed as she went to work. Her feet didn't throb as much as they did before Mike and Andi came in.

Shanna seemed to be making the transition well, with hardly a ripple. Patsy was doing better, too, and now maybe Ruark would find something to be happy about.

Dave had done this for her boy. She'd definitely have to find a way to thank him.

****

Ruark's backpack felt heavy as lead as he dragged his equally heavy feet in the direction of the music room. He hoped with all his heart that this independent study wasn't going to be lame.

On the other hand, it was better than study hall. Maybe. He could probably teach Mrs. Kelly about music. At least he could teach her about opera. Backwards, twice on Sunday, and blindfolded.

He'd been working on the Papageno arias from *Die Zauberflöte* for repertoire class. This year coming up, the main stage opera would be *Don Giovanni*. His teacher, Miles Maxwell, held the honor of being considered the best Don Giovanni in the world. This would have been his year. Ruark missed Max, missed the work, missed his friends. Nothing could take their place. Ever.

He stood and stared at the door handle to the vocal music room. To him, *vocal music* summed up the problem quite neatly. Vocal meant just making noise. Ruark *sang*.

The late bell rang, and he couldn't wait any more. He had to go in. He took a deep breath and pushed the door open.

Mrs. Kelly sat at the piano as he came inside the room. Her smile was big and looked genuine. "Ruark. Come on in and sit down so we can talk about what you want to study."

He slipped into a chair. "Opera."

"I figured out that much." Mrs. Kelly pulled a notebook and pen down from the top of the piano. "It's a big subject area. Want to narrow it down for me?"

Well, since she wanted to know, "I want to perform in an opera, with singers who are as interested in it as I am." And as talented, he added to himself. He didn't want to come off as stuck up.

Though, as Max always said, *if you don't blow your own horn, no one else will.*

"Okay." She tapped her pen on the notebook. "That's a big order to fill. That's something we'll have to work toward. I'm not sure we have enough students with enough skill for opera. Musical Theater, yes. Opera, not so much."

He shrugged. He'd known the answer before

she'd asked the question. He got a nervous, oogly-googly feeling in the pit of his stomach.

"What can we do in the meantime? You're already working on the Schubert for the next concert. District auditions are coming up. Let's pick an aria for that. I know you'll get an All State recommendation once the judges hear you."

"Sure." Ruark looked at the floor. "Whatever."

Mrs. Kelly was silent for a minute, then, she gave a noisy inhale. "I know it's not perfect, but it's a place to start."

He looked back at her. "I guess." Sudden tears stung behind his eyes. Oh, no. He would not cry. He swallowed and choked out, "It's just hard to know I used to have a goal, and friends who had the same goals, and now I don't have either."

"You still have the same goal you did back in Charleston. You want to be a professional opera singer." She stared at him. "You can make new friends. You *have* made new friends. Aren't you dating Cecily Brewster?"

Mrs. Kelly made him feel like a smear on a microscope slide. Like she expected him to say something about Cecily? Like she could read his mind and knew all about him.

Oh no, she couldn't tell he was gay. No way.

He squirmed in his chair, then just blurted, "I'm only taking Cecily out as a favor to Shanna."

"I see."

He'd disappointed her, he could tell. Probably she got mad because he really wasn't dating Cecily because he liked her and it was just the opposite. Time to change the subject. "I'm still not going to get into schools with good opera programs."

"That's not set in stone. We can work on material for conservatory auditions."

"I won't have the performance credits to get in." Ruark said. He knew he sounded like a brat, but he couldn't stop himself from opening his mouth.

Again, Mrs. Kelly sat in silence, then sighed. "I'm sure we can find some performance opportunities, if not in Addington, then in Boston. We can go online and find them."

He opened his mouth, ready to spout some lame excuse why that wouldn't work, then realized it might be a solution and it might be fun. Nodding, he said, "Okay."

Mrs. Kelly scratched some notes on her yellow pad, underlining something with two bold strokes of her pen. "So, let's get started on a list of arias for auditions. I can order scores after school today."

"I have some scores and some aria collections. I'll bring them into school tomorrow."

"That would be great," she smiled. "Let's get that list done."

Again, she looked at him like she could read his mind. He'd worry about that later.

Chapter Twenty-Two

"Hey, beautiful." Dave had taken a seat at The End Zone bar and pulled on Ainslie's apron strings as she cruised past the bar. "What's good tonight?"

She grabbed her apron and retied it. She couldn't help but smile. She'd hoped he'd come into the restaurant that night and there he was, with tousled dark hair and electric blue eyes, rumpled shirt and loosened tie.

He smelled faintly of soap and after-shave, clean and woodsy, but not too strong. She really had to be near him to catch the scent. Up close, it made her hormones buzz and jump like Mexican jumping beans in a hot pan. She had no choice but to lean in and give him a quick kiss square on the lips.

"Hm." He pulled her in by those apron strings and kissed her, teasing her lips open.

Her brain disconnected. Absolutely, totally went blank.

"Anybody got a fire hose so I can turn it on these two?" Bobby rumbled.

"Hey, Bobby." Dave pulled away from Ainslie but didn't let go of the apron. "How's it going?"

"It would go a hell of a lot better if you weren't mackin' on one of my waitresses."

"Sorry." Dave looked absolutely unrepentant, grinning like a pirate over a treasure chest full of booty.

Ahem. Ainslie did have some booty. She'd like to have less booty, but it was what it was. She felt herself blush as she moved out of Dave's arms. "Sorry, Bobby."

"Your order for table 20 is up."

"Oh. I'd better pick it up then." She hurried into the kitchen to get her order. She couldn't believe she'd forgotten it.

No more kissing high school principals at work, no matter how much she wanted to.

****

Dave watched Ainslie scamper off to pick up her food. He admired the way her sweet backside moved as she walked away. Whatever it was about her, Ainslie Logan had wiggled right into his heart.

Dave looked up to find Bobby staring at him.

"You want to explain just what the hell you're doing with Ainslie?" Bobby looked scary on a good day. Today must not be a good day, since Bobby looked more than ready to do some damage.

Dave bristled a little bit at what Bobby implied—that he was using Ainslie. "Back off, Bobby."

"She's a real nice lady who's gotten a real bad deal. Somebody's got to look after her." He drummed on the bar with calloused fingers the size of Volkswagens. "She's got kids." He took a swig of his cola.

"She's got great kids."

While it was nice that Ainslie had a knight in a kitchen apron, Dave took exception. *He* was going to be Ainslie's hero. *He* was going to be the one to take care of her and her children. "You've got nothing to worry about. I've got it all covered."

"Once upon a *time* you couldn't say anything nice about her, and now I catch you with your tongue down her throat? In the middle of a public restaurant. *My* restaurant." Bobby picked up a knife and cut a wedge out of a lime. He made it look dangerous. "She's not a plaything, and I'm just making sure you watch your step with her."

"Time's change." He met Bobby's gaze with his

own.

"Something tells me I'm gonna need to get out of the kitchen more often." Bobby looked past him.

Dave turned his head to see what Bobby was staring at. Chelsea stood there, studying her dupe pad like it had the cure for cancer written on it.

"I've got an order." She ripped the dupe off the pad and handed it to Bobby. "I need a couple of Coors Light," she told Spike.

Ainslie passed the bar while carrying a tray laden down with food. It looked too heavy for her. Clearly she was having a problem with it, though she had a smile plastered on her face. He wanted to take it off her shoulder and carry it himself. She shouldn't have to work so hard.

So what could he do about that?

He didn't know. He liked spending time with her, he loved talking to her. He loved touching her. Something loosened inside him when he was with her, something warm and soothing, a feeling which alternated with being turned on like he had stepped on a live wire.

But, still and all, she soothed him. She smoothed some the rough edges in his world.

He didn't want to wait any more. Time to step things up. But what to do?

Dinner at Hope's? He'd already done that.

Dancing? Okay, well, he guessed a high school dance wasn't exactly the most romantic place to impress her with his moves.

He could cook for her. Didn't feel quite right to him. She needed something unique, something romantic, something she wouldn't associate with anyone else. What could he do?

He smiled. He knew exactly who to ask. Grabbing his phone, he punched in a number.

****

"What are you asking me for?" Gina shook her

head, then pulled her red curls back into a ponytail and anchored it with a black hair tie. "I barely know Ainslie."

Dave had talked her into inviting him to her house, while he picked her brain about his Ainslie problem. Originally, just Ian had lived in this house, so there were books and newspapers all over. The Library of Congress probably didn't have as many books as Ian did. Now, many of the books were Gina's, and she had lots of them too. Since she was a huge fan of romance novels, that made her a romance guru, as far as Dave was concerned.

Plus, Ian taught French and wrote poetry. *He* must have picked up a few romantic ideas along the way. Dave looked over at him as Ian stirred some sugar into some tea. "Don't look at me, mate," Ian warned Dave. "I have no clue as to what a single mother of three would consider romantic."

Dave rubbed the spot in between his eyes. "I heard you swept Gina off her feet."

Ian and Gina exchanged a look that practically singed some of those books on the walls.

"See, you two are experts."

Gina sighed. "Okay. What does she like?"

He knew the answer to that question. "She was a big patron of the arts down in Charleston, so she likes that kind of thing. You know, artsy stuff."

"That's kind of a wide category. Want to narrow it down for me?" Gina sipped her tea.

"Well, I know she likes opera." Dave scratched his temple. "Here's the thing. Her ex-husband used to be richer than God. There's absolutely nothing I can do to out do anything he did."

"Her ex-husband is in jail. I don't think she's that much of a fan at this point, so don't worry about him." Gina pursed her lips. "The last thing you want to do is remind Ainslie of Bobby Lee Logan, wonder husband and dad."

"So what do I do?"

"Sandy told me she just really wants to spend more time with her kids. Arrange a date that includes them."

"That's hardly romantic." Ian pulled off his glasses and set them on the table next to him.

"The most romantic thing you ever did was put on a tee shirt that was too small and get conked in the head with a softball." Gina shivered and blew Ian a kiss. "Best marriage proposal *ever*."

Dave hoped he could get out of there without getting a cavity. "No way am I getting hit in the head. Next idea."

"You're awful bossy for someone who's asking for a favor." Gina checked out her manicure.

"It seems to me that you might start with doing something with her family. You know, movies, pizza." Ian snapped his fingers. "McDonald's. I once saw a single mother at McDonald's once. They were having a great time."

"Actually, the kids were terrors and spilled an entire cup of cola all over your lap." Gina reminded him. "No one was having a good time."

"Oh, yeah." Ian scratched his temple. "You might want to forget the McDonald's thing."

Dave ignored them. He wasn't taking Ainslie and her kids to McDonald's. "I don't want to give the kids the wrong idea. It's not fair to insert myself into the family when the relationship might not go anywhere."

"That's a consideration. You might as well stop seeing her now." Ian sighed. "Before anyone gets hurt."

"I don't want to stop seeing her," he grumbled. "I think I might be falling in love with her."

"Then the whole kids thing isn't a problem. Besides, it's too late. You've already inserted yourself into the family. So," Gina continued, "doing something with her family would be the thing. Or something with the kids so that she can have some fun time alone."

"It's a date, like as in two grown ups going out for some grown up fun and recreation."

"Or set up something where she doesn't have to worry about the kids, so she can relax with you. You've got feelings for her, let her know and go from there."

"She might not feel the same way about me that I feel about her."

"That's always a risk, isn't it?" Ian piped up. "There's a reason I got a concussion at a softball game." He shot Dave an accusing look. "If I recall, that was your idea."

"I was only trying to help you get back with Gina. I didn't mean for you to get a concussion," Dave mumbled.

"So why don't you talk to Ainslie and see what she likes to do." Gina nodded, looking pleased with her own advice. "See what she has to say."

Ian sighed. "That phrase drives me mad. You can't *see* what someone says. It's as if the words are coming out of her mouth in a cartoon bubble."

"Shush you." Gina rolled her eyes. "Don't listen to him. Pitch her a couple of ideas."

Ian grinned. "More softball. Get it? Pitch? Softball?"

"Ha ha." Gina turned back to Dave. "Let her decide." She nodded. "That would be best." She wrinkled her nose. "You know?"

"When I let you decide what was a good date, I ended up getting punched in the face, doused in beer and nearly arrested for a DUI," Ian pointed out.

Gina waved a hand in dismissal. "You had fun. Admit it."

Dave stood. "Thanks for the advice."

"I'm going to the ballet fund raiser thingy for

Ian on Tuesday afternoon, and Ainslie will be there. Want me to ask her?"

"No, I'll figure it out, thanks anyway. You've been a big help."

Ian also stood. "Anything to help the cause of true love. Speaking of which." He looked at his watch and waggled his brows à la Groucho. "Isn't it your bedtime? Don't I hear your mother calling?" Ian put a hand up to his ear. "Time for you to go home so I can do something about my own love life."

"Ian," Gina laughed. "That's rude."

"No, I need to get going." Really. As in fast.

Ian grabbed Dave's jacket and handed it to him. "Let us know how it works out. Later."

Somehow, Dave found himself on the other side of the front door. He heard a loud click as if a lock slid into place, then watched as the downstairs lights flicked out one by one.

Damn, he wanted a life like that, and it was just within his grasp. Ainslie was the one. As in, The. One. How could he help her realize that they would be amazing together?

He snapped his fingers as an idea came to him. He knew exactly the time and place.

Chapter Twenty-Three

Ainslie's stomach jumped as she pushed open the door to Esmeralda's, where the committee gala meeting gathered. As she closed the door, she took a moment to catch her breath while she looked for the rest of the committee.

Esmeralda's proved to be a lovely place, with peaceful New Age music, lots of plants and muted conversations. The walls were painted a soothing ecru, and the art on the wall, mostly scenes of nature rendered in calming pastel watercolors. Lots of potted ferns dotted the dining room windows.

Just like some of the places she loved to have lunch with her friends.

Bobby Lee would have hated it. *Hummpf.* One more reason to love it, as far as she was concerned.

She was glad for the time she'd taken to shower and change clothes after cleaning the Brewsters' house. She actually felt like she fit in, wearing a pair of light wool, pearl-colored slacks and a shell pink wrap-around blouse. She'd done her make-up, moussed up her hair and spritzed on a little Nocturnes de Caron.

It all put a little spring in her step as she scanned the dining room. Although this was one lunch, it was a boon to her soul. She would savor every minute.

Andi was already there, along with Hope Monahan, Gina Ross and... Was that Pamela Nelson at that table? The women all talked at once and laughed like girlfriends who had known each other forever.

Ainslie *so* missed having girlfriends. One of the real tragedies of her current situation was the loss of her friends. They had dropped her once Bobby Lee had gone to jail. She didn't blame them. Bobby Lee had stolen from just about everyone they knew. That was the main reason she'd relocated to New England.

This meeting would be an opportunity to meet people and do some things she loved to do. Ainslie fully intended to enjoy this meeting.

Hope noticed her first and greeted her with a big smile. "Ainslie! Good, you're here, we can start."

Ainslie trotted over to the table, her heels *click-clacking* all the way over the hardwood floor. The women all smiled at her when she slipped into the only empty place.

"Have you met my mother?" Andi asked.

"Yes." Ainslie smiled. "We've met. A lifetime ago."

Pamela smiled. "I remember. It's so good to see you again."

Pamela wore an elegant and stylish outfit. If Ainslie didn't miss her guess, Pamela wore Betsey Johnson, an unconstructed pair of silk slacks and a silk floaty tunic in peacock tail colors. Her hair impeccably cut and styled, her make-up flawless, it was easy to see where Andi's beauty and class came from.

Ainslie wanted to be Pamela Nelson when she grew up.

"Andi says you have a marvelous idea for the gala. I love the name and the concept."

"Oh, I didn't come up with it. Someone else did. It was a lot of work, but we made a fortune for the opera."

"It's a fantastic idea, this Mirror Mirror on the Wall Ball. The fairy tale theme is just genius," Pamela gushed. "I can't wait to get all the details."

She took a sip from her iced tea.

"Ian's very excited about it." Gina added.

Hope narrowed her eyes. "Not that I don't love *you* and all that, but why are you here and not Ian?"

"An unexpected faculty meeting got called. So, I'm your girl."

"I thought we wanted a man's input."

"The professor really doesn't know anything about this kind of stuff. Besides, it's mid-terms, and he has a slew of papers to grade." Gina grabbed for her ginger ale.

Liberating a breadstick from the container in the middle of the table, Hope pointed it at Gina. "This might be a good thing. Guys hate costume parties. Ian would only try to talk us out of it."

"He's shy," Gina said.

"I'm looking forward to tricking Mike into dressing like Prince Charming." Andi smirked. "I know just how to do it."

Gina snickered. "Mike is not Prince Charming. He's more like the Frog Prince."

Andi chuckled "Who are you going to get Dad to dress up as?" Andi arranged her silverware on the table in front of her, from shortest to longest.

"The Giant from *Jack and the Beanstalk.* He won't know in advance, not until I tell him what he's going to put on that night." Pamela took another sip from her iced tea.

The waitress came by with water for Ainslie. "Are you ready to order?"

Ainslie hadn't even looked at the menu. She didn't feel like she could eat a bite, her system was already in overdrive. Listening to what the other women ordered, she decided to go with the French onion soup. Hope had ordered it, so it had to be good.

Pamela put a hand over Ainslie's. "So, tell us what we have to do. I'm anxious to get going."

Ainslie took a sip of water and cleared her

throat. The girls watched her, faces lit by curiosity and anticipation. "So many operas and ballets are based on fairy tales and magic mirrors are part of that whole fantasy thing. So we commissioned artists to design mirrors, based on fairy tales, brought in some singers from the Charleston Opera to sing some arias, duets and such from the pieces." She shrugged. "We auctioned the mirrors, paid the artists the commission, and pocketed the difference, which was considerable."

Ainslie stopped to take another sip of water. "We made it as much of a fantasy as we could—a masquerade ball, dancing, the Opera Orchestra, amazing food. Tickets were pricey." Ainslie pursed her lips together and nodded. "Very pricey."

Pamela considered this. "Addington isn't Charleston. We can't price the tickets too high." She pulled a notebook out of her purse.

"That's right." Gina scribbled notes on a yellow legal pad. "Barrett U. is one of our target audiences. None of them are getting rich on what they're paid."

"The biggest expense was the orchestra. You could pare that down or get musicians to donate their time."

"We had a Jazz group last year," Andi reflected. "They were very good."

"Could we get them to donate their time?" Ainslie wondered. "We do need people to have money left over so they will bid on the mirrors."

Andi shrugged. "I can ask."

"So let's put you in charge of the music. That's your area of expertise." Pamela tapped a pen on her notebook.

The waitress returned with their lunch orders. Ainslie looked for a nametag so she could use her name when she thanked her. Since she'd become a waitress, Ainslie knew how nice it was when people didn't treat her like an anonymous servant.

The waitress put a bowl of baby spinach, along with smaller bowls of cheese, croutons and dressing in front of Andi. "Thank you, Clarisse," Andi said.

Clarisse set a grilled chicken Ceasar in front of Gina before delivering the Onion soup to Pamela, Hope and Ainslie. The melted gruyére smelled heavenly, all full of cheesy goodness.

Hope smiled as she shook out her napkin. "Thanks, Clarisse! It looks great!"

"Yes, thank you." Ainslie smiled up at Clarisse.

"Bon Appétit!" Clarisse sounded a little like Julia Child.

Looking at her watch, Hope said, "I've got to get back to the restaurant to begin dinner prep in about a half an hour." She swirled her spoon around in the molten cheese.

"Then let's talk about the food." Andi smiled at Hope. "We have to have the shrimp in puff pastry."

"Dear Lord, I am really tired of making those." Hope pulled a list out of her briefcase. "I put together a menu for you to look at."

Pamela took it and frowned. "It doesn't have the shrimp."

"I'm trying something different. It's a fairy tale inspired menu." Hope said. "I'm actually thinking of getting rid of standard buffet tables and co-ordinate the food into the decorations, like these bird nests made out of deep fried shredded potatoes filled with sautéed shiitake mushrooms. We can tuck them into trees, like so." She pulled out a picture. "Think of an Enchanted Forest. Baskets full of sweets, spinning wheels with gold wrapped confections. That kind of thing." She waved a hand in the air. "It's all there. I've made a copy for each of you."

Pamela picked up her copy. "That's going to take some planning."

"Oh, dear Lord, these look amazing." Ainslie had never seen such and innovative menu. "This certainly outdoes what we did in Charleston." She looked at Hope. "I really love it."

That got them off and running, making plans. As Ainslie was the one with all the auction experience, she ended up working with Pamela on choosing which artist's work would be featured and pricing the auction acquisitions. Pamela knew the artists to visit. As for Ainslie, she loved dealing with artists and planned to enjoy seeing the mirrors they'd come up with.

"Hello, ladies," Dave's smooth, deep voice came from behind her. "Are you done organizing the world?"

He dropped his hand on her shoulder and her nerve endings popped and fizzed. Her stomach jumped, her heart stuttered. She hadn't felt that way in a very long time. Not since before Bobby Lee went to jail.

Dave Mason seemed to have the magic touch.

She liked it.

"Just finished. Ainslie's ideas are fantastic!" Andi tipped her head to one side.

"Of course they are." He grinned at Andi. "She's amazing."

"What brings you here in the middle of the afternoon?" Hope closed her briefcase and stood.

"This." He grabbed Ainslie's hand and pulled her to her feet. "I'm kidnapping Ainslie." He kissed her quick on the lips. "Let's go."

She stumbled as he moved her across the room. "Wait! I haven't paid my bill yet!"

"One of the girls will take care of it. I'll pay her back later."

Oooooh-kay. "Where are we going?" She'd never been kidnapped before. It thrilled her to the tips of her toes.

"You'll see." Dave pushed the door open. The glare from the sun momentarily blinded her. By the time she got used to it, Dave had already dragged her to his car and opened her door.

Wait! "What about my car?"

"You can get it later." He closed the door and sprinted around the car.

"What about my babies? I've got to get home, they're expecting me!"

Sliding into the driver's seat, he grinned. "It's the middle of the afternoon. They're all home, right?"

"Well, yes. The twins are taking care of Patsy."

"They've got enough food and water to last the afternoon?"

"You make them sound like puppies. Yes, they've got more than enough food in the house."

Dave backed out of the parking space. "Then, you have some time for some grown up fun."

"Grown up fun?" Oh, boy. She squirmed a little in her seat.

"Yep. As much fun as you can handle. You're going to beg me for mercy."

She swallowed, then licked her lips. Her mind went blank. Mercy? She liked the sound of that.

"Now, sit back and enjoy the ride." He flashed her the crooked grin that always made her all wobbly inside.

"Where are we going?"

"Don't worry about a thing. I've got it all under control." His fingers tapped on the wheel as he maneuvered his car through traffic and out onto a tree lined road that led out of town. The leaves were starting to turn into a burst of color, yellows, reds, and stubborn greens while sun light danced and dappled the roadside.

They turned a corner, and a lovely old home came into view. White, with stately columns, a porch decorated with terra cotta pots holding brick-colored mums, it projected charm and romance. A porch swing hung to the right of the door. White gravel crunched under the car's tires. A deep green sign with gold lettering proclaimed it as the Inn at Foxwood Creek.

Dave cut the motor with a quick flick of his wrist. Leaning over toward her, he hooked a finger under her chin and brought her face in for a slow, melting kiss. "Hello."

"Hello," she managed to whisper. His kisses could destroy even an angel's restraint.

"C'mon." He kissed her again. "I can't wait to have you all to myself."

Oh, Lordy. Ainslie wanted the same thing. Trembling, she brought her hand up to caress his cheek. "What are we waiting for?"

He turned his face and pressed a kiss into her palm. It sizzled where his lips met her skin. "Let's go."

God, yes. She'd go wherever he took her, as long as he kept kissing her like she was the only woman in the world and precious as spun gold.

He helped her out of the car and up the steps to the front porch. They stopped at the door, and he gently kissed her hand, like a knight in seeking a boon from a princess.

An older couple greeted them in a room filled with shiny antiques and crystal vases filled with fresh, fragrant flowers. Dave smiled at them, then kissed Ainslie on the tip of her nose. "Be right back."

While he talked to the couple, Ainslie took a minute to try and compose herself. This had to be the most impulsive thing she'd ever done. Unless you counted that time she and Bobby Lee just up and got married, right after that after-pageant party on Donald Trump's yacht.

She'd been so young back then. Loving Bobby Lee had been different, so simple, no complications. Then he'd gotten involved with his schemes and hardly had any time for her or their children.

Dave was a whole 'nother kettle of fish. Her life consisted of nothing but complications. Three very big complications she loved very much. Yet the emotions she felt for Dave were new and exciting. She had her eyes open, even though a wild mash of tangled feelings tumbled through her every time she stood next to him. Kissed him. Held on to him.

She didn't feel like the good wife standin' by her man, or like someone's mom.

She glanced at Dave, still talking to that sweet looking old couple. Nothing about this compared. Dave was miles away from Bobby Lee Logan.

He caught her staring and smiled, then blew her a kiss. God, she felt a giggle bubble up inside her. She hadn't giggled since she was sixteen.

Dave moved back to her and put a guiding hand on her elbow. "We're on the third floor." He dangled a key, like a hypnotist with a shiny object. "Let's go."

There was no place else she'd rather be. She let him lead her up the stairs, her heart beating faster with each step.

Her skin didn't even feel like it belonged to her anymore. It quivered at this man's touch. She had no choice but to go along with it.

He fumbled with the key as he tried to open the door.

Actually, it took him five tries, not that she counted, to get the door opened. She may have imagined it, but his hand trembled to the same stuttered beat as her heart. Once in the room, he closed the door with his foot and hugged her tight, then pressed a kiss to the top of her head. She sighed as she sank deeper into his embrace.

****

Jesus, Ainslie was sweet in his arms. Soft, delicious. Dave nuzzled her hair, saturating himself with her scent, a combination of exotic flowers and erotic promises.

Delicious. Good enough to eat. They had time. He'd try that later.

He'd never felt this total urge to totally possess a woman before. To brand her as his. God knew, he'd tried. This thing with Ainslie ran miles away from anything he'd imagined he'd ever feel.

He held *his* woman in his arms.

Mine, he thought as he crashed his mouth onto hers. Patience didn't exist anymore, he felt in the mood to take. She more than met him halfway. Her mouth moved eagerly under his.

Her throat released a deep, warm hum of surrender. He'd never heard a sexier sound.

Cruising his mouth along the tender skin of Ainslie's neck, his hands found the tie of her pink blouse and undid it. She whimpered as he slipped it off her shoulders and down her arms, leaving goose bumps everywhere he touched.

He pulled back to look at her. Her beautiful big brown eyes were wide and her face had flushed into a rosy pink. Her tongue darted out to lick her red, kiss swollen lips. Sweeping her up into his arms, he kissed her as he carried her across the room to lay her on the bed.

Covered in a mountain of blankets and topped by a soft quilt, the antique bed nearly swallowed her up. He stretched out next to her, raised on one elbow so he could see how lovely she was.

He swept a hand over the delicate skin of her stomach and rejoiced when her breath hitched. Hesitating when he reached the fastener of her slacks, he asked, "Is this okay?"

"No," she whispered. "You're going too slow."

He snorted a laugh. She always managed to surprise him. "Let me do something about that."

Discovering he still had some patience left, he took his time, enjoying every gasp as she squirmed underneath his touch. He removed the rest of her clothes, peeling them off slowly, just to tease her, stopping every so often to savor the smooth, fragrant skin he discovered or an interesting freckle that he just had to press his lips against.

In his own good time, he left her quivering in her pretty white lace bra and matching panties.

He discovered he was definitely a white lace man.

She had surgical scars beneath her belly. They were almost covered by her panties, but not quite. He pressed his lips to each one.

She gasped. He kissed his way back up her body to catch any more gasps that might be right behind it.

She reached up and wound her arms around his neck, pressing her lace-covered breasts against him. Now impatient for the bra to be gone so he could feel her amazing, gorgeous breasts next to his chest, he reached for her.

"Not yet." She gifted him with a woman's smile, full of feminine secrets.

Her lips made a beeline up his throat, and she nipped at his earlobe, pulling a low growl out of him that practically roared from deep in his gut. He rolled over and pulled her on top of him.

Panting, trembling, her breasts and pelvis covered with that white lace, she straddled his lap. "One of us is overdressed." She gave him a sassy, seductive smile. Leaning forward, she gave him a long, slow, deep kiss. A tongue filled, excited beyond belief, soul kiss.

He felt his eyes cross in pleasure as she unbuttoned his shirt one button at a time, then gave the skin she discovered a small bite as she moved sinuously down his body. He didn't think he could be more aroused, but with each kiss, each nip, his erection grew larger and more eager.

****

Ainslie reveled in the warm, muscular torso she uncovered, loved the way he sucked in his breath at her touch. Dave Mason was seriously ripped, much more than she imagined a high school principal could be. Nearly crazy with the absolute thrill of it all, she loved the powerful feeling rushing through her blood.

Any coherent thought Ainslie had melted away as she rocked against Dave. She quivered against the long hard ridge pressing against his fly. She pushed against his eager erection. It leapt in response. She chuckled.

Time to set that bad boy free.

"Damn!" he gritted out between clenched teeth when she touched him. She glanced at his face, wanting to see what she made him feel. Dave's eyes glittered with impatience. "Touch me."

Go figure. She liked making a man beg.

She *really* liked it.

"Hang on, there. I'm taking my time with you," she said as she tortured him in return by carefully, *slowly* pulling down his zipper, inch by thrilling inch. Oh, my!

Dave Mason was very generously equipped.

He lifted his hips so she could free him, hissing as she slid his briefs down along with his khaki slacks. Eager moisture welled at the tip of his penis, and she used her thumb to run it over the impressively swollen head. Bringing her thumb up to her mouth, she tasted the salty liquid she'd discovered. Reaching to touch him again, he grabbed her hand, gently holding her at bay.

"Gah!" he choked out behind clenched teeth. Air sawing in and out of his lungs, his chest heaved as he grabbed her hand. "Keep that up, and I'm going to embarrass myself before we get started." He briefly closed his eyes, and when he opened them, they were the color of a storm at sea. "I need to see all of you."

A spear of embarrassment flashed in her blood. Please, God, let him like what he saw.

He seemed more in control as he repositioned the two of them and rocked against her pelvis. She couldn't resist him. She didn't want to. She'd give him anything he wanted.

He kissed her, as gentle as a sigh. "Let me. I need to see you. To taste you." His tongue lapped along her neck to that vulnerable place just behind her earlobe. "I want to hold you against me, skin to skin. Please."

And there went that whole begging thing again. She was helpless to say anything but yes.

With an expert flick of his fingers, she felt her bra open and its straps travel down her arms. The butterflies in her stomach fluttered with each downward slide of her bra straps. Ainslie raised her hands to hold her bra in place. "You didn't get so good a look the other night. I'm not sure you'll like what you see."

"What's this?" He kissed her. "All I'm going to see is the woman I'm in love with."

The air left her lungs with a huge *whoosh*. Her hands started to shake. "What did you say?"

He kissed her again, lips urgent against her mouth. "I love you. It feels like I've been waiting all my life for you."

"You can't!" Dear Lord, she was going to hyperventilate.

He pulled her closer, wrapped her arms around his neck, then pulled the lacy white cups of her bra away from her. "I can and I do."

"But..." Speech failed her. Those three little words meant so much to her, she wouldn't just bandy them about.

He nuzzled the side of her neck and chuckled when she wiggled. At his mercy, she could only hold on to his shoulders. She actually saw stars.

"You don't have to say anything, not right now. It's enough that you know how I feel." He lightly raked his fingers along her arms, causing little goose bumps to form on the goose bumps he'd already raised on her over-sensitive skin. Rubbing his erection against her pelvis, he made both of them moan, twin sounds of helpless pleasure.

"What if I can never say it?" Tears threatened whatever shards of composure she had left.

"Let me worry about that." He rocked his hips in a mind-stealing move, and she felt her eyes cross.

Going now on pure instinct, she leaned away from him and brought his skillful, amazing hands from her arms to cover her breasts. Her nipples stiffened against his clever fingers, becoming painfully hard. Exchanging his hands for his mouth, he licked and suckled at each hard peak. "You taste like heaven," he said in a reverent whisper.

Who could resist that? She wouldn't even if she still could. Panting, she gave herself up to him, trusting him.

His gentle hands, his greedy, hot mouth created rivers of pleasure to flow through her body. It danced from each nerve ending to the next, a molten tide to drown in. She gave herself over to exquisite sensation.

Dave flipped her on to her back and slid down along her legs while he took off her panties. He used his teeth to nip and his tongue to soothe as he loved his way back up to her. "What do we have here?" Parting her soft folds with wicked fingers, his breath gusted warmly against her sweet spot. Unable to breathe, anticipation riding her hard, she squeaked at the first testing touch of his tongue on her clitoris. She ran her fingers through his hair, holding onto him so she didn't fly off the bed. He was merciless, kissing, sucking, and licking her.

Gasping with need, she flexed her fingers against his head. Still torturing her with his mouth, he used one finger, then two, spearing them in and out of her body.

Then he stopped and brought his head up to look at her. His gaze intense, he held her churning hips still. "Like I said, heaven."

Returning to his task, he licked her some more, sometimes with the tip of his tongue fluttering against her bud, sometimes with the flat of it pressing it down. Mad sensations rioting from his intimate kisses, she felt her release coming fast. He moved his fingers inside her passage again and with one long suckle on her clitoris, she flew apart as wave upon wave of pleasure rode over and through her.

Dave leisurely lapped at her like a lazy cat, bringing her back to herself. "You are amazing. Do you always scream like that?"

"I don't know." She trembled as he kissed his way back up her body, stopping briefly to swirl that wicked tongue around her navel.

He braced his arms on either side of her as he bent his head to lave each of her diamond hard nipples. When she gasped, he just smiled. "Too much?"

"Oh, God."

He worked his way to her mouth and took possession with a deep, long, kiss. She could taste herself and jolted. She'd never been turned on by that, but since it was mixed with Dave's own delicious kiss, it aroused her all over again.

His erection got longer and harder against her still throbbing clitoris. "You're so beautiful, Ainslie." He whispered her name like it was a benediction.

She gasped and spread her legs further, so he could reach her more easily. He grinned like a pirate. "Like that, do you?"

"Unh," she replied, astounded as she felt the slow build to orgasm return. Had she ever felt this way before? Lord, it was amazing. Her head spun. "Please!"

He knew what she was asking. "Not yet," he murmured, his voice low and rough, abrading each and every one of her oh, so sensitive nerves. "I haven't spent nearly enough time here." Lowering his head to her breasts, he suckled, molded, teased, and tortured her nipples into painfully hard points.

Ainslie writhed beneath him and finally, *finally*, he moved to join their bodies. He reached for a condom, but she grabbed his wrist. "We don't need one."

Happy birthday to him! "I'll be as gentle as I can." He took himself in hand and rolled the broad head of his enormous erection, around the entrance to her body, opening her up so she could take him inside. "I'll stop if it's too much."

"It won't be," she promised. Her muscles, relaxed from her earlier climax, welcomed him.

Dave made a teasing shallow thrust, then another one, both not deep enough to satisfy her. She keened in supplication.

"Yeah, me too," he gritted out, and thrust deep, deep, soul deep.

"Oh, God!" Her breath left her in a whoosh. It had been a long time, and he was especially endowed.

Their eyes caught, and something snapped and crackled between them. "I do love you," he panted. He began to move back and forth. "You feel so good."

She wrapped her legs around his waist, pelvis rising to meet him, her inner muscles clamping along him, trying to take him deeper to that sweet spot high inside her. His big, warm hands gripped her bottom and angled her, impaling himself in deeper.

He moved in long, slow glides, each one stretching her and reaching further inside. "Oh, yeah," he muttered as she moved to take more of him, all of him, in. "You feel so good, baby." He thrust inside her, pushing until he was all the way in. "So good."

He slid back and forth inside her and again the exquisite pleasure/pain of orgasm built one on top of the other, stealing her sanity. She raced toward the final plateau, hovered there on the cliff, when wild waves of pleasure rolled over her in spasms, each one more powerful than the previous one, and she flew.

"Oh, God, *yes*. Now." Dave gritted out, his head back, every muscle pulled taut as he pushed deep into her, touching all the way to her womb. He came in great, scalding eruptions, filling her with heat, pulling her tight against him. With one last powerful thrust, he shuddered and jetted into her a final time as she clasped him deep within her body, holding him as tightly as she could.

Chapter Twenty-Four

"Penny for your thoughts," Dave murmured as he pulled Ainslie into his embrace.

She didn't think she had any coherent thoughts to share. Dave had befuddled her so well, she might never, ever think any thing again that didn't revolve around how good he made her feel. "Mm."

He chuckled and the warm sound enveloped her. He kissed her, and the hair on her head tingled where his lips caressed.

Dave had been so thorough in finding all her sweet spots, she didn't think she'd have any tingles left over. He was proving her wrong, his warm hands and mouth coaxing sublime aftershocks from her love-sensitive skin.

"You're so beautiful. Your skin is so soft." He slid his skillful hands down along her torso and rested it on her hysterectomy scars. "What happened here?"

She closed her eyes as a pang of apprehension rushed through her. Those scars reminded her constantly that she wasn't a beauty queen anymore.

That she might be all used up.

That she couldn't have children ever again.

They reminded her that she was old.

"There's nothing you can't tell me, love." Dave placed a light kiss on each of her eyelids.

Then, kissing her fingers, looking at her like he was studying her. "I do love you, and I want you to know how I feel. And, just so you know, I've never said those words to anyone ever before. It's enough that I know, for the time being. I can wait until you figure it all out. You're safe with me. So," he whispered, "tell me."

Ainslie's breath caught as Dave slid his mouth down her body, until he reached her scars. His feelings in his eyes, he lifted his gaze to her face.

She trembled like rose petals tossed in the breeze. Did she trust him, or not? With a sigh, she took the leap. "There were complications with Patsy's birth. I needed to deliver by C-section and after that, things were still dicey, and I had to have a hysterectomy." She looked him straight in the eyes. "I know you want to have children. I can't give you any, so maybe you should reconsider those *I-love-yous* and look for someone who can." Her heart beat like a kettledrum. "Give you children, that is."

He became very still, very silent. Without a word, he pressed his lips to each and every scar. "I don't need children from my body. I *need* you." He kissed the white lines crossing her belly again. "You and your children."

That was apparently that. He moved further down, down to the most feminine part of her, alternating kisses with little tantalizing nips. Parting her gently, he laid waste to what was left of her sanity, kissing and suckling on her clit.

Again. The man had no mercy.

Giving herself totally over to him, she moaned, the sound coming from deep inside her. She fisted her hands in the soft sheets beneath her, unable to believe she could do this again. Wave after wave built up, one on top of the other, crashing until she keened wildly. Panting hard, she shattered into his mouth one more time.

****

Like he had a map, he found and chased every pulse, every squeeze, every spasm with his tongue. Watching her face as he feasted on her, he relished every moan, every sigh she made.

The taste of her made him want her in ways she couldn't even imagine. He kept his extreme desires leashed, since he didn't want to scare her. It would kill him if he hurt her.

She didn't realize the power she had over him. He'd have to show her.

His hands cruised back up that amazing skin of hers to mold around her breasts, shaping them, gently abrading her rosy, pink nipples until they looked like raspberries crowning her breasts. "God, you're gorgeous. So responsive," he praised, "so sweet." He lightly nipped the nearest raspberry peak with his teeth, then laved his tongue in circles around it.

"Oh, my Lord." She threaded her fingers in his hair as he did the same thing to the other sweet peak. "Please!"

Anything. He'd give her anything she asked for. Every thing her heart desired.

She wiggled out from under him, pushed him onto his back and stared at him, her pupils dilated so much that hardly any brown was left. Her small hands reached between their bodies to touch his penis. He didn't think he could get hard again so soon after, but hey! He was game. So he put a hand on top of hers and moved it, showing her how he liked to be touched.

"That feels amazing," he chuffed a hoarse breath.

"Hm. What about this?" She moved her hand so she could reach more of him. She swept her thumb around the head and spread the moisture gathering there.

He growled. "You know I like that."

She laughed, the sound deep and rich, sweet music to his ears. "Just making sure." Without warning, she leaned down and swirled her tongue around the top of his erection as her hands fluttered along the length of it. She hummed as she moved.

Oh, God, baby! More, please.

It was his turn to thread his hands in her hair and hang on for dear life as she moved her mouth and tongue along and around him. He tried to hold still. His muscles ached with the longing to move in and out of that hot, sweet mouth.

Unsuccessful against her tender assault, he felt himself grow and swell, stretching her mouth and pushing against the back of her throat.

Too much! For both of them. He put a finger under her chin to stop her. She released his cock with a soft pop and licked him as he pulled out. Her tongue darted around her lips like she was trying to save the taste of him.

Feeling like a caveman, he flipped her and used his knees to part her, so he could take her again. "Condom," he grunted as he pulled her legs up to rest on his shoulders and snugged his hard-on between her thighs.

"We don't need one." Ainslie panted, then lifted her hips, inviting him in.

He leaned forward and put his weight on his arms and drove himself all the way into her. "Sorry 'bout this," he gritted out between clenched teeth. Hard and heavy, a little rough, he couldn't manage any finesse.

He frantically moved within her warm, soft heat, driven by the sounds of pleasure she made. Her muscles squeezed him, goading him on.

Without warning, she came apart in shattering waves, clenching his cock until he couldn't hold back anymore.

"Oh, yeah, me too." He drove his way home one last time and shuddered uncontrollably as he jetted into her, long, pulsing explosions that went on forever.

Chapter Twenty-Five

Ainslie sighed, snuggled back and spooned against him. She fell asleep while she cuddled in the safety of Dave's strong arms.

She woke with a smile on her face, and stretched, feeling like a well-fed cat napping in a sunbeam. She reached behind her to touch the reason for the way her body hummed, but found she was alone in the bed. "Dave?"

He leaned against the bathroom doorjamb, the devil's own grin on his face. "How do you feel?"

"Like a very satisfied woman." She stretched, gratified to see his gaze follow her every move. Her ears pricked up. "Is there water running in the bathroom?"

A long, slow smile stretched across his face. "I'm running you a bath."

"A bath?"

"Yeah, a bath. Don't tell me you don't like long hot bubble baths?" He chuckled. "You'd be the first woman I've met who didn't."

"Other women?"

He grin turned playful. "My sisters." He crossed his heart. "They'd spend hours hogging the bathroom."

"Just your sisters?"

"Yep."

"Why don't I believe you?"

"You're the suspicious type." He waggled his eyebrows.

Ainslie laughed. The sound just bubbled out of her. She felt ridiculously happy. Free.

He cleared his throat. "I love to see you laugh."

"Dave."

"Actually, I love everything about you." He glanced behind him. "I need to check the tub."

She ran her hands through her hair, imagining what a terrible mess it looked like. Glancing out of the lace curtains of the window, she realized that it was now nearly dark, and checked her watch. She should have been home hours ago.

Much as she wanted to stay, Ainslie didn't have time for that bath. She tried to stave off the panic attack that fluttered in her stomach while she started looking for her clothes.

"Hey, what's this?" Dave came back into the room. "What're you doing?"

"It's so late. I need to get home." She found her bra and wrangled herself into it.

"Hey." He sat on the bed and grabbed her hands and slid her bra back off. Again, goose bumps rose on her skin at his slightest touch. "I've got it covered."

"What?" She shook her head as if to clear it.

"I'm going to your house to watch your children." He kissed her. "You're going to stay here and take some much needed Ainslie time."

Ainslie time? She hadn't had Ainslie time in so long she forgot what it was. "I can't stay here and dump my children on you."

"I kidnapped you, and that means I made arrangements for the children. I'm going to go over and make sure they finish their homework and all that. All you have to do," he kissed her on the tip of her nose, "is relax."

"But it's such an imposition..."

"Don't you trust me to supervise your kids?"

"Of course I do, but what kind of example does it set for them?"

He took her into his arms. "They don't know what we've been doing here. I told everyone that I was giving you a day at the spa."

"The spa?" Lord love a duck. "You told them you gave me a spa day?"

"Yep." He nuzzled her hair, which tickled enough to make her squirm. "Please, let me do this for you." His eyes looked so earnest.

"What about my car?"

"I've made arrangements with Mike. He's going to bring it by later."

Her eyes widened. "Mike knows?"

"If I didn't tell him, do you think Andi and Gina could keep quiet about me abducting you? Those two are better than Perez Hilton when it comes to spreading gossip." Dave took her hand and kissed each finger tip. "Have I told you how proud I was of you, running that meeting? The ladies were hanging on your every word."

She felt a blush creep up her neck. "Dear Lord. What they must think of me."

"Is it so bad if people know about us?" Those beautiful blue eyes of his clouded over.

"No, but I'm really trying to keep my private life just that—private." She cupped his cheek in her hand. "Plus, I have to set a good example for my children."

"You are an *amazing* example for your children. No one can fault you a damn thing." His lips tightened into a straight line and a muscle jumped in his cheek. "If anyone says otherwise, I'll deal with them. Look, I'm picking up some healthy stuff from Hope's, so everything is all set. You're overworked and need a little break." He demonstrated how little with his thumb and forefinger. "Please. Let me pamper you."

Dear Lord, the man was her own personal Mephistopheles. "You're sure Mike's bringing my car?"

"It's already here." He pulled her hand up and

pressed his lips on it, in the barest whisper of a kiss. "C'mon now." He murmured against her lips. "The water's getting cold."

Tugging on her hand, Dave pulled Ainslie to her feet. He scooped her up and carried her to the bathtub like she was a princess in a fairy tale.

He softly rubbed his lips against hers, like Prince Charming would kiss Sleeping Beauty, waking her back to life again. Lowering her into the old-fashioned claw-foot tub, he watched her with real intensity. "This time is for you. Consider it a gift. I know single mothers don't get a lot of pampering."

He'd lit rose scented candles that flickered playfully with the light. Hot water, again gently scented with roses, twined around her, wrapping her in. One by one each muscle released into the warmth surrounding her. She sighed as she leaned back.

Dave began to massage her shoulders and neck. Pure heaven, she dropped her head forward, like a rag doll's, to give him better access. "Mm."

"Like that?" Dave whispered in her ear.

"Oh, yes," she breathed on a gusty breath. "Soooo good."

She reveled in the feel of his strong hands running so gently over her upper body, finding nerve endings she forgotten about.

The man had the magic touch.

****

Moving to the other end of the tub so he could massage her feet, Dave marveled at her soft, pliant skin. He started working on her right foot and chuckled when she moaned. "Should I keep going?"

"I'll kill you if you stop."

"So bloodthirsty." He nipped a toe. "I like that in a woman."

Her eyelids drooped as he pressed on a sensitive spot. "Oooooh. Right there. Ah, ah, yes. *Right* there. *God*, that feels good."

A flare of pride, of ownership flashed through him, that he alone made her feel such pleasure. He had all he could do to not join her in the tub for a lot *more* pleasure.

But, unfortunately, no. He'd set this time up for her so she could have a quiet evening, indulging herself. It seemed like a good idea at the time.

He didn't want to leave. But, he'd made a promise. Besides, he really wanted to spend time with her kids, time that didn't involve him being the principal.

After planting a kiss on each of her perfect little toes, he stood.

"Where're you going?" Ainslie swiveled her head to see him.

"Right here." He grabbed a couple bottles of ice-cold mineral water he'd stashed in a cooler earlier. Grabbing a blue tinted goblet, he set them beside her, on a table by the tub. He twisted the top off with a *fthwipp-szzzz* and poured the fizzing water into the glass. Holding it out for her to grab, he smiled. "Though this is probably one of the hardest things I've had to do, I'm going to leave you here now."

She looked like she wanted to say something, but he stopped her with a finger over her lips. "I want to get to know your children, outside of school." He kissed her, because she looked too delicious not to. "Give me this chance. Give *us* this chance."

Her muscles softened beneath his touch, the tension seeming to melt away in degrees. "You can't tell them the things you've told me today."

"Please. Like I'm going in there and announcing that I've spent the afternoon making love with their mother—that I'm in love with their mother." He didn't say the next part about how he was going to be their new daddy. That would come later.

"You promised healthy food, right?"

"The healthiest food on God's green Earth." He

crossed his heart.

"Well, for you that means nachos with extra beef."

"Honest, it's going to taste horrible, just like healthy food is supposed to."

She splashed him. "All the food groups?"

"Red meat, Wonder Bread, greasy fries, and high fructose corn syrup? Check, check, check and check." He ticked each one off with a finger. "Ooops. Forgot cancer causing preservatives and the six pack of Sam Adams."

"Not even a six pack of pop." Ainslie warned, a smile quirking up the left side of her mouth. "Juice or milk. Nothing else." She pursed her lips. "Well, and water. And the juice has to be the organic stuff I've got in the fridge."

She smiled and Dave felt happiness bloom inside of him. "Yes, ma'am." He saluted her with a crisp snap of his wrist.

She looked at him, then her mouth twisted into a half-smile. "I won't be long."

"I want you to take all the time you want."

"I won't be long," she stated in a voice that brooked no disobedience.

"Then you'll see I'm a man of my word. You will come home to children eating gruel and doing their homework."

She slipped a bit under the water and sighed, raising her rosy, flushed breasts slightly out of the water. "The gruel better be watery and really foul tasting." She grinned. "So it's just like what I serve up."

"Your wish is my command." His gaze took in her face, her body. She looked well loved and relaxed. This wasn't just a gift for her, it was for him also.

Man, he was so jazzed. His blood hummed and popped through him.

He loved putting that look on her face. He was determined to do it more often.

Like every minute of every day for the rest of his life.

Chapter Twenty-Six

Ainslie tried to relax. She really did. She finished her bath, got dressed, and wiped down the tub. She picked up the towels, cleaned off the table where Dave had put the sparkling water, and put the empty bottle and glass in the cooler.

She made the bed.

Plopping her hiney down on one of the chintz-covered chairs, she toyed with the idea of going shopping, but she didn't feel the need for being around lots of people. Didn't want to ruin her post-sex buzz. Her foot swung back and forth as she sighed.

As great as she felt, curiosity just wouldn't let her go. Her every thought revolved around Dave and what was going on at her home.

She looked at her watch and frowned. How long a wait would be polite? She didn't want to offend Dave by coming home too soon, but she was dying to know.

As much as she wanted a relationship with Dave, no way could she have one if her children couldn't deal with it. It would be difficult, but she would nip things with Dave in the bud.

A tremor of sadness ran through her at the thought of the loss of someone she could fall into forever love with. But her children had to come first.

Always and forever.

She sent off a quick prayer that Ruark, Shanna, and Patsy would be fine with it. More than fine.

Spectacularly fine.

The first difficulty would be slipping past the

lovely older couple who ran the inn. She and Dave had been a little noisy. There could be no doubt about what they'd been up to all afternoon.

No time to be embarrassed. No reason to be embarrassed, she decided. Who gave a damn?

Standing then grabbing her purse, Ainslie scooted out of the room and made a beeline to her car. She just had to see what was going on.

****

Well, the house wasn't on fire. Good sign, right? Ainslie's tires screeched as she pulled into her space in front of her tidy little rental house. Taking a deep, bracing breath, she marched up her porch stairs and opened her front door.

The mouth-watering aroma of braised beef and freshly baked bread met her as she stepped in the room. Silence reigned, except for Patsy's sweet little voice reading to Dave. He wore a pair of horn-rimmed glasses and followed along with Patsy's reading like a lazer.

Those glasses shouldn't be as sexy as they were. She felt her engine revving all over again.

Patsy curled up next to him, reading like it was her job. Shanna sat cross-legged in front of the coffee table, scratching out some math homework. Ruark sat apart from them all, at the computer, ear buds in while he wrote notes on some music manuscript paper.

Patsy and Dave looked up, identical grins on their faces, two peas in a pod. "Hi, Momma! Mr. Mason makes real good mac and cheese!"

That was all well and good, except for the fact that Patsy hated mac and cheese. "I thought you didn't like to eat mac and cheese."

"He put a secret ingredient in it which makes it *dee-lish-us*." Patsy squirmed off the couch and ran to get a hug. "He made it special for me 'cause I don't like pot roast." She made her icky face. Ainslie hoisted her up onto her hip and gave her a kiss on the top of her head.

Shanna unfolded herself from the floor and brought a paper full of equations over to Dave to look at. "Are these right? Hi, Momma." She rolled out a big yawn and stretched. "Did you have fun at the spa?"

Dave looked up from Shanna's paper. His eyes twinkled with mischief. "You look relaxed." His brow creased. "I did think you'd be along later."

"I skipped the seaweed wrap." She and Patsy exchanged little Eskimo kisses as she walked over to Ruark. Pulling off his ear-buds, she knocked gently on the top of his head, like she was asking to be let in. It was a game the two of them played when he was deep into his music. "Hey, Bub. What are you doing?"

"Theory homework." He tunneled his hand through his hair, then slid his eyes over to where Shanna sat, on the arm of the sofa while Dave helped her through some corrections.

"Looks tough," Ainslie didn't have the first clue as to what all those squiggles, dots and lines on Ruark's paper meant. It astonished her that she had a child who did. Pride in her baby boy filled her up to the brim.

"Not really." Ruark shrugged. "It's a lot of review so Mrs. Kelly knows how much I know and what I need to work on."

"I'll let you get back to it." Ainslie let Patsy slip down. "Why don't you run upstairs and get ready for bed?"

Patsy put on that famous pout of hers. "But I gotta finish reading to Mr. Mason. He won't be able to sleep if he doesn't know the end of the story."

"Good try, doodle bug, but I think Mr. Mason will do just fine if he has to wait another day or two for you to finish the story."

"Can he come back tomorrow so we can finish it?"

"We'll see. He might be busy."

Dave stood and walked over to her and Patsy. He pulled his glasses off and put them in his inside jacket pocket as he crossed the room. "You need to do what your mom says."

"Oh-kay," she sing-songed. "But you can't go until I come back down," she told him. Off she raced.

Ainslie's nerve endings started to tingle all over again the moment Dave got near her. He smelled as good as he usually did, that clean, woodsy scent, with no hint of eau de wild monkey sex, so he must have grabbed a shower after leaving her.

Shanna yawned lavishly. "I'm really tired. I think I'll go to bed."

"Got all your work done, pumpkin?"

"Yep, thanks to Mr. Mason." Shanna nodded at him. "Without help, I don't think I'd have been able to finish that math." Her lips quirked up in a little smile. "Math is *so* not my friend."

"You're welcome." Dave blushed, which just made him look more adorable.

"So, Ruark." Shanna sidled up to her twin. "Aren't you tired too?"

Ruark gave Shanna that disgusted look Ainslie knew he saved just for his sister. "No."

"But, you've got that big test tomorrow. You need to rest up for it."

"I don't have any such thing."

"'Course you do. How could you have forgotten about it? In history? Just the most important test of the term." She motioned with her head toward Dave. "You need your sleep."

"I haven't finished my theory homework yet." Ruark frowned at Shanna.

"You can do that tomorrow. Come on." She made a bigger motion with her head toward Dave. "I bet

201

Mr. Mason has to tell Momma all about Patsy's reading tonight. And we've got that monster test."

Ainslie rolled her eyes. Her little girl was not the most subtle person on God's green Earth.

Dave looked at his watch. "Actually, I've got to get going. I've got an early meeting with the superintendent and the chair of the school board."

"Oh, you can't go yet!" Shanna jumped into the conversation with both feet. "You need to wait for Patsy. You promised her you would. I'll go up and see what's keeping her." She scrambled off after Patsy.

Ruark released a heavy sigh as he slowly got to his feet. "I'm tired. And I guess I've got a big, huge, honkin' test tomorrow. Good night." He turned like he wanted to say something, but shook his head, then ambled off.

"Good night, baby." Ainslie wasn't fooled. He didn't have a test tomorrow. Loyal to a fault, he'd always follow Shanna, whether it was to protect her or join in her mischief. Their bond ran very deep.

"Well, we seem to be alone." Dave's voice felt like silk along her ears.

"As alone as it ever gets around here." She smiled at him. "Thank you for my spa day."

"I should thank *you*. I haven't felt this good in a very long time."

"You can repay me by sharing the secret ingredient in your mac and cheese."

"A good chef never gives up his secrets."

His intimate smile caressed her. He looked like he wanted to take her into his arms and kiss her, but she knew he wouldn't, not with the children about.

She had to clear her throat. "But how will I get Patsy to eat *my* mac and cheese?"

"Guess you'll have to keep me around."

"I guess I will." She reached out to smooth down

his shirtfront, but stopped herself. Her palms itched with the urge to touch him. "Patsy's going to want you to come back tomorrow."

He stroked his hand down her hair. "That meeting I have tomorrow is real. I can check in the evening after that if it's okay with you."

Ainslie wanted that so much, she ached with it. "Let's see how it goes. They may need time to process this."

"You're right, of course." His mouth turned up into a gentle smile. "You've done a really good job with them. They're amazing people."

Pride for her children flared within her. "They're my life."

Patsy came running into the living room and clambered up Dave to throw her arms around his neck. She clung there like a baby Koala on a Eucalyptus tree. Ainslie caught a whiff of soap and toothpaste as Patsy planted a sloppy kiss on Dave's cheek. She'd at least made a passing attempt at washing up.

"Thank you for reading with me!" Patsy burbled. "Can you come back soon?"

"That's up to your momma."

"Can he, Momma?"

Ainslie looked at the two hopeful, expectant gazes twinkling at her. Her baby looked so comfortable, so happy, so *right* in Dave's arms. How could any woman worth her estrogen resist the two of them together?

She felt something click inside her, like a key into a lock. It opened up a door to a place she thought long dead, but sensation after sensation flowed out, knocking her nearly breathless.

Her heart dropped in a dizzy free fall straight into love. It rolled through her in long, luxurious waves, stealing her soul as well as her reason.

She loved Dave Mason. *Really* loved him.

Forever loved him. She trembled with the force of it.

"You okay?" Dave's forehead creased as he looked at her.

Ainslie smiled. "Oh, yes. I'm better than I have been in a long time." She wanted to tell him how she felt, but right there, right then didn't seem to be the time, not with Patsy staring at both of them.

****

"You should probably stop eavesdropping on Momma and Mr. Mason." Ruark shook his head at Shanna, who was trying to hide behind the bathroom door while holding it out a crack.

"Oh, hush. I want to know what's going on." She swatted his arm. "Look at how Momma's looking at him. She's practically googly-eyed over him. I haven't seen her look this happy in a long time."

Ruark had to admit she *did* look happy. He took a deep breath and waited for the jealousy that usually filled him when it came to Mr. Mason, but instead something inside him unbent.

"Omigawd, Ruark! Look at this!"

Now just as curious as Shanna, he peered over her shoulder. Mr. Mason stood at the door and handed Patsy to Momma. Patsy wiggled out of Momma's arms and ran into the kitchen.

Mr. Mason took her hand, he kissed her palm and curled her fingers into it, like she could hold onto it. Momma said something to him, something that made his mouth make this brilliant, amazing smile.

He left, she closed the door behind him. She leaned her back against the door and sighed as she opened her fist to place it over her heart. "Isn't that just *the* most romantic thing you've ever seen?" Shanna cooed.

"Ew," Ruark told her, because it was expected of him. "This is our mother we're talking about." He thought it was pretty romantic too, but no way he'd tell Shanna he agreed.

"I think they're in love." Shanna turned to face him. "Wouldn't it be cool for the principal to fall in love with Momma? We'd never get in trouble, like ever."

"You're such a retard."

"Hey, it's already working for us. He got you that sweet independent study with Mrs. Kelly."

Whoa. "You really think it's because of Momma that he set up that course?" Ruark didn't know what to make of that.

"I don't know, but whatever." She waved her hand in dismissal. "Why him and Mrs. Kelly did it doesn't matter. It's done, and you like it." She surprised the hell out him by giving him a quick hug. "I can still cheer and all. It's only fair that you get to do all that advanced music stuff."

"I guess." It did kinda feel good to have someone else looking after them. Momma worked too hard. It didn't hurt that Mr. Mason was hot *and* a stand up kind of guy.

Someone good enough to be with his mother.

He took another peek as she sat with Patsy. His littler sister was deep into telling her all about her day. They both had their heads together and were laughing.

Just like they used to.

A huge sense of well-being settled on his shoulders. Shanna was right for once.

Shoot, even a broken clock had to be right twice a day.

Chapter Twenty-Seven

"Slow night?" Gina and Ian Ross sat at one of Ainslie's tables. They both grinned up at her as she brought menus over.

"Not much going on, I guess." Ainslie had spent most of her evening sitting at the bar, making a list of ways to get Dave alone. Now that she was in love with him, she wanted to let him know in the most romantic way possible. "Can I bring you something to drink?"

"A Bass Ale for the professor, and I'll just have a club soda with a wedge, not a slice, of lime, please." Gina leaned her arms on the table and braced her chin on her hands. "So, where'd you and Dave go off to yesterday?"

"Mike didn't tell you?"

"No, he didn't." Ian rubbed a hand down Gina's back. "It's been driving her crazy."

"The rat. He wouldn't even tell *Pamela*! No one can resist Andi's mother, especially Mike. I bet she could find Osama bin Laden, get him to tell her all his secrets, and then thank her for being a good listener." She tapped a finger on the table. "But Mike wouldn't budge."

"Good man, Mike. Anyway, Gina's been itching all day to get down here and get the story." Ian chuckled. "So here we are."

"So, where'd you go?" Gina's voice dripped innocence.

"A Bass Ale and club soda, wedge not slice, coming right up." Ainslie turned to go to the bar.

"So not fair!" Gina called after her.

"That's right," Ainslie called back over her shoulder. She and Dave had made lovely memories yesterday, and she clutched them to her tightly. Later, when her feelings weren't so new, maybe then she could share, but not right now.

Spike put Gina and Ian's drinks on the bar in front of Ainslie. "I haven't even ordered these yet."

"It's what Ian drinks and Gina's staying away from alcohol." Spike leaned forward to whisper. "I got a bet with Bobby for ten bucks that says she's pregnant."

"You think so? Hm." Ainslie glanced back at her table. Gina and Ian sat with their heads together, smiling, their fingers wrapped together, their eyes for each other only.

Spike tapped her on the arm. "Maybe you can trade information."

"What?"

"Tell her where you and Dave went yesterday in exchange for her telling you she's pregnant."

"Dear Lord." Ainslie shook her head as she put the drinks on a small round cork lined tray. "You can't be serious."

"I'm dead serious. I got a bet with Bobby. If he's right, I'll never hear the end of it."

Ainslie laughed. "Sorry. You're going to have to wait for her to tell you."

"Okay, be that way," Spike grumbled.

Ainslie shook her head as she walked up to the table. "Maybe you two should get a room. Are you ready to order?"

"Is that what you and Dave did? Get a room?" Gina looked hopeful.

"Good try. A lady never kisses and tells." She delivered their drinks onto the table without spilling even a drop, then pulled out her pad and tapped on it with her pencil. "The soup of the day is minestrone."

Ian snorted a laugh. "I'll have the chili and cornbread." He snapped the menu shut. "What do you want, darling?"

"The grilled chicken Caesar, please." Gina muttered from out of a pout.

Ainslie picked up their menus. "Thanks! I'll be right back with your food."

She put the order in then came back out and leaned against the bar. Chewing on the end of her pencil, she pulled out her list.

"Did you find out anything?" Spike kept her voice low and obviously tried to make it not look like she was keeping tabs on Gina and Ian.

Ainslie hugged her list to her chest. "Gina ordered the grilled chicken Caesar."

"Well, keep trying." Spike waltzed away down to the other end of the bar where a couple of new customers perched on bar stools.

Ainslie pulled out and looked at the small pad of paper holding the ideas of ways she could tell Dave she loved him. A small smile lifted the corners of her mouth as she circled one of her ideas with her pencil.

Dave Mason wasn't the only one who could manage a surprise or two.

Chapter Twenty-Eight

"Hey, Ruark. Scooch over."

He looked up from his *Die Zauberflöte* score to see Shanna and Cecily gazing at him expectantly, holding trays of inedible food. He sighed. There was no getting out of this, so he moved over a seat.

"Thanks!" Cecily scooted into the chair next to him while Shanna sat across from him.

Shanna put her bag on the empty seat next to her. "I've gotta save a seat for Alden."

Ruark choked on a piece of tomato he'd just forked into his mouth. *Fab*ulous. Just the person he wanted to pal around with. Maybe if he could make himself puke they'd go away.

"So," Shanna chirped to Cecily, "Are you going to the party Saturday night?"

"I would, but I don't have a date yet."

Shanna the Subtle struck again. Ruark met Shanna's gaze. Yep, she expected him to ask Cecily to a party filled with kids he hated. He had to do something about this Cecily situation, because he was *so* not her boyfriend, but not here, not now. As usual, he'd do anything to avoid a scene or embarrass his sister.

He bit the bullet and manned up. "Would you like to go with me, Cecily?" Shanna's foot connected with his shin. "I'm sorry I didn't ask you sooner. I've been busy and forgot."

Cecily smiled and shook her shiny, perfect hair over her shoulder. "That's okay. I'd love to go with you."

Alden muscled his way into the chair next to

Shanna. He'd piled his lunch tray with enough food for five kids. "Hey, babe." He kissed Shanna's cheek.

That puking idea was looking better and better with each passing minute.

Luke, another guy from the tenor section in chorus, walked by. He was pretty hot and looked a little like that actor who played the sparkly vampire in *Twilight*. Ruark thought they might play for the same team. It definitely looked like Luke wanted to sit with him. However, when he saw Alden, he passed on by as fast he could.

Ruark wished he could do the same thing.

Well, that sucked.

"Right, Ruark?" Shanna sounded exasperated.

He looked up to find Cecily and Shanna staring at him, like they had asked him a question. Alden wore his usual douchey smirk.

"I'm sorry, I wasn't paying attention."

Shanna rolled her eyes. "We wanted to ask if you want to go to a movie tonight. Cecily and I want to see *Bring It On Fifteen: Spirit Fingers Forever*."

As if. But, wait... "If I go, who's gonna watch Patsy? Besides, it's a school night. We're not supposed to go out on school nights."

Shanna scrunched her nose. "I forgot about Patsy. Thanks for saying you'll mind her."

Oh, yeah. She hadn't forgotten diddley. "You can't go to a movie on a school night."

"I'll make sure she's home before your mom gets home," Alden assured him

Oh, yeah, that made him feel just fine and dandy.

"Please, Ruark? Let me go. I promise I'll be home *way* before Momma comes home. I'll do your chores for a week if you help me out."

He caved, but not because of the chores, though that was sweet. He just wanted to make them stop nagging him. "Whatever. But I'm not taking the fall for you if Momma comes home early."

"Deal." Her mouth blossomed into a huge smile.

"I wish you could come." Cecily stuck out her bottom lip. "Priscilla swears it's an awesome movie."

As if Priscilla's opinion really mattered to him. "Sorry. Someone has to stay home with Patsy."

Her face brightened. "Maybe you could bring Patsy with you."

Alden scowled at Cecily. Clearly he didn't like that idea.

"No. She's got to go to bed early." Ruark knew he had his get out of jail card right there. Never had he loved Patsy more than at that moment.

The warning bell chimed. *Thank you, Jesus.* He stood. "I gotta get to the music room. I'm outtie."

As he scurried to dump his tray, he knew he'd also have to get rid of that asshole Alden for Shanna's sake. Sometimes she could be really stupid.

This was one of those times.

Out of the corner of his eye he caught Luke watching him. Butterflies flew into his stomach and raised a mighty ruckus.

Please, Jesus, let Luke be gay.

****

Dave loosened his tie as he sat in his office chair. Hills of files covered just about every inch of space on his desktop. He glanced at his computer where his Word of the Day screensaver glowed. Clicking a key, he brought up his schedule. He had back to back meetings. His stomach growled. Too bad none of the meetings involved food.

Wait. There was a new appointment at 4:00 P.M. A very interesting appointment. His heart gave him a little kick. He buzzed Mrs. Rockland.

"Yes, Mr. Mason?" His secretary's voice sounded a little tinny over the tiny speaker.

"You added an appointment with Mrs. Logan at

4:00?" There was that kick again.

"Yes. She called and asked to see you, something to do with the twins. Should I call her back and re-schedule it? I know it's your only time to catch dinner."

Food or Ainslie? No choice. "No, let's leave it where it is. I'll catch something at the vending machine in the faculty lounge."

A sigh gusted out of the intercom. "I don't think stale fake cheese and peanut butter crackers count as lunch."

"Sure they do." He felt a grin grow on his face. "They're the perfect food in one small package: dairy, protein, carbs and nuclear orange dye #56."

"You need to think about your health. You're not getting any younger. Do you have any other questions?"

"No. You know, why don't you take off early." He didn't want Mrs. Rockwell and her bionic hearing in the adjacent office.

"What?"

"You've put in a lot of extra hours lately. You should go home early." *Please.*

"Um, okay." She sounded dubious. "Do you want me to do anything before I go?"

"No, I'm all set."

"Shall I leave your door open?"

"Yes, please."

"Well, good night then." The intercom clicked off.

He leaned back in his chair and enjoyed the hum of anticipation running through him. Seeing Ainslie would be a bright spot in an otherwise crappy day.

The part about the twins gave him some worry. He didn't think there was anything seriously wrong. He kept a pretty close eye on them and hadn't heard or seen anything out of the ordinary.

Maybe there was another incident in the locker

room. He grabbed his cell and speed dialed Mike.

"Kelly."

"Hey, Mike, anything happen with Ruark Logan in the locker room?"

Dave could almost hear Mike scowl. "Not that I know of. Why?"

"Ainslie called and set up an appointment to talk to me about the twins."

He could actually hear Mike grin. "Ainslie? Maybe she just wants a little office booty call."

"Of course your mind would go there. I don't think booty calls are her style."

"Well, you can dream. Anything else?"

He certainly could. "No. I'll let you know if there's any locker room stuff you need to know about."

"Thanks." Mike ended the call.

Dave thought about calling Andi, but she'd be in the middle of a rehearsal with the madrigal group. Checking his watch, he felt his heart bounce around like a soccer ball in Spain. Two hours until Ainslie came.

A different image of Ainslie coming flashed in his mind. He felt himself harden at just the memory of being inside her, feeling her wet around him, hearing the erotic noises she made, tasting the delicate skin of her beautiful breasts, that lovely contrast between pale skin and puffy, raspberry colored nipples.

Her unique scent of woman and exotic flowers.

Heaven.

His desk phone rang. Taking a deep breath, and counted to ten so his voice would be steady before he answered it and shoved all thoughts of Ainslie aside.

****

It wasn't a booty call, per se. All she was doing was bringing food to the man she loved because she knew he didn't have a lot of time to eat because of meetings.

And, well, to tell him she loved him.

It wasn't the most romantic of venues, but they had so little alone time, and she needed him to know how she felt.

So she'd run home and showered. She'd have loved to dress up, but she had to get to The End Zone right after and wouldn't have time to change. She did her make-up a little more carefully than she usually would and again raided her stash of vintage *Nocturnes de Caron*. Squirting a mist of lilies and jasmine in the air, she walked through it so the scent didn't announce her presence or gag everyone within a ten-mile radius.

Besides, it was the perfume she wore when they'd made love, and she wanted to remind him of that.

Personally, she didn't need a reminder of it. Every moment was etched in her memory.

She'd picked up a Daveburger and fries from Bobby and had the take-out bag tucked discreetly in a tote bag. She did her best to make sure she looked like a parent coming to discuss her children with the principal, not a woman with stars in her eyes and a song in her heart paying a visit to her lover.

Her delicious, amazing, incredibly handsome lover. It made her all hot and squirmy just remembering all the delightfully wicked things they'd done together. She couldn't wait to do them again. All her life she'd been conventional, then notorious, but never shameless. Until now.

Sweet Jesus. She should not be at the mercy of her hormones, not at her age and with her situation.

It's just that it felt so damn good. She felt, well, happy.

And young, giddy with love.

No one sat at the desk in the outer office, but the door to Dave's office was ajar. She felt a smile bloom on her face and tapped on the door.

"Come in," Dave's baritone rumbled from the other side. She shivered at the sexy sound. The man could make a dead woman jump up and sing hallelujah.

She pushed the door open. "Hey."

He looked up from the file he wrote in and a smile spread slowly across his face. Taking off his glasses, he tossed them onto his desk, then stood. "Hey."

She held up the End Zone take-out bag. "I brought you food." She took a couple steps into his office.

Dave met her halfway. Sniffing like a dog on the trail of a juicy bone, he brought her further into his office. "Smells like a Daveburger." He took the bag, then went to close and lock his office door. "Let's do this the right way," he said as he put the bag on his desk. His warm, skillful hands now free, he gently framed her face with them and kissed her.

Lovely. His lips, now so familiar to her, swept over her mouth once, twice, three times before he deepened the kiss. Her body softened and melted into his, helpless to do anything else. Surrounded by the woodsy scent of his aftershave, filled with the exquisite taste of him, coaxed by the warmth of his hands, she gave herself over to him.

Her lover. Her man.

He lifted his mouth from hers. "You don't know how much I need this today."

"I remember you said you had meetings into the night. You must be hungry."

"I am," he said. "For you." He kissed her again. "Only for you."

"I love you," she blurted, unable to keep her feelings to herself a moment longer. Never had the time seemed so right for her to say those three little words.

Dave went very still in her arms. After a moment, he looked her straight in the eyes. "You're sure?"

Her heart beat, knocking into her ribs. She smiled at him. "I've never been more sure of anything in my life."

"Thank you, God." He picked her up and swung her around in a circle. Landing her on the edge of his desk, he spread her legs open with his thigh and made a place for himself between them. She grabbed hold of his tie and brought his amazing mouth down to her level and opened up for his kiss.

Pulling her right up against him, he crashed his mouth down onto hers. The kiss was greedy and demanding, possessive, crackling like electricity down a live wire. He framed her face again and kept on kissing her and kissing her and kissing her. Her heart in her beat a hard, erratic rhythm, and she clung to him, kissing him back, all lit up by the love she felt for him.

Smiling, Dave murmured "I love you. So much." Heaven was in that smile. He looked at her, his eyes warm and filled with magic.

She leaned in against him. "I think I've loved you all along. It just took me this long to believe it. To believe you."

"I've believed in you all along."

"Even when I was spilling food in your lap?"

He laughed. "Well, maybe not then. But once I got to see the real you, it only took me a little while to fall at your pretty little feet."

She brushed a strand of her hair off his shirt. His heart beat strong and true under her hand. "I've got to get to work. I'm almost late as it is."

"I'll explain things to Bobby."

"No, you won't." She slid off the desk, the full body contact thrilling. She just had to kiss him. "Now, I really have to go. Bobby's onion rings wait for no woman."

Dave stared at her for long moment, his blue eyes the color of a stormy sea. One of the corners of his mouth lifted in an adorable half smile. "Let me walk you to your car."

"No, that's okay." She motioned to his burger. "You better eat before it gets cold, or, well, colder."

"I don't want to let you go."

"You've got those meetings, remember?"

"Wish I didn't."

"Are you pouting?"

"No!" He adjusted his tie and cleared his throat with a gruff *harrumph*. "I never pout. Manly men don't pout."

"And you're a manly man?"

"Didn't I prove that yesterday? Like four times?"

"Mm." She went on tiptoes to plant a quick kiss on his lips. "Yes, you did."

"Okay, then. Just remem—"

His desk phone exploded with a strident jangle.

"Damn." He rounded his desk to answer it. "Mason."

Ainslie went to the door and unlocked it. Then she crooked her fingers into a little wave and blew him a kiss. He scowled, clearly not wanting her to go, but they both had work. She unlocked his office door and let herself out.

Free. She felt able to breathe easy for the first time in a long time. Once Ainslie thought she'd never be able to love and trust a man ever again. Dave Mason had changed all that. Maybe she had another chance at happiness after all.

Chapter Twenty-Nine

"When do you think Shanna's gonna come home?" This must be the fiftieth time Patsy had asked Ruark that question.

He put his own concern aside and put his patient, everything's-cool face on. "Soon." He hoped. "The movie can't go that long."

"She's gonna get in trouble, ain't she?" Now Patsy looked less worried and more fascinated about the prospect of Shanna getting in trouble.

"I hope not. Momma will ground her, and you know how mean Shanna gets when she's grounded." God, wasn't that the truth. They'd pay for days. Shanna had a way of sharing the misery.

"I guess not." Patsy put down the book she'd been reading to Ruark. "But she shouldn't have gone. It's a school night."

And wasn't Ruark worried about that. Shanna had been sucked into Cecily and Alden's world and acted just like them most days. She'd turned into someone he almost didn't know anymore. There's no way Shanna would have deliberately disobeyed one of Momma's rules down in Charleston.

He wanted his sister back.

Twin bright lights poked through the living room window, swerved crazily then stopped. A minute or two went by, then Shanna opened the front door.

She was a mess. She'd clearly been crying, for awhile it seemed, judging by the puffiness of her eyes. Two rivers of black mascara flowed down her cheeks. Her arms clasped tightly across the middle of her stomach. "Don't say anything," she scratched out of a closed throat. "It was a sad movie."

Bring It On Fifteen? A sad movie? No. A pitiful movie, yes, but not a sad one. "Patsy, go get washed up for bed right now." He didn't want Patsy to hear whatever Shanna had to say.

Patsy ran off without a complaint. For once. Good. Ruark turned to look at his other sister.

She looked terrible. He'd never seen her so undone. Her hair was sticking out all over the place, and she had it pulled forward into her face. As for her face itself, what he could see of it, was blank, like she was in shock and her eyes filled with despair. He began to feel the same way. Their twin bond, so unconnected lately, came zooming back to him, like being hit by a truck. He swallowed and it hurt his throat. "So you going to tell me what really happened?"

Shanna clutched her sweater around herself tighter. She started to rub her hands up and down her arms, then winced when she brushed over a place high on her biceps.

A sinking feeling descended upon Ruark. "Did Alden hurt you?"

She snuffled back some newly threatening tears. "No. He wouldn't hurt me."

"I don't believe you." That sinking feeling was quickly morphing into anger. "Show me."

"Ruark, please," she begged. "Just leave it alone. I'm okay. Really."

"Then prove it to me. Show me your arms."

"Ruark, stay out of it. Let me handle it."

"Show. Me. Your. Arms." Though he hated his father, he did a good imitation of the old man's do-what-I-tell-you voice. "Or I'll tell Momma what you did."

They looked at each other, at an impasse. Then something passed between them, a remnant from the time when they knew each other's thoughts as well as their own, when they'd had a special language only they could understand.

Shanna slowly slipped her sweater down her arms. Leaking out from her tee-shirt sleeves, huge purple bruises in the shapes of huge hands marred the pale, delicate skin on her arms. She sobbed.

"Son of a bitch," True, pure rage bubbled up inside him. "I'm gonna kill him."

"Please, Ruark, you're only gonna make it worse." Shanna plopped down onto the sofa and hid her face in her hands. Her shoulders shook as she sobbed.

He sat down next to her, his angry hands shaking. Wanting to touch her, but not knowing how, he carefully clasped his hands in his lap. "What happened?"

She sniffed and kept her gaze fixed on the floor. "It was all my fault."

"Alden holding you hard enough to give you bruises? I don't think so."

"Really, Ruark, it was. He wanted to, you know, do stuff and I, it didn't feel good and I...I tried to stop him." Her voice trickled down to a whisper. "He said if I loved him, I'd let him do what he wanted." She swiped at her left eye.

"Bullshit." Ruark *was* going to kill him. "If he loved you, he wouldn't force you to do anything you don't feel good about."

Shanna started sobbing again, in deep, hard, wracking spasms. He reached out a hand and gently stroked her hair and hissed when she flinched.

Alden had left a nasty hickey on her neck. It looked like he'd tried to suck all the blood out of her, like a damn vampire or something. It sure didn't look like it had felt good. It looked like Alden deliberately tried to hurt her, to punish her. Ruark didn't think he could hate Alden more. Sick freak.

And they called being gay sick? Stupid, stupid bastards. A horrible thought blasted into his brain. He didn't want to know, but he had to ask.

"Did he hurt you anywhere else?" Ruark clenched his jaw, bracing for the answer.

She swiped her nose with the back of her hand. Her whole body trembled. He was about ready to jump out of his skin until she shook her head no.

Thank God. He let out a breath he hadn't realized he was holding. "We should call Momma. Those bruises look serious. Maybe you need to see a doctor."

"No!" She lifted her head and swiveled it to look at him. "I told you, it's my fault!"

"You really need to tell her. She'll know what to do."

"Don't! I don't want her to know!"

"At least you should…"

"No!" She jumped off the couch. "Promise me you won't tell her!"

His heart beat in savage painful bursts as he stood.

"Stop asking me questions! It's my business. It's my fault. I'm a bad girlfriend. Other girls would let him do all that stuff and they'd like it." She hung her head. "He said I didn't love him because I didn't want to, you know. He said there was something wrong with me because I don't really like it."

No. Just no. "He's hurt you before."

"Not really." Shanna sounded choked. "It always kind of hurts when he, you know, kisses me and stuff. Everyone says it feels really good, but I hate it. There's something wrong with me."

Alden'd been hurting her all along. Why hadn't Ruark seen it? Guilt sifted into the stew of ugly emotions he already felt. He'd known Alden was bad news. He should have paid closer attention. "There's nothing wrong with you." He watched what was left of her composure just disintegrate. "He's an asshole and a bully. He beats people up just for the fun of it." Ruark was ready to cry himself.

Jesus. Shanna was so tiny and Alden was huge. He could have done some serious damage.

"He told me I was a tease, like I led him on and stuff." Tears welled in her eyes. "He told me he's gonna tell everyone he broke up with me because I'm a slut. That's what he told Cecily when he texted her."

"I won't let him say one wrong word about you."

"You can't stop him. It's probably all over Facebook by now." She put a hand over her mouth.

"Cecily should…"

"He's gonna get Cecily to kick me off the cheering squad."

"Cecily is stupid. Besides, she's supposed to be your friend."

"Not any more. She does what he tells her to. Everyone does. She texted me that her mother won't let her be friends with me anymore because Momma is their cleaning lady."

Son of a bitch. "You're better off without a friend like her."

"I won't have any friends anymore. Cecily is telling everybody right now what Alden said about me. That I'm a tease and a slut." Shanna shuddered. "Her mom is going to fire Momma, and it's all my fault." Waves of tears took her over. "Momma's gonna hate me. I'm such a failure."

"Momma will never hate you. You know that." Ruark's stomach lurched. Momma fired? Damn them all. "It's not your fault. I won't let anyone talk smack about you or Momma."

"I don't want to talk about it anymore." Shanna's breath sawed out in huge noisy pants. The sound made him more and more mad at Alden. "I think I'm gonna throw up." She pushed past him and ran to the bathroom.

Ruark watched her, feeling helpless, lost and furious.

Well, if Shanna wouldn't do anything about it, Ruark would. He'd beat the truth out of Alden and make him pay for hurting his sister.

He was so caught up in his confusion and righteous indignation, he didn't realize Patsy had been hiding and had heard every word.

Chapter Thirty

The next morning, Ruark managed to get out of the house without his mother seeing him. She was busy with Shanna, who wouldn't get out of bed because she felt too sick.

It actually made his plans easier. He jammed his backpack in his locker and headed for the gym.

Gunning for Alden.

He didn't care if he got thrown out of school. He didn't care if he got the crap beaten out of him by Alden. The bastard couldn't skate away from what he'd done to Shanna.

Ruark's kicks squee-geed as he marched down the hall. That scent of the mystery lunch of the day wafted woefully from the cafeteria. Mrs. Kelly stood in the doorway of her room, nodded at him, but he just walked on by.

Alden stood with his friends underneath the score sign. Ruark didn't think. He launched himself at Alden as hard as he could, pushing him down to the floor and against the wall. Alden's head connected with the floor with a satisfying *thunk*. Then, without a word, Ruark brought his fist back and punched Alden as hard as he could. The yelp of pain Alden gave was totally worth it.

He'd had the element of surprise, and had gotten a few good belts in, but that was no more. Alden's buddies pulled him off and held him so that Alden could use him as a punching bag. Pain exploded in his face and his gut.

"What the hell! Stop that right now!"

Ruark dimly heard Mr. Kelly explode on the

scene. The kids holding him dropped him on the floor. "He threw the first punch, Coach." Alden yelled.

"Quiet!" Mr. Kelly ordered. "Chelsea. Go get some wet towels."

Mr. Kelly dropped to his knees next to him. "Ruark. You okay?"

He was so obviously not okay. His nose hemorrhaged blood and it ran down his face and back into his throat. He gagged on it. Pain radiated in sharp bursts from the places Alden had punched him. He could barely breathe due to the blood.

"Can you stand up?"

Absolutely. Even if it killed him, he would walk away from this. Without help.

Well, a little help. Mr. Kelly helped him to his feet, but then Ruark shook his arms free. "I'm okay."

The student teacher came back with the towels. Ruark took them and gingerly pressed it to his nose.

"He just came out of nowhere and ran me down." Alden complained. "I wasn't doing nothing to him. He's crazy."

"You three. Up to Mr. Mason's office right now. If your story checks out, maybe, just maybe, I won't bench you on Friday. But as of right now, it's not looking good. What were you thinking, three against one?" Mr. Kelly pointed his finger at them, "Don't plan on practicing today."

"He started it. He threw the first punch," one of the kids, Kevin, whined.

"Mr. Mason's office. Now."

Ruark heard them leave. He kept his head high as he took one shuffling step forward.

Mr. Kelly studied Ruark's face. "I'm taking you right to the nurse's office so we can make sure you don't have to go to the E.R. You want to tell me what that was all about?"

Ruark wasn't about to tell Mr. Kelly. For all

Ruark knew, he'd take Alden's side. Mr. Kelly barked out a couple of orders to the student teacher and left her to deal with the custodians and other kids.

He wasn't sorry, and he wasn't going to apologize. Even if his mother tried to make him, he wouldn't do it.

A real man stood up for what's right. He protected his family.

"Okay. You can tell Mr. Mason. Come on, kid. Let's get you checked out." Mr. Kelly walked beside him all the way to the nurse's office.

****

Ainslie's day added up to quite possibly the strangest day she'd had in a long time. Shanna was at home in bed, too sick to go to school. It seemed to be a very mysterious malady, although Patsy swore that Shanna had been throwing up.

Speaking of whom, Patsy had several bad dreams during the night and ended up sleeping with Ainslie. She didn't keep up her constant stream of conversation on the way to school, instead being oddly silent. Ruark managed to slip past her so Ainslie hadn't even *seen* him this morning.

She pulled her car up in front of the Brewster's house, in the spot they designated for her. Grabbing her stuff, she walked up to the door like she always did.

Oddly, Mrs. Brewster met her at the door. Handing Ainslie an envelope, she said, "Your services are no longer needed. This is the last of the wages we owe you. Good bye."

"Wait!" Ainslie shook her head as she looked at the envelope and then back at Mrs. Brewster. "Is there a problem? Did I do something wrong?" If she had, she couldn't remember it.

"There is no place here for you anymore. Perhaps you can use this free time to keep better

226

track of your tramp of a daughter."

"I beg your pardon?" No one called her daughter a tramp.

"You are no longer welcome here." She closed the door, right in Ainslie's face.

Her daughter? A tramp? Her daughter was no tramp—Ainslie knew that for sure. How dare that Brewster woman say otherwise?

What in holy hell was going on? Obviously, something was really wrong. She got back into her car and high tailed it home to talk to Shanna.

****

Dave juggled his briefcase, coffee, and breakfast sandwich as he tried to open his office door. Running late, he had ten minutes to meet with Joe L'Amore, the new superintendent, about the budget. Something had to go, and these money meetings were never pleasant.

He'd just managed to get in the office when his phone rang. Tossing the briefcase onto his chair, he dropped the bag with the sandwich on to the desk. He was hanging on to the coffee, phone call or no phone call. "Mason."

"Yeah, Dave, it's Mike. There was an incident in the gym a couple of minutes ago and I've got Ruark Logan here at the Nurse's Office. He's pretty beat up."

"Be right there."

"Alden, Kevin, and Leo are on their way up to see you. Leo and Kevin were holding Ruark down so Alden could use him as a punching bag. Throw the book at them."

"I'll be right there." The bottom fell out of his stomach. God damn! Dave headed out his door. "Mrs. Rockwell," he said as he passed her in the hall, "Can you please call Mr. L'Amore and tell him there's a situation with some students, and I can't meet with him? And Alden Bradford, Kevin Baldwin and Leo

Campanello are on their way up here. Make them wait here until I get back."

"Of course." She sat at her desk and immediately picked up the phone.

"Thanks. And after that, please call Mrs. Logan and see if she can come down here. There's something up with Ruark."

The fear eating at his every step had a different edge to it. He just wasn't going to check on a hurt student. He was going to check on a kid he very much felt to be his own.

Ruark was sitting in a chair holding a cold compress to his nose. They had his shirt off and bruises bloomed into large, fist shaped marks. The nurse was checking to see if any ribs were broken, and the kid winced every time she pushed. If Dave didn't miss his guess, Ruark was also getting a pretty impressive black eye. Why would anyone beat up Ruark. Someone better have some answers.

"What happened?" Dave looked at Mike.

Mike's jaw couldn't clench any tighter. "I don't know. Ruark won't say anything. When I got there, Leo and Kevin were holding Ruark so Alden could use him as a punching bag."

Son of a bitch. "Three against one? I don't care what happened, they're suspended."

Mike nodded, his eyes grim. "That's what I thought would happen. I'm sure some time cooling their heels on the bench will give them a new perspective on good sportsmanship."

Dave looked at Ruark, but the kid wouldn't look at him. "I've had Mrs. Rockwell call Ainslie, let's hope she reached her."

Mike nodded. "I've got to get back. My first period class already started."

"Right." He stared at Ruark, willing him to look at him. "I'm going to my office to hear what the other guys have to say. Your mom should be along, as soon as Mrs. Rockwell reaches her. Are you sure you don't have something to say to me?"

Ruark peered at him out of his good eye. "Don't call her. Please."

"Too late." He turned to the nurse. "Please keep me in the loop here."

"Of course, Mr. Mason."

Ruark stared at him, defiant and though his face was beaten, his spirit was not. Violence was not the way he handled things. He was far too sensitive for that. Something important had happened and had driven him to this.

Dave wouldn't rest until he found out the truth.

Chapter Thirty-One

"Shanna? Shanna, sweetie, I'm home," Ainslie called out the minute she stepped in her front door. A nasty stew of emotions swirled inside her. Anger, confusion, and most of all, fear.

What in the world had happened?

Shanna didn't answer, but as Ainslie dropped her purse onto the table by the door, she thought she heard Shanna crying softly. Heart stumbling with worry, she pushed the door to her daughter's room open.

Shanna lay on her bed tucked up into a ball, weeping like her heart was broken. Used up balls of tissues littered the bed as Shanna cried her eyes out. She rushed right over to her and pulled her into a hug. "Beautiful girl, what happened?"

Shanna flinched, like she was in pain, when Ainslie touched her arms. Her heart stilled and for a moment, she forgot how to breathe. "What's going on here, sweetie?"

Shanna let loose. Incoherent through her violent sobbing, she flung her arms around Ainslie's neck and just let go.

Rubbing her back, her hair, Ainslie held on to her baby tight, rocking her and crooning low sounds meant to soothe. Fear swirled around her.

When the storm had subsided, when Shanna's sobs had dwindled to hiccups, Ainslie tried to get her to repeat the story. "What happened, pumpkin? You know you can tell me anything."

"I really messed up," Shanna snarfled.

Ainslie reached to move Shanna's hair out of her

face. She saw the lurid bruise on Shanna's neck and had to bite her tongue to keep calm and quiet, even as her blood turned icy cold. "You need to tell me right now what happened. I promise you won't get into trouble."

Face red and blotchy, Shanna shuddered. "I'm sorry, Momma. I snuck out to a movie last night with Alden, only we didn't go to the movie, we just dropped Cecily and Priscilla off, 'cause Alden didn't want to see it."

"Okay." *Calm, blue ocean,* she told herself. Shanna didn't need her flying off the handle.

"He…" Shanna swallowed, sounding like she was forcing a rock down her throat. "He took us to the Quarry Overlook, you know, where all the kids go, so we could, like, you know, just be alone and stuff." She looked so ashamed.

"And stuff." Dear Lord. Her heart beat like a hammer on an anvil. "Is that when he hurt you?"

"It was my fault, Momma. All my fault." She grabbed for another tissue. "I don't really like to do all that stuff, 'cause it always kind of hurts, you know? But he's always telling me that if I was a good girlfriend, I'd like it when he does that stuff."

"What kind of things does he pressure you to do?" Could this get any worse?

"He'd like me to let him do everything, but I won't. I just let him go, you know, like part of the way. Then he gets mad and calls me a tease." Shanna started crying again.

"Is this the first time he's hurt you?" How had she not noticed? She should have made sure Alden was on the up and up. She hadn't because he came from a wealthy family, and she cleaned his house.

She should have known better. Guilt and shame covered her like a heavy blanket. "You have to tell me, sugar."

Shanna shook her head. "He says it hurts

because I don't know how to do anything right, like there's something wrong with me."

Ainslie looked down to see her hands were shaking. "There's nothing wrong with you. He shouldn't touch you and hurt you. He's the one who's wrong."

"There's more, and I'm so sorry, Momma! He broke up with me, and now he's telling everyone I'm a slut and a whore. Cecily won't be my friend, and she's on his side, and she says she's gonna make her mother fire you." She broke down again, this time her arms around her momma's neck and her face against her shoulder.

Cecily hadn't wasted any time, had she? "It's just a job, baby. I'll get another one." She smoothed her girl's hair. "You're the most important thing right now."

Ainslie held on to her daughter like she'd never let go again. She wanted to cry herself, and tears did well up in her eyes, but she would be strong for her baby.

The phone rang. She ignored it, because she couldn't, *wouldn't*, leave Shanna right now.

****

Dave looked at the three boys sprawled in his office chairs. He could usually keep his cool, distance himself from the situation, but this felt so different. He had a personal stake in this.

He felt outraged to see how casual these clowns acted. Well, they'd learn soon. "Sit up."

When Dave used that voice, no one disobeyed. The boys sat up.

"So, what happened to make the three of you gang up on one kid who's only half the size of one of you?"

"He started it," Leo said. "Alden was just minding his own business, and Ruark came in and attacked him."

"That's when you decided that three of you were needed to take care of the situation?"

"What do you want me to do? The freak attacked me." Alden's argument might have held more water if there had been more damage to him, other than his pride.

That pride was going to take another beating. Right. Now.

"So you, captain of the football team, needed help to take care of one skinny kid who doesn't know how to fight?"

Alden's face turned bloody red. "It wasn't like that. The kid was crazy."

"It's too bad you couldn't walk away from it. All three of you. Doesn't give me much hope for the future of the football team. And here I thought you guys were going some place this year."

"We are!" Kevin blurted. "This is the best team in years."

Dave raised an eyebrow. "Think you're going to the championships this year?"

Kevin looked surprised, then nodded. "We've got a shot."

Dave went in for the kill. "Well, the team may have a shot, but you guys are benched for the rest of the season."

They started to protest, but Dave held up his hand. "Fighting is against the code of conduct you all signed when you joined the team."

"That's not fair! You can't bench us!" Alden yelled, his face turning a violent purple.

"Quiet!" Dave sliced the kid with a glance. "You sit there and mind your tone of voice."

"But Ruark started it! It's not our fault." Kevin glowered, eyes hot and angry.

Dave ignored the comment. "Here's the rest of it. You have in school suspension for the rest of this week and all of next week. You can't go to any school activities. You come to school and you go home. And if you ever touch Ruark Logan again, I'll make a case for expulsion, right after I call the police and have the D.A. charge you with assault. Got it?"

The boys didn't answer.

"You look at me. I didn't hear you. Got that?"

They nodded, their movements jerky, their eyes hot as they met Dave's gaze.

"Good. Go get your stuff and come right back here. Mrs. Rockwell is calling your parents and having them come pick you up. Come back tomorrow to start your in-school suspension."

The boys lurched out of their chairs, and it looked like Alden wanted to kick his, but he pulled back.

Wise move.

Boys gone, Dave sat behind his desk, picked up a pencil and snapped it in half. Still furious, he took another pencil and repeated the process. Not much better. He buzzed Mrs. Rockwell. "Have we reached Mrs. Logan yet?"

"No. She doesn't answer her home phone or her cell."

Well, that wasn't good. "Please keep trying, okay?"

"Absolutely."

He sat back and worried. Following a hunch, he checked the attendance list. Shanna Logan was marked absent.

Not good. Not good at all. Something was very, very wrong. Time to see if Ruark was ready to talk.

****

Ainslie got Shanna calmed down enough to try drinking a cup of tea. Toast would come later, if she could keep the tea down.

Those were the easy things to do. The ordinary things. Child's sick—feed her tea and toast. Familiar territory.

234

Talking to Shanna when she was so ashamed of herself felt harder to do. No time like the present. "You have nothing to blame yourself for. Real men don't hurt women."

Shanna shook her head. "I thought he loved me. I'm so stupid." She gestured wildly. The teacup and saucer nearly fell out of her hands to meet the floor.

"You are not stupid." Ainslie saved the teacup. "Some men are just really good at saying what you want to hear, even though it's not the truth." She took Shanna's cold hands into her own. "That's on them."

"Is that what happened with Daddy?" Shanna's chest rose and fell with uneven breaths. "Is that why you didn't know what he was doing?"

Ainslie sighed. Shanna deserved the truth. "Yes. I believed exactly what he wanted me to believe."

"That's why you married him, then? You didn't think he was a crook?"

She cursed Bobby Lee. No child should have to say her daddy was a crook. "He wasn't doing anything bad when I first met him. He was so handsome and so very tuned in to what I wanted." She shook her head. "I was young and foolish, and so full of myself because I was Miss South Carolina."

"Are you sad because you married him?"

Good question. "No, because I wouldn't have you, and Ruark, and Patsy, if I hadn't married him." She sighed. "I'm more mad at myself because I let him fool me and take advantage of all our friends and family."

Shanna cocked her head to one side. "I let Alden fool me. I wanted to be popular and have the best boyfriend and be in the top clique." More tears gathered in her eyes. "How could I be so wrong?"

Ainslie passed her the tissue box. "Next time, you'll know better and make better choices."

"There's not going to be a next time. I don't ever

want a boyfriend again."

Ainslie smiled. "You will. Some man will come around, and you'll take your time getting to know him, so you don't get hurt."

"Is that what you're doing with Mr. Mason?"

The phone jangled again. Saved by the proverbial bell. "Hello."

"Mrs. Logan. This is Mrs. Rockwell from the high school. Ruark's been in a fight, and we need you to come down to the school."

****

Dave had his hand ready to push his door open and leave to see about Ruark in the nurse's office, but the damn phone rang again. He picked it up.

"Mason." It was his boss. His new boss. Addington Schools Superintendent Joe L'Amore. "I hear you've had some excitement over there."

"Nothing we can't handle."

"When do you want to go over the budget, then? Does tomorrow at 7:30 AM again work?"

Dave glanced at his blotter calendar. "That works."

"I'll set it up with Mrs. Rockwell." L'Amore cleared his throat. "You should know, I've already gotten some calls."

Dave just bet he had. "I'm sure you have."

"There's some concern that you're involved with the mother of the boy who initially attacked Alden Bradford."

"That has nothing to do with it. Ruark Logan will receive the same punishment the other three boys got."

"Good. I've got your back for now, but we'll talk tomorrow." L'Amore hung up.

Dave stared at the receiver as he replaced it. It hadn't taken long at all for Alden, Kevin, and Leo's parents to call the superintendent to complain. They'd probably put all the School Board members

236

on speed dial.

Tough. He stood by his call. He hoped Ainslie would feel the same way.

What the hell had happened to make Ruark attack those boys?

That was the $64,000.00 question.

Chapter Thirty-Two

"Do you need more ice?" The school nurse asked.

Ruark nodded. His left eye throbbed like a mofo, he was pretty certain that Alden broke his nose. At least it had stopped bleeding. They didn't think any of his ribs were broken, but they hadn't ruled out any of his internal organs being bruised.

It was all worth it.

"Excuse me, but I think my son is here?" Momma stood in the doorway, looking like some kind of avenging angel. "Ruark." She barged right on in when she saw him. "What happened to you?"

"He got into a fight this morning," the nurse told her.

"A fight?" She sat right next to him on the little bed he already sat on. "Let me see your eye."

Her gentle fingers combed through his hair. He closed his good eye so she wouldn't see him cry.

"We checked him out as best we could. I don't think his ribs are broken, and he's got some nasty bruises on his torso. You might want to get those checked out," he heard the nurse tell his mother. Momma stopped stroking his head as she stood. "I don't think they're serious, but things can come up later on. I'm afraid his nose *is* broken."

"Who did this to him?" Momma's voice vibrated the same way it had when she found out his father was an embezzler and threw him out of the house.

"They're dealt with."

Ruark opened his eye to see Mr. Mason come into the room.

"They? There was more than one?" Momma

looked furious. Her eyes shot fire as she turned to face Mr. Mason.

"Yeah. Look, why don't you take him home, and see if you can get him to talk about why he took it into his head to single-handedly attack Alden Bradford this morning." Mr. Mason raised his hand like he was gonna touch Momma, but he stuffed his hand in his pants pocket instead.

Momma turned back to look at Ruark. "You attacked Alden Bradford?"

He shrugged. She gave him that stare that made him worry that she could read his mind.

"Can I take my boy home now?" was all she said.

"Of course." Mr. Mason said. "Just sign him out here."

Momma didn't need to be told twice. "Come on. Let's get you home."

Ruark slowly got to his feet, still determined to walk out of there without help. Momma followed him.

"Ainslie." Mr. Mason's voice was quiet as he called Momma's name.

She stopped to look at him. "I've really got to get home, Dave. There's a lot more you don't know."

"May I come by later on?"

Momma sighed, the sound gritty as it left her throat. "Yes. Please. I'd really like you to."

"Good. I'll bring food."

"Of course you will." A bunch of the tension seemed to drain out of her as she looked at him.

"Do you need someone to pick up Patsy?"

"No. I'm going to swing by the elementary school and pick her up now."

"Okay. Call me if you think of anything you need."

Mr. Mason's voice was low and rumbly. Reassuring. It made Ruark feel kind of warm inside, the good kind of warm inside. Safe. Protected.

"I will. Come on, baby. Let's go home." Momma gave Mr. Mason one small, last smile.

It wasn't until they got to the car that Momma said anything else. "You did this for your sister, didn't you?"

"Shanna told you?"

"After Mrs. Brewster fired me because of my tramp daughter, I went home. You should have told me last night when I got home from work."

His good eye started to leak again. "Someone had to defend her, and she wouldn't let me tell you."

"Oh, sugar." Her voice got soft again. "Let's go home and figure out what to do next."

****

After a stop at Hope Monahan's to pick up some comfort food, mostly soft stuff that Ruark could eat without hurting himself, Dave headed for Ainslie's.

It felt good, like he was going home. To a family.

His family.

Which right now was in turmoil. He was going to find out why and then be a part of the solution. Not because he was the principal of the damn school, but because he was part of the family.

He took a minute to look at the tiny little rental house Ainslie and her children lived in. He'd love to move them to a bigger house, with a yard and a fence.

Patsy would love a dog.

And...He was getting way ahead of himself. Focus on the task at hand. Fix the trouble, save the family.

He knocked on the front door. Technically, officially, they weren't his family yet. He'd work on that.

Ainslie came to the door. "Oh, Dave! I'm so glad to see you." She held out her hands. "Let me take those take-out bags for you."

"How are things?" Stepping inside, he let her

take the bags then shrugged out of his blazer.

"Better now that you're here. Come with me to the kitchen." Opening one bag a crack then sniffing appreciatively, she hummed. "This smells wonderful. Is it from Hope's? Thanks for bringing it."

"No problem. I just had Hope put in a little bit of this and that. And a lasagna. I figured soft foods would be easier for Ruark to eat. Speaking of which, what happened?" He couldn't wait to get the whole story. It had gnawed at him all afternoon.

She pushed open the kitchen door with her foot, then caught it with her hip as it swung back to close. He recognized the move from The End Zone. "Do you have to work tonight?"

After placing the bags on the counter, she turned to face him. "No. I called in. Bobby understood totally, thank the Lord."

"He should." Dave stepped closer to her and pulled her into his arms, an embrace more meant for comfort than arousal. "Is this okay to do here?" Even though she loved him, she might not be ready for her kids to see her with him."

She wrapped her arms around his waist and lay her head over his heart. "Yes."

He kissed the top of her head. "Where are the kids?"

"Ruark and Shanna are in their rooms. Neither is in any shape to do anything strenuous. Patsy is in my room. She's so upset by the whole mess."

"Of course she is. Can you tell me what happened?"

Ainslie pulled away from him and plopped down onto a chair. "Short story?"

He sat as well. "Sure." He imagined he'd get the long version later.

Ainslie pursed her lips and studied a spot on the kitchen table. "You know that Shanna's been dating Alden Bradford."

"Yeah."

"Well, it appears that he gets…God, I can barely say this." She shook her head as she looked at him.

He took her hands in his. Hers were icy and trembled. "Take your time."

"No, I think I need to get it out all at once." Her chest heaved as she took a deep breath. "Alden's been pressuring her for sex, and he doesn't exactly have a gentle touch. She snuck out last night to be with him and came back with huge bruises. If I'd been here, I could have…"

"No." Anger sifted through him to settle in his stomach and churn there. "No could haves. Alden is responsible for his own actions."

However, Dave wished he could have gotten in a few punches of his own.

A horrible thought made his stomach churn faster. "Did Alden, uh…" *Shit. How to ask this delicately?* "Hit her? Assault her sexually?"

Ainslie shook her head. "No," she whispered. "She says not. Just that he's rough…" She choked. "When he touches her." Looking him in the eyes, she took a deep breath. "She blames herself. Says it's her fault, that something's wrong with her because she doesn't like it when he…" She choked again. "When he kisses and touches her. Dave." Ainslie sniffed. "He left bruises on her arms and her…her breasts where he grabbed her. She's got a monstrous sucker bite on her throat."

I'm going to kill him. Bare hands around Alden's throat, twisting until he had bruises on *his* fucking throat.

She must have seen the violence in his eyes. "Please, Dave, not here. Not now. Shanna needs some calm. Peace."

"That explains the incident with Ruark."

Ainslie nodded. "He was so mad. I've never, ever known him to be violent. But there's more, and here's where I need your expert advice."

"Okay."

"Alden has turned all the kids against her, telling them what a slut and tease Shanna is. It's all over Facebook, Twitter, all of those things." Despair colored her face. "It's like it was back when we had to move from Charleston, after Bobby Lee went to jail. The kids have been brutal."

"There's a school policy against cyber-bullying. Can she cut and paste the posts?"

"Oh, I don't know. I don't even want her to look at those awful things. There's more."

Jesus. What else?

Ainslie slipped those cold hands of hers out of his and swiped at some tears welling in her eyes. "They're telling their parents all these lies, to the point where I've been fired from one cleaning job. At least that I know about. There're probably more."

Son of a bitch. "You don't want to work for them anyway."

"Of course I don't, but Shanna feels it's her fault I got fired."

The kitchen door opened, and Patsy stood in the doorway, eyes wide. Ainslie pulled herself together in the time it took her to stand. It was impressive. Picking Patsy up, she nuzzled her child's hair. "Hey, Doodlebug. Are you hungry?"

Patsy nodded.

"Well, lucky for you, Mr. Mason stopped by and brought us some goodies. Want to see what he brought?"

Dave watched Ainslie take care of her daughter. He pulled his cell phone out of his shirt pocket and went into the living room. He had a lot of phone calls to make.

****

"Mr. Mason's here." Shanna quietly closed the door to Ruark's bedroom shut. "What do you think he's telling Momma?" She sat on his bed with a bounce.

Ruark shrugged and sat up, wincing as his ribs complained about the change in position. So Mr. Mason was here. Ruark figured he'd be in trouble for starting the fight. "He's probably here to tell Momma I'm being suspended."

"I am so stupid! I've ruined everything!" Shanna grabbed a tissue from the box next to his bed.

"Please don't cry again." Really. Please, don't cry. He couldn't stand to see her tears. "Nothing is your fault. You didn't make me go after Alden. That was my own idea." He'd do it again in a heartbeat.

"Momma got fired, and Cecily probably hates you now like she hates me."

"Trust me. Cecily hating me is a relief."

"But you did ask her out?"

"Only because it was important to you."

Shanna frowned. "You must have liked her a little bit."

His shoulders felt burdened down like two acme anvils had fallen on them. He was tired of the effort of staying in the closet. Ruark sighed and made a decision. He'd carried this secret for so long, and he ached with the weariness of it. If he couldn't be honest with his twin, then his life really wasn't worth living. "I didn't like her. I don't like girls that way. I'm gay, Shan."

Chapter Thirty-Three

"What?" Shanna's eyes bulged like a cracked out Chihuahua's. "Are you serious?"

"Very." Ruark tried to gauge her reaction. He hoped he hadn't made a mistake. Too late now. Little rusty claws of fear grabbed hold of his throat.

Shanna just looked confused. "How long have you been gay?"

"All my life." He willed her to be okay with this. *Please, Jesus.*

She shifted on the bed. "No, I mean, like, when did you get gay? When you got into all the music school stuff?" She put her hand on top of his.

"It's not something you catch, like the flu." He shook his head.

"How did you know, then?"

"I don't know. I just did." He switched their hands so his was on top. Desperation nipped at him with sharp, pointy teeth. He had to know how she felt. "I hope you're okay with this. I love you. I *need* for you to understand."

"I love you too." She gave him a peck on the cheek. "It's cool. I'm just surprised. I wish you'd told me sooner." Her lips drew across her face in a straight, tight line. "I never would have asked you to date Cecily if I'd known. That's another thing I screwed up. I'm so sorry!"

Relieved to have his twin know about him and be okay with it, he needed her to feel relieved too. He wasn't going to let her blame herself for Cecily. "You didn't screw up. I could have told you."

"Yeah, you could have." She frowned. "Do you

think I'm gay too, because we're twins?"

He would have smiled if his mouth didn't hurt so much. She could be such a ditz. "I think you'd know by now."

"Maybe that's why I don't like it when Alden touches me."

"You don't like it when Alden touches you because he hurts you. You're not gay."

She furrowed her brow as she thought about it. "Well, I sure don't want any boy to touch me again. Ever." Biting her lip, she asked, "Does Momma know?"

"No. I wanted to tell her, but then our sperm donor went to jail." He grimaced. "No time has felt right. I didn't want to stress her out even more. She's so busy, working herself to the bone for us."

"You need to tell her. I'll go with you." Shanna nodded. "I know I didn't want to tell her about Alden, but I'm glad I did. She made me feel a lot better." She grabbed another tissue and wiped her nose. "I thought she'd be mad at me, but she wasn't. I think she'll be okay with us being gay."

"This is different." Ruark shook his head. "And you're not gay."

"No, it's not different at all. She loves you. If you don't tell her, I will."

"You're really bossy, you know that?"

"It comes in handy sometimes." Rubbing her hands on her lap, she stood up. "Maybe we can tell her now."

"No. After Patsy goes to bed." He *so* didn't want to explain what being gay meant to a six-year-old. Never mind having her see Momma have a bad reaction to his revelation. He didn't know what he would do if his mother couldn't accept who he was.

"It's no good keeping secrets from Momma. Look what happened when I did." Shanna rubbed her arms up and down.

"If you keep beating yourself up, I won't tell Momma."

She flashed him a weak smile.

"It's all gonna be okay," he tried to reassure her.

He hoped with all his might that he was telling her the truth.

****

Ainslie re-wrapped the lasagna Dave brought for the kids and put it in the fridge. There was still a lot of it. They'd be eating it for at least a week.

Now that she was losing cleaning jobs, money was going to be too tight. All five of her clients had called to tell her that her services were no longer needed. Thank goodness she still had The End Zone.

Dave left earlier to take care of some calls. She missed him. He said he'd be back.

She counted on it.

She'd made Patsy a grilled cheese and read with her. Now Patsy was tucked away in bed. Neither of the twins had made an appearance, so next on Ainslie's to-do list was to check on them. She knew they were both holed up in Ruark's room.

She loved them so much. Her heart almost couldn't hold all the love she felt for them.

She damned Bobby Lee to hell and back for deserting their family.

Ainslie would blame this whole situation on him if she could, but the fact was only she held the blame. Remorse slogged over her in thick, sludgy waves. She closed her eyes as they filled with tears. Why hadn't she noticed something was wrong with Shanna?

She wiped her eyes, staunching those tears. She had no time to wallow in guilt. Her children needed her.

She had only taken one step when the twins walked into the kitchen.

Oh, dear Lord, the bruises. Ruark looked like

he'd gone ten rounds with a 'roided up heavy weight boxer. Shanna had her bruises covered up, but Ainslie knew they were there all the same. Both children marked by the same monster. She tamped down the sudden burst of rage that rushed through her. The twins didn't need any more ugly emotions today.

The two of them held hands like they'd done when they were little. They always touched each other every chance they could. Her heart hitched a beat as she smiled at them. "Hey, babies."

Shanna gave her a ghost of a smile. "Hey, Momma."

"Are you two hungry?" Ainslie asked.

"I'm not hungry, Momma." Shanna actually turned a shade of pale green.

"Do you have a minute to talk?"

Ruark's voice stayed level as he interrupted them, but she could tell he was nervous. She also didn't miss Shanna squeezing his hand.

"I've got all the time in world for you." She smiled at them. "What's up?" She motioned for them to sit. "Are you sure you aren't hungry? Mr. Mason brought us a year's worth of take out from Hope Monahan's."

"Mr. Mason did?" Ruark sounded surprised. "I thought he was here to punish me for punching Alden."

"No. He just brought food. Are you sure you aren't hungry? There's lasagna. It's killer." She really hoped they were hungry.

"Okay." Shanna pulled Ruark into the room and pushed him into a chair. "I'm not hungry, but Ruark might be."

"I'm not."

Ainslie ignored them and pulled the lasagna out of the fridge, slapped a couple of wedges on two plates and put them into the microwave. Inhaling deeply to calm her nerves, she smiled and turned to look at her children. "Okay." She sat down next to Shanna. "What's up?"

Shanna looked at her brother. "Ruark has something to tell you."

"Shanna." Ruark shook his head. "I can do this myself."

"Go on already." She pushed his shoulder. "I'm all set to tell if you don't."

Ainslie felt her heart clench with every word of their banter. "What's going on?"

A moment of silence.

Shanna pushed Ruark again and made a snort when he didn't react. "Ruark has something to tell you," she repeated.

What more secrets could they possibly throw at her? Pulling on her best beauty pageant face, she folded her hands on top of the table. Summoning all the restraint she could, she said, "Don't keep me on tenterhooks. I won't judge, I promise. Please just tell me what's going on."

The twins looked at each other. Ruark was clearly pained, Shanna seemed large and in charge. The two of them were playing some strange game of chicken.

Shanna said, "Okay." She looked Ainslie straight in her eyes. "Ruark and I are gay."

Ruark rolled his eyes. "I'm gay. Shanna only thinks she is because she doesn't like it when Alden touches her."

"I could be gay," Shanna complained. "You're gay, and we're twins."

Gay. Whatever Ainslie had expected them to say, being gay was not even on the list. Not even *near* the list.

Her stomach lurched as she absorbed what they were telling her. Was this the reason for the bullying? Kids were killing themselves because of being bullied for being gay.

Lord help her. Was Ruark thinking about hurting himself like those other boys? The blood rushed out of her so quickly that she felt lightheaded and heard a loud buzzing in her ears. The horror of it chilled her to the bone.

"Shanna, just...Stop, okay? You're not gay, no matter how much you want to be." Ruark raised his head to look at Ainslie. "But I am, Momma." He stuck out his chin, daring her to disapprove.

"But you still love him, right, Momma?" Shanna put a protective arm around Ruark.

"Of course I do!" She jumped out of her chair and put her arms around both of them. "There's nothing you can do, or say, or be..." She kissed the top of first Ruark's head and then Shanna's. "That could make me stop loving you."

"I told you." Shanna kissed her brother on the cheek, then stood. "I'm tired. G'night, Momma."

"G'night, doodle bug." She kissed her beautiful girl on the cheek, then sat in the chair Shanna had vacated. "So, now, tell me about you." She smoothed out a place where Ruark's hair stuck out.

He looked at her. "I'm gay."

Like she hadn't heard him the first time. "Is that the reason you've been bullied?"

"I don't know. I mean Alden and those guys throw around words like gay and faggot as general insults, but I don't think they really know. The new kid with the hick accent, I'm just the target *du jour*."

She studied his face. This was no time to beat around the bush. There were too many tragic stories about suicide because of bullying out there. "Have you been thinking about hurting yourself?"

He shook his head slowly. "No. I wouldn't do that."

Relief ran through her like warm summer rain. Thank God. "How long have you known that you're gay?"

"A while." He shrugged. "A few years, anyway."

A few years? "And you've been keeping it a secret all this time?"

Nodding, he looked down. "Yeah."

"Why didn't you tell me sooner?" Appalled at herself for not noticing it, she almost didn't want to hear his answer. "Didn't you think I'd understand?"

"I don't know. I guess I figured *you* would understand, but then you'd tell the great Bobby Lee Logan, and I just didn't want him to know." Ruark swallowed. "I knew he'd be ashamed of me."

"Oh, baby boy." She gathered him into her arms, being careful not to hurt his ribs. "You must have felt so alone." She rested her chin ever-so-gently on the top of his head. "I'm so sorry."

"It wasn't that way in Charleston. All my friends at school knew. We all knew about each other."

"And then I uprooted you and took you away from them." She was the worst mother in the world. "I'm so very, very sorry."

He disentangled himself from her arms and sat back. "It's okay."

"Well, I'm so glad you finally trusted me to tell me." She smiled. "How did you get Shanna to keep your secret for so long? She usually blabs right away."

"I told her about an hour ago."

"She kept quiet a whole hour, huh?" Ainslie sighed. "That must be a record. Does anyone else know?" His eye and nose looked like they were swelling up again. She got up to get him some more ice.

"My teachers at my old school. And Max."

Max, his private voice coach and his teachers at his school in Charleston had seen this before Ainslie had. She handed Ruark the ice pack she'd put together. "Put this on your eye again, sugar."

"You're not mad, are you?" He winced as he put the ice on his face.

"No, sweetie. I'm not mad, not at all." Just at herself. "I'm happy you came out to me. I wish you'd trusted me sooner. I just wonder how I didn't see it myself."

"I'm a pretty good actor."

"Honey, I spent all those years doing beauty pageants, and trust me, they are chock to the brim with gay men. Remember Uncle Rudy?" Rudy had been her best friend and stylist for years. Bobby Lee had robbed him blind, which really put a wedge between her and Rudy, to say the least.

Ruark smiled a real smile. "I think he's how I figured it all out."

"Did you tell him?"

"Yeah, but I begged him not to tell you. Momma?" His smile faded. "I don't want to go to school tomorrow."

"Neither you nor Shanna are going tomorrow." Actually, they were never going back if Dave couldn't ensure their safety.

She trusted him to do just that, to protect her children from those bullies. That didn't mean she could just hand the whole mess over to him. The school part, yes. But she'd make sure her children were happy and knew they were loved. They would never feel the need to keep secrets again.

Chapter Thirty-Four

Dave checked out the time on his cell phone. To call or to stop by and tell Ainslie about the arrangements he'd made with Joe L'Amore and Mike in person, that was the question.

Not too late to go and tell her face to face, he decided. Maybe the twins would still be up, and he could brief them on the need to copy bullying private messages and wall posts.

His need to see Ainslie also factored into the decision, so it really didn't take much convincing to go and talk to her, hold her in his arms. Maybe steal a kiss or two.

Or three.

He pulled out his cell phone to call her and make sure it was all right to come back.

She picked up on the second ring. "Hello?"

As usual when he heard her sexy, southern belle drawl, all the knots in his stomach disappeared, replaced by a warmth that spread from his heart. "Hey, Ainslie. It's me I've got news."

"Dave, hi. What kind of news?" She sounded tense, her worry palpable, even over the phone line.

"If it's not too late, I'd like to come over and tell you in person. Is that okay?"

"In person. Is it that bad?"

"No. I've spent a lot of time with the superintendent, and we've worked out some strategies." He smiled. "And I'd really like to see you again tonight."

"Strategies." She sounded tentative. "Okay." A sigh gusted across the phone lines. "I'd like to see you too."

"Great! I'll be there in a few."

"Drive carefully."

"I will."

****

Ainslie took a quick look at herself, using the shiny side of the toaster as a mirror. *Eek*! What a trainwreck!

Not wanting Dave to see her looking that dreadful, she bustled to the bathroom to wash her face and take a comb her hair.

Forget a comb. She'd need a rake to fix this mess.

Too late, she thought as she heard her doorbell jangled.

The bell didn't jangle as much as her nerves did. She really hoped he had good news. Her hands trembled as she reached for the door knob.

One minute she trembled as she let Dave in, the next she was in his arms.

He kissed her. That incredible jolt she felt from his warm, firm lips always surprised her.

"Hey," he said when they came up for air.

"Hey." Her words fluttered out, breathy and quiet.

"Why don't you let me in, so I can tell you what's going on."

"Oh, yes, please." She pulled him in and shut the door. "Do you want anything? Coffee? Tea?"

"No, I'm good," he said as he settled himself on her couch. He tugged on her hand. "Join me."

She didn't resist, dropping onto the couch beside him. "How bad is it?"

"As far as school goes, it's okay." Dave loosened his tie. "All the boys have gotten suspended, I can't fix that. Alden and crew have to come to school and do their work in the detention room. They're benched for the rest of the football season. They can't practice with the team, nothing. Ruark can spend the suspension at home. I'm sending a tutor to go over his work with him."

Panic clomped through her composure on hob-nailed boots. "I don't have the money to pay a tutor!"

He put a hushing finger up to her mouth. "The school is paying the tutor, so don't worry about it."

"What about Shanna? High school is so full of mean girls."

"That's true." He rubbed the heel of his hand. "We've got a few things to put into place to address the harassment."

"I'm not going to send her to a school where she's not safe." No way would Ainslie budge on that.

"Let's keep her home at first. She can use the tutor we're sending for Ruark. However, we'd like to get a restraining order for bullying at school and the cyber bullying, but we need her help."

"What do you need?" Ainslie would make it happen.

"We need her to copy and paste all her e-mails, private messages from Facebook, tweets, whatever. Do you have caller ID?"

"Yes." She'd gotten it in case Bobby Lee tried to call the children from prison.

"Good. Don't answer any calls from the other kids and forward any harassing texts to me."

"She doesn't have a cell phone. We only have the one, which I usually have."

"Okay. That makes it a little bit easier." He took her hands. "You've got to trust me."

"I do. This all just makes me so upset." She shook her head. "Why didn't I see what's going on?"

"You can't beat yourself up. Working two jobs to put food on the table and pay the rent is exhausting." He leaned forward and gave her sweet, quick kiss on her cheek.

"There's so much I missed. Things I should have

seen, secrets they were keeping."

"Kids this age do their best to keep secrets. They're very good at it. You probably wouldn't have seen anything, even if you were with them 24/7."

She sighed. Should she tell him about Ruark?

No. That was Ruark's story to tell. Changing the subject, she asked, "Are you sure you don't want any coffee?"

He smiled gently and without thinking, she ran a finger across his mouth. He caught her hand and pressed a kiss into her palm. "No, thank you."

"Momma? I thought I heard..." Shanna walked into the room. "Oh. Hi, Mr. Mason." She took a step back.

Shanna looked more than a little afraid.

Dave stood and helped Ainslie up. "I just came by to talk to your mother about tomorrow."

"Do I have to go?" She didn't have to add the words "to school."

"I'll let your mother tell you all about it." He looked at his watch. "I should go anyway. I've got early meetings. Let me know if you need anything, anything at all."

"We will," Ainslie said as she walked him to the door. "Thank you."

He kissed her, brief enough for propriety, long enough, he hoped, to make her miss him. "Good night."

"Good night." She watched him bound off the porch, then closed the door. A sense of serenity filled her, warmth rising from her toes to the top of her head. "Come here, baby. What do you need?"

"You like Mr. Mason."

"Yes, dumpling. Very much. He's a good man, someone you can count on, or else I wouldn't bring him around here."

"Are you going to marry him?"

Where did that come from? She frowned. "Well,

for one thing, he hasn't asked yet. And it's too soon to make a decision like that."

"Okay." Shanna frowned. "Do you, like, really, really like him?"

"Yeah, I really, really like him." She sighed. "But it doesn't matter how much I like him. If you, Ruark, and Patsy don't like him, then that's it. The three of you come first, forever and always."

Ainslie opened her arms, and Shanna flowed into them. "Everything is going to be okay, pumpkin." She rubbed her hands up and down Shanna's back. "Just trust me. You'll see."

Shanna snarfled back some tears. "I love you, Momma."

"I know, I know, sugar. I love you, too. Nothing's going to hurt you ever again. I promise."

"Cross your heart and hope to die?" Shanna looked up at her.

"You know it, doodle bug."

****

Three days later, Dave took a deep breath before knocking on Joe L'Amore's door. All set for this showdown with the parents of the kids who were bullying Shanna and Ruark, he couldn't wait to take them on.

Ainslie had gotten right to work and gotten the harassing texts and private messages. They were just what they needed to enforce the school's policies regarding punishment for the cyber-bullying.

He knocked on the door. Joe told him to come in, so Dave pushed it open. "Hello," he said to the room in general.

Stone dead silence from the parents. Joe smiled, stood, and gestured to the only open chair. "Thanks for coming, Mr. Mason."

"I wouldn't miss it." Settling in the chair, he pulled the kids' files out of his briefcase. Brody Carpenter, the school's attorney, sat in the chair next to Dave's.

The air hung low and stagnant, like a dark, toxic cloud. The parents of the kids glowered at him, as if they were cats left out in the rain. They most likely felt they didn't need an attorney, since Elliot Bradford was one.

What did they say about lawyers representing themselves? That they have fools for clients.

Dave felt pretty sure they would prove that theory today.

Joe L'Amore shredded his throat with a room clearing *humpf*. "Okay, we're all here. So, here's how this is going to go. Mr. Carpenter will go over the reasons the boys got benched for the season, as well as why the girls have been taken off the cheering squad. You'll have a chance to present your issues, then we'll hear Mr. Carpenter's response."

He pushed his glasses up his nose and then held up the School Code of Behavior, which every father, mother, guardian and student signed every year. "You've all got the document outlining the rules and expectations, yes? And a copy of all your signatures acknowledging your compliance, yes?"

"I don't think we need to go into all this. I'm sure the matter can be cleared up very quickly." Hank Brewster said.

"I'm sure you want to spare the Logan children any embarrassment." Elliot Bradford folded the Code of Behavior in half and slid it into his briefcase, without giving it a glance.

"This year we added a cyber-bullying policy to the other policies about student harassment," Carpenter said. "The rules are clear, and there is a zero tolerance clause, for the children's safety. Now, what I have here are some copies of threats being made to Shanna and Ruark Logan, along with the signed statements from witnesses who came forward to tell us about the physical harassment against

Ruark Logan in the boys' locker room. Then there's the destruction of property, the willful destruction of an iPod."

He passed out an envelope to each of the parents. "All the documentation is there. Take your time going over it." Carpenter stood there like a sentinel guarding a fortress.

Bradford barely glanced at the envelope. "Let's cut to the chase. Our kids are being made scapegoats in a situation the Logan kids initiated. And they're getting away with it because their mother is sleeping with Mason here."

Dave inhaled a sharp breath. His hands balled into fists at his sides. Every muscle in his body quivered with restraint. He bit the inside of his cheek to keep from defending Ainslie and her children. It more than chapped his hide to stand back and let Brody Carpenter do the talking.

"The punishment for Ruark Logan is correct according to the student code. He started a fight, he got suspended. End of story." Joe L'Amore sat back in his chair. "Shanna Logan has not violated one word of the code. She is, however, the victim of some serious cyber-bullying, by your children, as evidenced by the documents we've given you."

"Further, Ruark Logan is the victim of not only cyber-bullying, but actual attacks on his person, as well as the loss of his personal property." Carpenter held up an envelope like the ones the parents had received. "It's all here. Now, if you're not willing to make sure your children leave Ruark and Shanna Logan alone, both here and on the internet, and phone, you'll leave us no choice but petition the court for an order of protection to insure the Logan children's safety. Failure to comply will mean expulsion from school."

"You can try." Elliot Bradford smiled, baring a wealth of pointy, sharky teeth. "I'll get a judge to dismiss it right away and then sue the school for defaming our kids' reputations, and a host of other things." He stood.

"So be it." L'Amore stood. "We will enforce every word of the Student Handbook, as well as the Sports Code of Conduct to the letter. We stand behind Mr. Mason's decisions regarding the in-school suspensions, as well as the restrictions regarding the football team and cheerleading squad." He looked at his watch. "Are we done here?" he asked Brody Carpenter.

"I believe we are."

Bradford turned red in the face, nearly knocking over his chair as he lumbered to his feet. "This is nowhere near done. No football means no playing in college, which is unacceptable. You'll be hearing from me."

Noisy chairs scraping across the floor accompanied their march out Joe L'Amore's door.

"I'll go down to the courthouse to get the wheels in motion for the orders of protection, just to be prepared." Brody looked at Dave. "We've got the evidence, and it'll stick, so don't worry."

"Thanks Brody." Dave stood as Brody did. "I'm grateful for the back-up."

"It's in the job description." Brody gave Joe and Dave a sharp salute and left.

"Right." Dave looked at Joe. "Thank you."

"Like Brody said, it's in the job description. You did yours by enforcing the code of conduct to the letter. I hope this helps the Logan kids feel safer."

"Me too." Dave nodded. "Me too."

Chapter Thirty-Five

One good thing about losing all her cleaning jobs, Ainslie thought as she sat down at a table at Hope's restaurant, was that she had more time for meetings and errands for the Mirror, Mirror On The Wall Ball. Today she needed to take care of some last minute details with Hope Monahan.

It kept her busy enough that she didn't drive herself crazy with all the drama surrounding Shanna and Ruark. They were both back to school, restraining orders soundly in place, thanks to some threatening Facebook posts and private messages.

It used to be that school drama stayed at school. With Facebook, the bullies could harass you 24/7. It was reassuring that Addington High had a stern cyber bullying policy and that they enforced it, no matter who the bully was.

Thanks to Dave, the school superintendent Joe L'Amore, and the school lawyer Brody Carpenter, her children felt safe enough to go back to school.

The cool, serene atmosphere at Hope's soothed the rough edges of her composure. The hostess led her to a small table and Ainslie sat and absorbed the peace.

She really admired and liked Hope. Hope had built an at home kitchen catering business into one of the best restaurants in New England, all on her own. There were rumors Hope was going to be a judge on some new reality cooking show.

Well, if any one could make it happen, Hope could. She had more energy than the Tazmanian Devil.

"Sorry, I'm late!" Hope said as she slipped into the table. "I'm trying out a new dish for the Ball, and I want to test run it tonight. Did Renee bring you something to drink?"

"No worries, I'm all set." Ainslie reached into her bag and pulled out a pen and a notebook. "I'm just trying to finalize some details and show you photos of some of the mirrors the artists are donating, in case you want to imitate some of the food in the colors of the mirrors." She pushed a file folder across the table.

"Ooooh, I've been itching to see some of these." Hope pulled her glasses out of her chef's tunic and put them on. "Aren't they charming!" She pointed at one done in blue and green decoupage with mermaids frolicking along the frame. The artist had imbued the mirror with whimsy and humor.

"That's my favorite," Ainslie said.

"They're all wonderful." Hope shuffled through the photo book. "I want them all!"

"Good. Let's hope someone feels like you do and we make a lot of money on them."

Hope closed the book. "You do good work."

"I was on so many committees in Charleston, I got a lot of practice. And I love to do it."

Eyes direct and honest, Hope nodded. "I'm wondering if you'd like to work for me, as an event planner. I've put the restaurant into that Best Tastes of Addington competition." She wrinkled her nose. "It's going to take a lot of time, and I won't be able to really give the catering part of the business the time it deserves. I need someone I trust to handle that part of Hope's. I think you're perfect for the job."

Uh, wow! Her brain couldn't form a sentence to save her life. She forced herself to focus. "I can't give you any references, except for Bobby. Are you sure you want to hire me?"

"I wouldn't have asked if I didn't think you could do the job."

"I'm flattered." Excitement zapped through every synapse she owned.

"It will be pretty much a full time job, 'cause even when I am around, I can't consult with everybody who wants us to cater their event, its gotten that big. I need someone who knows how to plan and execute big events as well as the smaller ones. It'd be mostly day time, with some nights to oversee some of the bigger events."

Oh, my stars and garters. Full time? She could quit The End Zone to do something she really loved to do, but more importantly, be with her children at night. "I'd love to be your event coordinator."

Hope grinned. "Excellent! Come on back tomorrow, and we can go over details, and you can sign the paperwork." The pager hooked on Hope's belt buzzed. She looked at it and swore. "I'm sorry, I'm needed back in the kitchen."

Standing, Hope held out her hand to Ainslie. Ainslie stood on rubbery, unsteady legs and shook hands with her new boss. "No problem. When do you want me to come around for the paperwork?"

"Tomorrow, in between lunch, while we're prepping for dinner, say about 3:00."

"That sounds great." She'd have to make arrangements for someone to pick up Patsy, or to leave her in aftercare a little longer.

A job that didn't involve the backbreaking work of cleaning, that didn't mean dealing with hauling beer and nachos until her feet throbbed.

A day job meaning she could be a better parent to her children.

She couldn't wait to tell Dave. She punched in his phone number.

"Mason."

"Hi, Dave."

"Ainslie, hi! What's up?"

"Hope Monahan offered me a full-time job as her events coordinator."

"That's great!" Ainslie could tell he was smiling by the sound of his voice. "Are you going to take it?"

"Oh, yeah, I'm going to take it."

"Congratulations! We'll have to celebrate later on."

She licked her lips. "My thoughts exactly."

****

"Andi wants me to dress up like the frog prince." Mike scowled as he popped a pretzel into his mouth and bit into it with a huge crunch. "The freakin' frog who needs a kiss to turn back into a prince." He shuddered.

He and Ian had caught up with Dave at The End Zone. They were all sitting at the bar, Mike and Ian complaining about the Mirror, Mirror on the Wall Ball.

"It's not easy being green." Ian stared into his pint of Guinness. "Gina wants us to dress as D'Artagnan and Constance." He shrugged. "It's not a fairy tale, right? But that's what she wants."

Mike took a slug of his Heinekin. "You need to find one of those boa covered hats the Three Mouseketeers wore," he said to Ian.

"Musketeers, not Mouseketeers." Ian corrected. "I think I can find a hat without feathers." He frowned. "At least I hope I can. I can go to the theater department at Barrett and see what I can borrow."

"You're lucky you don't have to go, Dave." Mike toasted Dave with his beer. "Whose idea was this costume ball thing anyway?"

Spike looked up from the glasses she was washing. "I do believe it was Ainslie's idea."

"Don't make me hurt *you* for criticizing Ainslie." Dave gave Mike his hairiest eyeball.

"Heh. That means you're going then. What humiliating costume is she making you wear?" Mike grumbled.

"I don't know. We haven't talked about it." They'd had a lot of other stuff to do, like celebrate her new job, that didn't really require conversation.

"I heard her talking to Andi, and I think she's going as Cinderella, since she already has a ball gown or two and a tiara left over from her beauty pageant days." Spike grinned and snapped her fingers. "You should go as Prince Charming."

"That sounds like a splendid idea!" Ian looked positively giddy at the prospect.

"Makes me feel the frog thing isn't so bad." Mike rubbed his chin. "Does Ainslie have an extra sparkly tiara for you?

"Maybe she'll have one of those shiny sash things for you to wear. You'll look soooo cute." Mike sat back in his chair and linked his hands behind his head.

Ian snorted. "Adorable, even."

"Don't forget the jaunty little jacket and the white leggings. Do they make lacey white leggings in your size?" Mike clapped Dave on the back. "Oh, and those puffy pants with those slits that are a different color, the real short poofy ones. What do you call those pants?"

"Breeches." Ian nodded. "He should also have a cod piece. Maybe a sequined cod piece. You know how the royalty love their bling."

"Oooooh." Mike pretended to swoon. "You'll be the belle of the ball."

"Okay, okay. You can stop now." Dave plucked a pretzel out of the bowl on the bar and threw it at Mike. "If Ainslie wants me to dress up as Prince Charming, then I'll dress up like Prince Charming."

Mike grinned. Ian glowered.

Dave shrugged. "You guys are making fools of

yourself for Andi and Gina, just to keep *them* happy. Why can't I do the same for Ainslie?"

Mike held out a hand in front of Ian. "Told you. Pay up."

Ian grumbled as he pulled out his wallet. "Why couldn't you have waited three more weeks?" he asked Dave.

"You guys made a bet on me and Ainslie?"

They both looked at Dave with *well, duh* looks on their faces. Of course they'd made a bet.

Dave shook his head. "I'm so glad you're tracking my love life, like little girls tweeting about Justin Bieber."

"Just let me know when you want to go out picking colors for the wedding and all that crap." Mike signaled Spike for another round of beers.

"God, Mike." Dave rested his elbows against the bar. "You're really a pain in the ass."

"That's true," Ian added as he looked at Mike. "You're a *huge* pain in the ass."

Spike put the new round of beers in front of the guys. "*Prost!*"

Mike and Ian held up their glasses. "To Dave. Good bye, Freedom," Mike toasted.

Mike was such a faker. He loved being married to Andi. Ian would die for Gina. Neither of them were fooling anybody. Dave held his glass up and saluted Ian and Mike with it.

They drank deep, beer glugging down their throats, the fizz pricking their throats as they swallowed. Dave figured he'd never had better friends.

As for asking Ainslie to marry him, he'd have to wait until her kids were ready for it. As much as he wished it could be otherwise, it felt like Shanna, Ruark, and Patsy just weren't ready for a new daddy.

Chapter Thirty-Six

"Are you going to marry Mr. Mason?" Patsy moved her peas around on a plate, thinking Ainslie wouldn't notice that she wasn't eating them. Her baby girl should just learn that Momma sees and knows all.

Wait! Marry Dave? Where was that coming from? What a question. "Why do you ask, baby?"

"He's over here a lot, and he's doing a lot of stuff to take care of us." Using her fork, Patsy smooshed the offensive peas in a green gooey mess.

Shanna and Ruark looked at Ainslie, eyes wide and sparkling, like they were trying to see into her brain.

"It's a little early to think about getting married. It's good to take these things easy. Slow, so we can figure out if it's the right thing to do."

"Would you marry him if we weren't around?" Shanna tended to say what the three of them were thinking.

"That's a silly question."

"Would you?" Ruark asked.

"It's not an option." Ainslie looked at their expectant faces. "We're a family. It has to be right for all of us. And besides, he hasn't asked me, so it's all a moot point."

"What's a moo point? Does Mr. Mason have a cow?" Patsy asked as she spread a layer of mashed potatoes over the smashed peas.

"No, a moot point is something that's not important to what you're talking about."

"Okay." Patsy frowned, clearly disappointed that

Dave didn't own livestock.

Ainslie sighed. "Let's drop this, okay? Let's just enjoy having Mr. Mason as a special friend."

Her three meddlesome children exchanged serious looks. They must have talked about this.

Lord love a duck. What next?

****

Dave sat back in his office chair as he tossed his reading glasses on his desk. He hadn't seen Ainslie for days, not an acceptable situation.

One he'd remedy tonight by stopping at The End Zone.

His desk phone trilled. He scowled as he looked at his watch—4:30. The last thing he needed was an interruption making more work and delaying his trip to The End Zone.

Please don't be a crisis. "Yes, Mrs. Rockland?"

"I have three students sitting here in the outer office, wondering if you have time right now to see them."

"Of course." Resigned, he tightened his tie, but didn't roll down his sleeves.

And gawked as Mrs. Rockland opened his door for Ruark, Shanna, and Patsy to walk into his office. Whatever he expected, it wasn't this. "Hey. What's up?"

"We want to talk to you about Momma," Ruark said.

His stomach hitched. "Okay. Is there anything wrong?"

Patsy heaved a very big, very dramatic sigh as she sat in one of his office chairs. "Yep. We want you to be our daddy and marry our momma, but she says she can't 'cause you have to ask her."

"So, we came here to tell you that if you want to ask her it's okay with us," Shanna added.

"Um." Suddenly incapable of speech, a high pitched buzz drilled through Dave's brain. Marrying

Ainslie and being a father to these three amazing kids was his fondest wish delivered to him on a silver platter.

"Gawd, Patsy." Shanna glared at her sister. "We weren't going to put it out there right away."

Patsy stuck her tongue out at Shanna.

Ruark shook his head. "Fighting like this in front of Mr. Mason is sure going to make him want to marry Momma." He looked at Dave. "I apologize for my sisters."

"It's okay, no need to apologize." Dave could finally think again. "Does your mother know you're here?"

"'Course not." Shanna shook her head. "She'd just up and die from embarrassment if she knew."

"You can't tell her. She'll ground us *forever*," Patsy pouted.

"Patsy has a good point." Shanna pursed her lips. "Can you ask her to marry you without mentioning this little visit?"

Ruark sat and put his elbows on his knees, then dropped his head into his hands, the picture of despair.

Dave took a deep breath. He didn't want to mess this up. "Maybe your mother doesn't want to marry me."

Patsy nodded her head so hard her curls bounced in a frothy tangle. "She does want to marry you. Why won't you ask her?"

"Is it because of us?" Shanna added. "You don't like us?"

"Of course I like you." Dave's heart began to beat in heavy thuds—*ka-thunk, ka-thunk*.

"We promise we'll be really good. We'll clean our rooms and not leave dirty dishes in the living room and do our homework right away after school." Patsy looked like a baby owl, eyes wide and unblinking.

Ruark stood. "What we're trying to say is that

269

we want Momma to be happy. We can tell she loves you, so we want you to know we won't stand in the way. That's if you love her back and all."

"Well, uh, I do love your mother, and I love you kids. I think it's great that you love your mom and are looking out for her." He held up a finger. "But you have to promise me that you'll let me take it from here. Can you do that?"

"Yep." Ruark looked at his sisters. "Let's jet."

"Thanks for listening to us," Shanna nodded.

Patsy grinned. "I'm glad you're going to be our daddy." She lifted her arms to be picked up.

So Dave picked her up.

She puckered up and gave Dave a kiss. "Thank you."

Dave set her down and watched her scamper off after Shanna and Ruark. His heart still stuttering, he sat down in the chair Shanna had been sitting in.

Ainslie's children wanted him to be their father. Intense pride rolled through him. Maybe he should start passing out the cigars.

His heart unclenched and a gentle warmth took over. Looked like he had some plans to make.

Chapter Thirty-Seven

Ainslie loved the way her silk Lanvin gown swished and frothed as she moved across the room. Pink as pale and fragile as a June peony, the dress bared her shoulders, and champagne colored tulle bloomed to frame her neck, shoulders and cleavage. Ainslie had sheathed her arms in long, white gloves and had perched her most elaborate and sparkly beauty queen tiara on her head.

She'd sprinkled a light, tasteful smattering of glitter across her cleavage, along with a tiny touch of her beloved *Nocturnes de Caron* behind each ear. *Bibbidi Bobbidi Boo!* Instant princess.

She sighed as she took stock of the room. Strategically placed trees strung with hundreds of multi-colored, twinkling fairy lights created an enchanted forest. Whimsical mirrors waiting to be auctioned appeared here and there, reflecting the lights of the trees. Wisps of the sounds of musicians warming up teased her ears.

She loved to dance. She hoped she'd have someone to dance with.

Dave Mason. She wanted to dance with Dave.

He'd been non-committal about attending, claiming that work might keep him from the Ball.

She suspected it was the whole costume thing. Andi and Gina told her their husbands had done nothing but complain, creating outlandish excuses to try and get out of it.

Speaking of whom, she noticed them near the bandstand talking to Hope. Andi made a very elegant princess, in a rich gold colored gown and plain gold crown on her head. Gina looked lovely in a yellow gown with hoops and panniers. The dress was so wide, she had trouble getting through doors. She piled her curly red hair on top of her head, with long curls that escaped to flirt with her shoulders.

As for Hope, Little Bo Peep had never looked so good. She'd curled her hair into fat ringlets and topped them off with a white mop cap. Her blue dress was very short and puffed out over a stiff petticoat. A tight bustier covered a white, puffy sleeved peasant blouse. Her sheer white hose and black stilettos showed off a whole lotta leg. Hope handled her shepherd's crook like it was a weapon.

This Little Bo Peep had her some dangerous teeth.

Andi spotted her and beckoned her to join them. Ainslie felt a smile bloom on her face. It was so nice to have girlfriends again and a brand new career doing something she loved. No more cleaning lady. No more waitress.

The girls toasted her as she joined them. Hope handed her a glass of champagne. "We're having a toast to us because we are made of awesome."

"Seriously." Gina said. "We rock hard."

Ainslie laughed as they all clinked glasses.

She had to pinch herself to make sure she wasn't dreaming.

****

"Here's the codpiece." Ian held out a totally ridiculous athletic supporter, decorated with some sequins glued to it."

"I'm not wearing that." Dave shook his head. "No way, no how."

Ian laughed.

"Are you sure this is okay?" Dave looked at himself in the mirror, from the front, then moved to the side.

"Actually, that outfit really makes your ass look

fat." Mike tipped his chair onto its back two legs. "Huge, actually."

Dave gave Mike the one finger salute. "Ha fuckity ha, ha, ha. This from the man rocking a frog suit."

"The gold crown on top really goes well with the fluorescent green webbed gloves and flippers," Ian added.

"You've got a point." Dave looked at Mike and crossed his eyes. "Ribbit," he croaked.

Mike's eyes narrowed. "At least I'm not a sissy. Wearing that? You should change your name to Nancy. What do you think, Ian?"

"Yeah, Nancy's ass is huge."

"Hugest ass I've ever seen." Mike chuckled.

"It's why, it's beautiful." Ian cocked his head and turned his head toward the ceiling. "What's that I hear? Is it the weeping of angels?" He looked back at Dave and Mike. "I do believe I heard the angels cry."

"Yeah, yeah, funny, funny." Dave adjusted the fake sword at his side and the red banner across his chest. Even though he felt stupider than he had ever felt in his entire life, he was going out, in public, in this outfit.

His plan had a few flaws, sure enough.

He'd just have to make it work.

****

"See how the artist used silver and gold filigree to achieve a fairy tale atmosphere." Ainslie stood near a set of mirrors, ready to sweet talk people into bidding on a mirror. "I can imagine Rapunzel sitting in front of it, combing her hair."

The ballroom sparkled with fairy lights in a forest of trees and greenery. Champagne fizzed while the guests danced, nibbled on Hope's amazing food, and surveyed the mirrors on auction. Ainslie would tap dance if she needed to close the sale.

"It would look so sweet in Jenny's room," the

woman told her husband.

"She'd break it in two weeks." The husband crossed his arms across his chest.

The woman looked at Ainslie. "Don't mind him. He's always grumpy." She reached a finger to trace the filigree. "My Jenny loves fairy tales. How do I get it?"

Ainslie smiled and reached for a clipboard. "Just fill out this little form and put it into the box here with the other bids."

The woman grabbed the clipboard. "How much do you think I should bid?"

"The minimum bid is $375.00. The artist's other pieces have gone for anywhere between $800.00 to $1,500.00."

After signing her bid with a flourish, the woman put the bid in the box. "Thank you."

"No, thank you! Your gift to the Addington Ballet Theater will help us immeasurably." She ratcheted up the wattage in her already bright smile. "I hope you win!"

The woman winked. "Not as much as I do. Come on Ed. Let's get you some food." The pair moved along.

Going on tiptoe, Ainslie scanned the room. So no sign of Dave, Mike, or Ian.

She hoped so much Dave cleared his work schedule so he could make the ball, she ached with it. He did admit he had a costume, but wouldn't say a word about it. Curiosity scooted up her spine then danced down again.

The man definitely could keep a secret.

"This is going so well," Andi said as she came up to Ainslie. "I think we're going to make a mint for the ballet."

Ainslie turned from looking for Dave to smile at Andi. "I hope so." She slid her eyes back over to the entrance to continue watching for Dave.

"If you're looking for Dave, he's with Mike and Ian." Andi wrinkled her nose. "Mike is not going to get here any earlier than he has to. Dressing in costume is *so* not his thing."

"Am I that obvious?"

"Yes, but only from those who share your predicament." Gina said as she joined Andi and Ainslie. She tugged the off the shoulder neckline of her yellow satin ball dress. "I've gotta say, Ian had some very interesting questions for me."

"Oh, really." Andi raised her eyebrows. "Do tell."

"Crazy stuff." Gina shook her head. "Like how to get sequins to stick to an athletic supporter."

"What? No way!" Andi laughed. "You're kidding."

Gina's curls bounced as she nodded. "Yes, way! It's God's own truth. He wanted to know if he had to use glue or could he get away with scotch tape."

"Oh my God." Andi looked like she was going to faint. "Frog princes don't need sequined supporters, right?"

Gina shook her head. "Only if he's going to hop around all night. I know my guy's costume doesn't need sequins. It's got a lot of gold braid and maribou trimming. Sequins would definitely be overkill."

Andi took a deep breath. "Maybe it's for Dave."

"What kind of costume would need a sequined supporter, anyway?" Ainslie shook her head.

"Damned if I know." Gina looked sad, but the twinkle in her eyes said otherwise. "But whatever it is, it can't be made of good."

Ainslie's mind boggled.

She turned to watch the doors again, her heart sounding loudly in her ears. Something in the air had changed.

Then her heart stopped when she saw Dave enter the ballroom with Mike and Ian. Mike had dressed all in a fluorescent green, long sleeved turtle neck, webbed gloves and green make up on his face. The crowning touch was a pair of green flippers on his feet instead of shoes. Ian wore a dark blue velvet coat over leggings and boots. The coat was be-ribboned with a ton of gold braids and his huge hat was trimmed with more maribou than a Frederick's of Hollywood mule. He had a fencing foil attached to his belt, and it kept getting in the way when he walked.

And Dave. Dear Lord, he was Prince Charming come to life.

"Wouldja look at that," Gina breathed. "God, they're so cute."

"Do me a favor and don't tell Mike he looks cute." Andi grinned.

"Okay, I'll say he looks adorable." Gina grinned.

"And please don't say *ribbit* to him. It'll make him crazy."

Ainslie couldn't tear her eyes away from Dave. He could have been lifted off the page of a fairy tale, a perfect prince. Dressed in a dark blue coat and black breeches, a red sash across his chest and a sword at his side, he looked ready to slay dragons and rescue damsels.

Nary a sequin in sight.

When he stood before her, Dave reached for her hand and brought it to his mouth for a gentle, thrilling brush of his lips. "You look amazing, Cinderella."

She sighed in delight. "You look so handsome." Wait. "How did you know I was coming as Cinderella?"

"Spike." Music floated around them, the tune sultry and slow. "Dance with me."

Ainslie followed him onto the dance floor and into his arms. His arms felt warm and strong around her as he twirled her around the dance floor. "You dance very well," she breathed.

"My mother made me take ballroom dancing classes. It ended up being a good way to meet girls."

"Oh, really." She angled her chin to look up at him. "You're full of surprises."

He cocked his head to one side, love shining brightly from his eyes. "You don't know the half of it." He pulled her tight against him.

She sighed as she melted into the warmth of his embrace, the steady thud of his heart against her body. Her skin felt extra sensitive, prickling as the air around them sparked and crackled.

"Penny for your thoughts." Dave looked at her, a question in his eyes.

Did he look worried? How odd. "I'm thinking about how perfect tonight is." She smiled. "About how much I love you."

Something flickered warmly in his gaze as he studied her face. Though the music still played, he spun her to a stop.

And then, oh dear Lord, he went down on one knee in front of her. She looked at his face, that handsome face, those beautiful blue eyes and saw the love there.

Love for her.

He took her left gloved hand and kissed it. "Ainslie Logan, I love you so much, there are times I can't breathe because of it." He let go of her hand to pull a small black velvet box and flip open the top.

Her breath caught in her throat as the diamond ring in the box reflected the light and made it dance. She couldn't find her voice, couldn't move.

"What I really want to ask is will you marry me? I'll do anything you want, anything you need."

"All you have to do is love me and the children."

He shifted his weight on the one knee on the floor. "Not to be unromantic, but if you could give me a yes, my knee will be forever grateful."

"Just your knee?" She still couldn't believe what

she was hearing.

"My heart, my body, my brain, my left small toe—whatever you want, you've got it."

"And my children?"

"Trust me, they're good with this."

"I think there's a story here."

"There is, but I'll tell you after you say yes." Dave gave her the smile she loved the best.

"Well, then, I better say yes." She reached out to touch his cheek. Pulling up on his arms so that he stood in front of her, she trembled as she gave him her answer. "Yes, I'll marry you."

That's when they noticed that the music had stopped and everyone in the room was watching them. The crowd on the dance floor clapped and hooted with approval.

Next thing she knew, Dave snatched her up into his arms and spun her around.

Dave set her down and kissed her, a soul kiss full of love and promise. She kissed him back, with all the love and trust she felt for him.

After tugging off the glove of her left hand, he put the ring, a classic solitaire, on her finger. "This is forever. I mean it. I'm not ever going to let you get away."

"As if I'd let you." She grinned.

Dave led Ainslie into a private little corner of the room.

"We've got a lot of plans to make." Ainslie felt light-headed and dizzy with the thrill of it all.

"Good thing we know a professional event planner."

A laugh bubbled out of her. A new job, a proposal from the most wonderful man she'd ever met.

A new life. "I never thought I could be this happy again."

Dave kissed her, a deep claiming kiss, which

made her toes curl. "I plan to keep you this happy for the rest of our lives."

"Me too." She stared into his blue, blue eyes. "I love you so much!"

He smiled. "Me too, baby." He kissed her again. "Me too."

Epilogue

Ruark looked around the small chapel where Momma would marry Mr. Mason.

Correction. Dave. His soon to be step-father.

He was Dave's best man, how cool was that? Shanna and Patsy were standing up for Momma.

There weren't a lot of people there in this pretty little white clapboard church. No stained glass, the old windows let the sun in to light up the sanctuary in this warm golden light. Actual beeswax candles gently scented the air. They wanted a small wedding, because Momma had been there, done that with the huge wedding the first time around. So, just family and friends. Dave's family was pretty chill, even though there weren't a lot of them. The crew from The End Zone was all at the wedding, since Bobby closed the restaurant for the day.

And, speaking of friends, Ruark had taken a big step and asked Luke, the hot bass from chorus, to be his date. Luke was sitting in the pews right now, third row, with Mr. and Mrs. Kelly.

It felt good to be out of the closet. Really good.

It wasn't perfect, but it was getting better.

"It's time, kid," Dave said as he put his hand on Ruark's shoulder.

Ruark's heart bumped against his ribs as they stepped up to the front of the chapel, as the organist pumped and wheezed out Beethoven's *Ode to Joy*.

Dave wore the goofiest, lovesick look on his face, as he looked toward the back doorway.

Ruark followed Dave's gaze, and looked to the back of the church, where Momma, Shanna, and

Patsy started the short walk down the aisle. He heard Dave suck in a breath, probably in awe of how beautiful Momma was in an elegant winter white tea length dress.

They'd let Patsy pick her own dress, an over the top pink number with sequins on the bodice and a full puffy, layered tulle skirt.

And, yeah, he had to admit Shanna cleaned up pretty well, in a deep blue satin dress.

Like he couldn't wait to touch Momma, Dave moved halfway up the aisle to travel the rest of the way with her. Their matching smiles shone brighter than the sunlight streaming into the sanctuary. They kept their hands clasped together as they made the forever kind of promises.

From where Ruark was standing, the future looked pretty damn good.

A word about the author...

Doreen has wanted to be a writer her whole life but took a detour into being an opera singer and choral conductor. She realized that maybe she should spend more time writing when creating the back stories for her operatic roles was more fun than actually singing them. Plus her romance-lovin' heart couldn't take all the dead bodies littering the stage at the end of the performance. She is still an active conductor and is regularly found waving her arms around in front of singers.

Thank you for purchasing
this Wild Rose Press publication.
For other wonderful stories of romance,
please visit our on-line bookstore at
www.thewildrosepress.com.

For questions or more information
contact us at
info@thewildrosepress.com.

The Wild Rose Press
www.TheWildRosePress.com

To visit with authors of The Wild Rose Press
join our yahoo loop at
http://groups.yahoo.com/group/thewildrosepress/